WikiJustice

Jack King

ISBN: 0986787132
ISBN-13: 9780986787133
Goat Path Publishing 2012

For Elizabeth, with love.

PAGE INTENTIONALLY LEFT BLANK

"The killings of your Bureau, while justified by crimes committed by the victims, were not regarded by you as punishments. You looked upon your victims as social ills, the extirpation of which would benefit society."

Jack London, The Assassination Bureau, Ltd.

"I directed [...] the director of the CIA, to make the killing [...]"

Barack Obama.

PAGE INTENTIONALLY LEFT BLANK

PROLOGUE

The speaker's deep and pacifying voice, combined with paper-white hair, made him appear older than his forty-four years would have it. Those who never saw him before were startled by the contrast of the first impression against the youthful, velvety-smooth face, and probing eyes. His crispy white shirt, bright-blue eyes, and frail body, set against the sky-blue background, were all the markings of an angel. An angel of justice in the world besieged by evil.

Setting his inquisitive gaze on the camera, he spoke in his trademark soft, yet well articulated voice. "Welcome to our second annual court of the people's opinion, where the voice of the 99% shall be heard, and reckoned with, by the 1% — that narrow caste who usurp their privileged position to wreak havoc and misery on the rest."

The broadcast was streamed over the Internet in a wide range of video formats in order to accommodate an audience of users, many of whom were subjected to restrictive bandwidth or various other limitations set against their wallets, or freedom of access, as imposed by their service providers who operated in servitude to their more or less oppressive regimes. The broadcast was shown in the English language — the native tongue of the online community, though not of the speaker, whose lisping accent reminded of his Latin provenance. Live voice-to-text transcript, in user-selectable language, followed his words at the bottom of many computer screens. His calmly delivered words, coupled with self-assurance, reaffirmed in every mind that what was about to commence was necessary and based on just principles. His voice poured out of a growing number of speaker-phones in innumerable, and continuously growing locations. His electrifying eyes reached deep into the eyes of every viewer, as though he was not speaking to faceless masses, but to each one individually. His moving persona projected the impression that the speaker might transcend the confinement of the binary code and materialize outside of the screen — such was the persuasive power of anticipation of his annual appearance. It was the culmination of years of injustice, and the awaiting of the opportunity to right what was wrong, to take charge where institutionalized justice had failed, or favored the privileged few. Here was the embodiment of all the pent-up expectations and hopes of the untold masses whose voices could not be heard, of the intimidated, the bullied, the hurt, and those who were cheated, whose trust in public institutions was broken, who found no recourse through the established channels — those, which were supposed the serve and work for the people, but acted against them.

Countless sets of eyes were glued to the screens, as the speaker continued. " Let us begin by recapping the procedures. I shall like to remind everyone — those who will judge, and those who will be judged today — that these proceedings are not about vengeance. It's about justice, plane and simple. We have not gathered here to cast conjectures, or to settle grievances, but to view cold facts — the documentation, whether written, or recorded, of the misdeeds of those who stand trial today." His voice paused momentarily, as the blue background suddenly came to life with images from the previous edition of the online poll. Every computer screen split in two, vertically, with one side showing the speaker, who continued to narrate the changing images that appeared on the other side. The images showing scanned documents, and photographs, flashed in rapid succession, and came to a pause on the likeness of uniformed figure sporting chiseled facial features, small cold eyes, and slim lips. The speaker described the case of the man who was tried exactly a year ago to the day. "Meet Col. Manuel Ramirez. His case is presented here for instructional purposes. As the chief of the secret police of Colombia, he was charged and found guilty, by people just like you, of organizing death squads that killed labor organizers, and farmers. The case brought against him was supported by documents leaked to the whistleblower portal, and sporting his signatures on kill orders; video footage of a raid on a village, whose inhabitants, including women and children, were killed indiscriminately, was instrumental in the online community finding him guilty." Hyperlinks to documents, images, and video files followed his words. "Peruse the evidence online, or download it to view at your later convenience. Similar material will be made available today, and pertaining to public office holders, or corporate executives, who turn against the broader public interest. You shall see documents such as these, where police officers use brutality to quench peaceful protesters, where politicians lie or use force in order to further their private agendas, or where corporate bosses sponsor violence to silence regulators and activists. You shall see cases of documented abuse, of corruption, and harm inflicted on the meek. Use this evidence wisely. Consider it carefully, as you cast your votes for every individual or a business entity named in the documents. For each charge you shall have two options: Guilty, and Not Guilty. Choose the appropriate option according to the evidence and your conscience, taking to heart the fundamental principle of the law, where no one is guilty until proven so. Keep in mind that no local or extraterritorial law applies to the judgment that you, the people of the world, shall cast, but rest assured that no jurisdiction shall remain indifferent to your voice, for no one, regardless of the position they hold in society, stands above the law of public opinion. The judgment day has come."

1

The online trial brought together an unprecedented number of participants from across the world, totaling millions. It was a remarkable accomplishment on the part of the organizers, who received no prior coverage in the corporate media. The phenomenal success of the event was due, chiefly, to years of germinating anger, and the people's desire for change. The fallout of the trial could not be ignored, as it indeed was not, when two months later the media from around the world broadcast the message, when commentators of all stripes and agendas filled the airwaves, and the Internet outlets multiplied the gist of it as only free and uncensored medium can: Two high-level politicians were killed in apparent mob attacks that were inspired by the online trial in which they were tried and found guilty. The more conservative spectrum was filled with outrage of the killings, and condemnation of those who facilitated them, whereas the more liberal, while not lacking on the former sentiments, were not above pointing out that said victims of lynching, after being found guilty, had called, publicly, for the assassination of those who made the trial possible, as well as for sever penalties for those who participated in it. The press, the media, and the World Wide Web we abuzz, with comments ranging from insightful, to the most outrageous. One name was on everybody's lips, and at the tip of everyone's proverbial quill, or fingertip tapping on a keyboard, as it were. The man at the center of all the buzz was the white-haired Angel of Justice, the man who founded the site that hosted the online trial. Who was he?

"Who is this man?" was the question asked by the editor-in-chief of one of the major British print and online dailies.

His researchers went to work, and in a short time furnished him with an impressive portfolio of insight into the life of the most sought-after man on the face of the Earth. A panel consisting of the newspaper's editorial board, investigative journalists, and the board of directors assembled in the action room to hear the scoop. The importance of the meeting was highlighted not by the persons taking part in it, but rather in the measures taken to shield the conversation from unintended ears and eyes — no mobile telephones were permitted inside, and white noise-emitting devices were activated in the room.

The senior researcher reported, "Damian Allende is the son of an Argentine couple who were forced into exile following a coup in their country. They spent eight years—"

"Wait, which coup?" The editor-in-chief was a man who paid attention to detail. He acquired this trait the day he ate his teeth, literally, when they were smashed and shoved down his throat by the butt of a rifle belonging to an officer of a military junta that seized power in Chile. A young journalist then, he was covering the unfolding events in that country, and, inexperienced that he was, he considered it his journalistic prerogative and duty to confront an officer who took away his camera, tore out the negative, and smashed it against the bloodied pavement. Later years of covering conflicts around the world had taught him that one does not confront men wielding power. One documents their actions, meticulously, and publicizes them to as wide an audience as possible.

"Umm, the last one," replied the researcher, her eyes scanning several white sheets of paper. The paper felt awkward in her hand, unnatural for someone whose entire personal and professional life revolved around a smartphone, or a tablet computer. She continued when no further inquiries were made, "The family spent the next eight years moving places, never settling in one permanently. For young Damian the forced exile was the catalyst for his later activism."

"What do you base this on?" the editor interjected. He liked to keep his staff on edge, especially the interns, frequently reminding them about the importance of not taking guesses, or making assumptions, and thus perpetuating rumors and gossip — all those things that ran rampant in cyberspace, but did not qualify for consideration by a respectable news outlet. He subscribed to the old, and disappearing, school of journalism that distinguished between facts and opinion.

The researcher replied confidently, while waiving the sheets of paper in her hand, "Taken verbatim from Damian Allende's personal blog; according to his own words, from an interview he gave awhile back, when visiting the city of his birth." She quoted, "Living in different countries, among different cultures, had allowed me to watch all the familiar themes from a different perspective. It made me realize that a different world was possible. When we returned to Argentina, and found out that the junta *disappeared* my aunts and uncles, I knew that a day would come when those responsible would be made to pay for their crimes."

One of the members of the board said, "A clear case of personal vendetta." He was a man responsible for the influx of funds necessary to operate the online news portal, but not well versed on the inner workings of journalism.

The researcher exchanged glances with the editor, in the latter's eyes a sign to go on.

The young woman continued in a voice gradually turning impassioned, and betraying a level of sympathy for the subject, "In pursuit of the truth behind the abduction of his family members, Damian Allende taught himself the computer skills necessary to break into government and military databanks, and though he was not successful in uncovering the fate of his relations, he learned a valuable lesson. He found that governments, whether tyrannical impostors, or those chosen in free and democratic elections, are prone to excessive secrecy. He came to realize that some of this secrecy is often justified in being kept out of the public's eyes for the sake of the broadly, if seldom clearly defined, reasons of national security, while much of it serves no other purpose than to shield the excesses committed by those in power. In later years, as a freelance journalist, Allende was instrumental in the formation of the first truly independent news organization in his country. From there on it was only a step to funding several media transparency organizations and government watchdogs, culminating with the online court that's on everybody's lips these days."

"Sounds oddly familiar." The comment came from the same board member.

His words were seconded by another, "I say! It sounds like something we heard from the anonymous founders of the whistleblower portal."

Another added what chilled the others to the bone, "Which also happens to be the source of the leaked classified documents we received, and published on an exclusive basis."

The editor-in-chief found his audience sufficiently engaged to come to the point that prompted him to convene the meeting. He sent his researcher a silent signal, and when the woman closed the door behind her, he said, "Ladies and gentlemen, our organization finds itself in a precarious position. I think we all understand the implications of a decision made in this very room, some years back, when we agreed to publish the first batch of classified files that were leaked to the whistleblower portal. We researched the facts contained in the files, and ran extensive editorials around them, turning diplomatic, military, or intelligence jargon into stories our readers understood and cared about. We determined then, and it holds true to this day, that it was in the public interest to make available the documents that our own, as well as other governments, would rather keep locked up in deep vaults, away from public scrutiny. We've done nothing to reproach ourselves with; we went above and beyond journalistic principles of objectivity, while trying to accommodate the government's requests to withhold some information from publication, namely that, which could endanger the lives of our spies and military personnel serving abroad. Some of our readers called it censorship. Nonetheless, even they appreciated that we published the material at all, given the pressure not to. Let me reiterate — it was the right decision. Unfortunately, it brought us to the conundrum that we face today. Unbeknownst to us the whistleblower portal that has been our source of the classified documents, appears to be tied to Damian Allende's online trials. If we are to believe Allende, millions of *jurors* from around the world took part in casting judgment in the cases of individuals, and corporations, that were charged by the founder of the trials with various, apparent misdeeds supported and documented by the leaked files. This resulted in hundreds of guilty convictions of public officials, from corrupt small town cops, to prime ministers and presidents. Unfortunately, the crowdsourcing venture, while undoubtedly interesting in its novelty, and from many different perspectives, be it journalistic, political, sociological, or psychological, has taken an ugly turn. Following the results of last year's trial, a man was lynched by a mob in a small village in Colombia, apparently in response to having killed many of their relatives in a death-squad raid some years back. A week ago two men convicted in this year's trial were murdered in an apparent act of vengeance, or skewed sense of justice. Their killers left notes around the bodies, claiming to have been prompted to conduct the assassinations in response to the results of the online trials. One of the victims was a United States Senator, who pushed for legislation that allowed the sales of arms to an allied Middle Eastern dictatorship that used the weapons to quench the popular uprising during the Arab Spring. More importantly, perhaps, he was also his party's candidate for the U.S. President. The second victim was a Londoner, a British 'merchant of death' — an arms dealer who helped facilitate the sale of weapons. Again, what is even more important, he made significant financial contributions to the Senator's campaign for presidency. Political implications of their machinations aside, we come to the inevitable question: Are we, the primary media outlet that published the classified documents that supported the charges brought against the accused, are we responsible for the outcome? Such voices have been raised, and at the highest levels, and we must respond to them."

After a period of silence that followed the words, one of the members of the board suggested pragmatically, "Our readership, traditional and online, has skyrocketed since we began the publication of the leaked documents."

The editor-in-chief was not surprised by such oversimplification. He said, "The allegations leveled against us go beyond readership and revenue."

"Everything we do comes down to it, though."

"As long as it's done without jeopardizing our integrity, which is responsible for a loyal readership base."

Another board member asked, "The authenticity of the leaked documents is beyond question, is it not?"

"Naturally."

"And your own policy to limit opinion, and focus on cold facts, has been observed?"

"I stand by it. We pride ourselves on having a progressive readership base, for whom we deliver the news. We are not the newsmakers. We report the facts, sometimes fortified with context and expert evaluation. That's not the issue."

"What is, then?"

"After the killings we've been accused of not publishing alternative documentation in support of the actions convicted in Allende's trials."

"Are we their legal council?"

"Nonetheless, it's been construed as subjective reporting."

"All reporting is subjective, if only by the constraints imposed by space limitations in print, or bandwidth of the online version."

The editor did not reply immediately, his eyes scanning the faces of the board members. *They are right*, he thought to himself. Nevertheless he wanted firm commitment from them, for what he was about to propose required unanimity when the proverbial shit would hit the fan.

"We cannot escape the inevitable accusation of bias, perhaps even of collusion," he said.

The members of the board exchanged glances. Their faces lacking expression, they apparently were of the same opinion, expressed by one of them, "It is the fate of all independent media. Slander of bias is the first sign that we are doing a good job. It's an unmistakable sign that we are getting under the skin, that we are chipping away the pillars of the status-quo, that we are not sleeping with the establishment. This is what our readers expect of us."

That's some statement from a corporate executive, thought the editor. Out loud he said, "It is all true, yet we must be prepared for what is coming our way, and trust me when I say it, for I have been in this business long enough to know the interaction between the powers that be and the news media. We are going to have to answer for what we have published. We've released classified government documents that were used to justify the killing of a member of a U.S. senator, and it makes no difference whether he sat on the committee that finances and arms murderous regimes, or whether he sang in a church choir."

"We did what the news media should, but what most refuse to do. We did our job, which is not dictated by the politicians and corporate interests, but by an obligation to serve our audience. They are the only ones we owe our existence, and thus our allegiance, to." The words came from one of the investigative reporters, a young and still idealistic man who hoped to be handed the biggest case of his career.

"Philosophical implications aside, we must look at the facts. And the facts suggest that the document-leaking portal and the online court are somehow related," said the editor-in-chief.

"What if they were?" asked a board member.

"Damian Allende founded his online court precisely because of the failures of the justice system to deal with what he calls institutionalized crimes," chimed in the chief investigative journalist.

The editor-in-chief picked up on the last statement. He said, "Which may explain why we are being attacked for fuelling the flames of the mobs. Naturally, we've put our technical department on the job to find out whether a connection exists between the whistleblower portal and Damian Allende. So far they were unable to make the connection, other than to confirm the use by Allende of the documents stored on the document-leaking portal. This means nothing, of course, for anyone can access these documents, whether a journalist, or a reactionary, and distribute them around. What is at stake here is not the fundamental freedom of speech, but the very real possibility of complicity with murder. We must tread carefully. If those two portals are somehow connected, and used to justify lynching, then we must distance ourselves from their agenda, yet find a way to continue to serve our readers and the public at large."

"What do you propose?" asked a member of the board, the others' faces seconding the question.

"First and foremost — we must determine whether there exists a connection between the two portals."

A board member sneered, and said, "We've already tried it." He shot a cold look to the investigative journalists.

"The investigation was inconclusive, but that is not surprising," the editor-in-chief defended his journalists. "Our source at the whistleblower portal, who provides us with the early scoop, wished to remain anonymous, which is understandable given the rush for his head. The founder, or the founders, of the portal, did a remarkable job at covering their tracks. They had every reason to — their predecessor, the eponymous document-leaking service, was attacked and shut down by authorities, its founder persecuted. The current whistleblower portal is regularly attacked by intelligence services, some of which originate in countries of very questionable judicial values, where law and order are terms known only from imported television shows. Nonetheless, we must determine whether the connection exists."

"If we don't? Do you suggest we stop publishing the material obtained by the whistleblower portal?"

"It is newsworthy in itself, and as such publishing it is our mandate."

"And if such a connection exists?"

"We are subject to British law. We cannot aid murder."

"No, we cannot; that privilege is reserved for the lawmakers," murmured the elder of the investigative journalists.

His younger colleague could not help a chuckle.

A board member responsible for the flow of funds for the online edition disregarded the irony. He said, "Yet we must find a way to continue reporting on these stories. Our coffers depend on the material from the whistleblowers. It brings more audiences than a Royal wedding."

Other board members giggled. They had a good reason to rejoice, for they filled the niche, a huge gap really, left by the corporate media, by providing the public with the news and material no one else wanted to touch. They proved that a lot of people were keenly interested in issues vital to their country and the world at large, and not merely fixated on celebrity gossip.

"What do you propose?" someone asked.

The editor-in-chief replied in one breath, "To conduct an investigation in such a way so as not to jeopardize our source."

"What do you need?"

"I'd like a dedicated fund to conduct a deep, yet discreet, investigation, one that cannot be done through the document-leaking portal, one that can only be achieved by getting close to Damian Allende."

Everyone in the room exchanged glances. One of the board members expressed what was on everyone's mind, "Well, then, go ahead. Send your best investigating journalists. Our coffers and our readers will be better served if we can continue to publish the leaked material. Do you have such a journalist on staff, someone who can deliver the goods?"

The backs of the two investigative journalists seated at the table straightened. Each wanted to be taller, more visible.

"I do," said the editor. "I have the only person who can get close to this most wanted and most elusive man in the world."

2

"This man must be stopped," said the Secretary of State. Her bloodshot eyes cast furious looks about the conference room. Her entourage, consisting of aides, advisors, secretaries, and a whole slew of lick-ass groupies, nodded obediently. Standing behind their boss they looked down on the other big shots who occupied the seats around the elongated table, and who were surrounded by their own yes-men.

"Damian Allende is a foreign national," reminded the Attorney General.

"Who has publicly stated that he does not intend to ever set foot on American soil," added the Director of the Federal Bureau of Investigation, in his voice a trace of regret of a crucifier who missed the chance to nail his victim to the cross.

The State Secretary would not have it. "He has organized a forum for murderers who target our military personnel, diplomats, and public servants, and you suggest that we ought to send him an invitation?"

"I'm afraid it makes no difference where he resides. The classified documents he used to target our people were not hosted by his servers. We'd have a better shot at dealing with the owners of the whistleblower portal, against whom we could invoke the Espionage Act for distributing our classified government files. It's quite different with Allende, whose service is but an engine for exchange of opinions."

"Opinions that demand blood of our civil servants!"

"He is smart enough to avoid such language, and it is allowing him to win the PR battle."

The highest-ranking woman in the administration pushed back in her executive chair. She was not surprised by the answer, after all similar questions raised about the whistleblower portal and its anonymous founders, who hosted and distributed classified government documents, had yielded no results either. She merely acted a rehearsed part when she said, "This meeting was not convened to discuss what cannot be done, but how to end the charade. She turned to face the huge monitor that hung on the wall behind her. She then nodded to one of her assistants, who pointed and clicked a small remote control unit. Images appeared on the screen. The Secretary remarked each one, as they changed. "Take a good look at these photographs. These are faces of our civil servants who were subjected to the mock online trials. More than half were found guilty. Guilty. Guilty. Guilty. Now, look at this. This is the body of Senator Warmaker, who was found guilty by the mob, and then gunned down. The cheering mob called it justice."

A long and eerie silence followed her words. The atmosphere in the room was charged, quiet before the storm, with the expectation that something was about to happen. No one said anything, for everything had been said in the days following the assassination, and yet no conclusions were raised.

At last a voice could be heard. It was quiet, barely above a whisper, a voice so unbecoming of a military general who dropped the uniform to serve as director of the Central Intelligence Agency.

"The line between justice and revenge is very thin."

Suddenly everyone in the room understood that whatever initiative would be raised today, would come from him.

The Secretary of State shot him a long gaze, and turned to the Attorney General, in her question the last effort to explore legal options. "Can we count on our international partners?"

"Appropriate requests were dispatched, but the outlook is not promising. I'm afraid other jurisdictions face the same conundrum that ties our hands."

A quiet anticipation followed his words. It was broken by one of the impatient young aides, who wanted to appear tech savvy.

"We could shut down Allende's website."

"We'd tried it with the whistleblower portal," chimed in someone from the Attorney General's troupe. "In effect, almost overnight, thousands of clones were set up on servers around the world. Taking down any of them led to further multiplication."

The woman nodded, as though appreciating the answer.

She said, "What it boils down to is that this, the most powerful nation on the face of the Earth, is losing the PR battle, as the Attorney General mentioned, to a single self-proclaimed judge of morality, while our public servants are sitting on death row." She flicked her fingers and her assistant immediately clicked on the remote. The presentation started with the screenshot of the now familiar main page of Damian Allende's portal, followed by mug shots of various members of the administration, from the Secretary of Defense, to the President of the United States. Each photograph was hyperlinked to files stored on the whistleblower portal, and bearing the signatures of the officials shown on screen. It was the same presentation used by Damian Allende, only the sound was muted.

The woman said in a grave voice, "This is not only a PR matter. It goes further than simple embarrassment of having to display our dirty secrets and not be able to do anything about it. These faces," she pointed to the screen, "are faces of the next candidates for assassination. All of us, as we sit at this table, and some who cannot be here today, will be subjected to Allende's next kangaroo court. Are you still insisting that we have no recourse?" She cast cold looks around the table.

Before anyone could reply, and as though on a signal, a mobile phone rang in the room. One of the Defense Secretary's aides answered it; he listened for a while, his face suddenly turning pale. He ended the call, approached his boss, and leaned as though to convey a message meant only for his ears, but delivered in a voice that everyone could hear. "Mister Secretary, the chairman of the Hegemonton Corporation was shot dead at the footsteps to his headquarters."

Short-lived consternation was followed by commotion and enlivened exchanges among the entourages whose smartphones suddenly became abuzz. The head of one of the largest military contractors was assassinated. With Hegemonton being one of the major contributors to the late senator's presidential campaign, it became evident that the chairman's murder was not a coincidence. Any doubts were removed by a reminder that Hegemonton appeared on Damian Allende's list of corporations who were charged with actions contrary to the interests of society.

The aides and assistants blabbed in disarray. Only their bosses remained seemingly unmoved; they said nothing, but their eyes expressed what could not be dressed in words. They exchanged glances with each other, and each directed their staff to leave the conference room. The call could not have come at a more opportune moment to ensure that these blabbermouths would have a correct recollection of the meeting should their testimony ever become required.

"It highlights the urgency of our plight," the Secretary of State said after the staff left the room.

The others said nothing. They listened, after all the woman was the highest official in the room, and she had a plan.

She hissed through her teeth. "I repeat — something must be done about Damian Allende."

"We don't know that it is Allende's doing," said the Director of the FBI. His voice offered no contradiction, his only intention was to receive clarification of the woman's intentions.

"Oh, shut up, Bill!" The Attorney General exploded. "I too am tired of our inability to prevent this man from making us look like fools. Sadly, though, there's nothing you or I can do to stop him."

"But there is someone among us who can do something." The Defense Secretary made the encouraging remark.

All eyes turned to the man of the quiet voice, the newly appointed Director of the Central Intelligence Agency.

The Secretary of State asked, "Can you do something?"

"I can do something. I can turn the situation to our advantage, but it will require unanimous approval of all who are gathered here."

He described his plan.

A long silence that followed his words was broken by the only woman in the room. She said, "I admit these are rather drastic and bold measures, but given the economic and political crisis in our country, and around the world, only boldness can be the guarantor of stability and unity that are so needed. Does everyone agree?"

All eyes turned to the Director of the FBI — the only one among the conspirators, whose position was not yet clear. His joining the plan was necessary for the plan's success on the domestic level.

The Director of the Federal Bureau of Investigation nodded his head.

All others breathed with relief.

The Secretary of State looked directly into the eyes of the men who were gathered at the table, from one to the next.
She summarized the meeting in an assertive tone, "What we have discussed today may be read as cruel, perhaps even treacherous, but make no mistake — it is necessary, and I have no doubt that history will show that we did it for our great country. May God bless America."

3

Reykjavik, Iceland.

Damian Allende ended the connection in his Internet-based communication suite. He has been a busy man in the months since the online trial, and in the past week in particular. Calls for interviews with the media were coming day in and day out. He had answered many, from the corporate television networks, to online activist portals. He was the most sought-after man on Earth, and in the binary lanes of the Internet, but he did not like the attention he was receiving. Personal exposure was never his intention when he set out to launch his project. He wanted to highlight the injustices committed by those who had broken the public trust. They were the ones who should be answering questions, not him, but the reaction of the media was quite the opposite. Damian was angry, even though he was not surprised. The reaction of the media — jumping on the sensational and the gory, while omitting the crux of the story — was what prompted him to launch his online trials in the first place. Had the media done their job, had they kept an eye on the public servants, and the corporations that influenced them, had they provided a window into the workings of the governments, then services such as document-leaking portal, would not be necessary, because the public would have all the facts necessary to draw conclusions and demand accountability. This went for the, so-called — democratic states, as well as for the ones ruled by tyrants, nearly all of whom were, in one way or another, propped up by the democratic, the enlightened, the developed, the civilized, the advanced countries, whose citizens would not permit the excesses had they had all the facts of the dealings of their elected officials. The calls that he was receiving now were proof that the media had lost all sense of that public service. It was not just that they concentrated on the sensational alone, but that they sought it in all the wrong places. All the explosive news they could ever want was within their reach all along — within the corridors of power. Yet instead of pursuing that line, they chose to display their contempt for the public by going after him, worse — by turning his work into mental junkfood, by concentrating on the effects, instead of the causes of his activism. Still, Damian did not despair. Having long ago lost all hope in the mass media, he believed that the audience was not as gullible as the media bosses thought them to be — the number of people who participated in his project was proof enough that he was right. The single-track interviews that he gave in the past two months, portraying him as some sort of a vengeful monster, a traitor, or even a terrorist, had failed at their attempt to shoot the messenger. They made people curious. And people flocked to his portal en masse.

Damian stood up from his makeshift desk and approached the window. He looked down to the copse of trees that marked the boundary of his new property. He hardly had the time to get to know the house so generously provided by his supporters. So many times he looked out the window, so many times he was tempted to go out, to smell the ocean breeze, the smell of rotting leaves, to touch the grass, to feel the dew on his skin — all that which most people considered the real life — and day after day he remained at the computer, though not entirely removed from life, the lives of others, the countless people to whom he dedicated his talent and his time. The only signs that life existed outside of his project, were the changing leaves outside his window, and even then he only realized the passage of time when the trees became a sea of gold. He was like an author working on a book, for whom all outside stimuli become subdued, and the book becomes everything, the only lifeline. Damian's lifeline was his project. His mind never rested, constantly working out the many aspects of the online trials, even in his sleep. His friends used to joke that it was his conscience that kept him awake at night. It was not, he would reply, it was the collective conscience of all those people for whom his portal became the only vessel to express their anger and frustration. It was the conscience of the untold millions who demanded justice, who awaited resolution to fresh and old wounds, the pain, and the suffering caused by greed, corruption, and lies — all that which makes the foundation of any public office, and goes unchecked. Two years had passed since he set out to build his project. It was the brainchild of anger and frustration witnessed during Damian's years in exile, a decision reconfirmed by the whistleblowers' portal failure to affect change. Hundreds of thousands of classified documents were leaked, all documenting disregard for justice and the rule of law, files pointing at those who made decisions and policies that caused harm, pain, and suffering, and yet not one of those guilty were made to pay, not one policy had changed, and not one journalist asked — When will this end? This was when Damian stepped in, and said — It stops now. He founded his online portal to raise awareness, and to give voice to the voiceless, to those who were always at the receiving end of all the erroneous or downright evil policies, but who hardly ever were asked if they mind being tramped upon. He struck a chord with the masses from day one. His first online trial, intended as a poll of public opinion, was attended by more people than he ever expected, so much so that his servers crashed under the heavy weight of the traffic. This year he was better prepared, and the funding drive has allowed him to purchase additional servers and bandwidth to turn his project into a truly Global Court of Justice. Participation exceeded all expectations. People flocked to his portal from all corners of the Earth, from countries rich, and poor, from countries of established democratic principles, and from those suffering under the boot of tyrants. Such was the hunger for justice and fairness that were in chronically short supply.

The online court proved a success. Damian Allende had every reason to be proud of himself. Yet his eyes were far from smiling this morning. While he had achieved what he set out to — he had opened the eyes of millions, and filled the hearts of millions more with hope — Damian was not a happy man. He had no private life to speak of, and while many could lay such claims, for Damian it was a source of deepening and unrelenting heartache. The more visible was his public persona, with his face appearing in more newspapers, shown on more television screens, and whispered in reverence, or shouted with anger from more and more radio stations, the more he longed for something else. Something was missing from his life: His name was not on the lips of the one person for whom he cared the most.

Damian returned to his desk, where next to the laptop computer stood a framed photographed, that of a young woman caught in a natural, unstudied pose. It was a candid photo of his only daughter, the one person in his life whom he loved with all his heart, and whom he had not seen in a very long time. Damian did not suffer the affliction of so many busy parents, too busy with their work to spend time with their children. Far from it — Damian would have given up plenty for a minute with his girl, alas the circumstances were such that it was not up to him. He picked up the photograph, and was struck by a thought: Why was it not up to him? He approached the window, with the photograph in his hand, and studied his daughter's image in natural light. His thumb caressed the hair that was the color of drying summer hay, and his eyes locked with the pearly-blue eyes. It was not enough, no longer enough. He gazed outside, where the trees shed their leaves, and where he witnessed the aging of the Earth. Damian straightened his back — slightly hunched from the countless hours in front of the keyboard — and suddenly a smile graced his slim lips, the first smiles in a long time. He realized that he did not want to die like those leaves — pretty and admired by strangers, but unseen by the close ones — and it occurred to him that what was important to the millions around the world, for whom he devoted his life, must not be exclusive of his own needs and desires.

Damian made up his mind, and returned to his desk. He sat down in front of his laptop computer, and pointed the cursor to the keypad of the VoIP communication suite, where tens of new messages had accumulated in the short amount of time that he was away, and, instead of reading them, as was his custom, he started to key in a number for a mobile phone. He was making a phone call, the most difficult call in years, one that he hoped would help make amends with his daughter.

4

The editor-in-chief opened without much ado, "The board has approved funds for a top-priority, and a very sensitive investigation."

Sparks in the woman's eyes resembled reflections of the sun in an inkpot. She knew that something major was brewing in the office, where the buzz could not be contained. To be invited to the boss's office at a time such as this meant that she was factored in to whatever was taking place. From the way the editor stood up to shut the door behind her she knew that it would be something extra special. She realized it was her chance to broaden her scope of assignments, and she was determined to get this one no matter what.

The editor added, " I immediately thought of you."

She would have gloated six months ago. Today she only nodded her head. Having started two years ago as an intern, she quickly made her mark, became noticed, and was assigned her own desk. Granted — the local events scene was not much on a grander scheme of things, but given that it was published in the world's second most popular news portal, it was not a mean feat either. She was given free reign over a range of topics and took full advantage of it, without raising jealousy among senior editors who scoffed at the seemingly insignificant role the local news played in a news portal that was regularly read by visitors from around the world. With practically no oversight, and no one to set guidelines, she was left to her own. And she let it all out — she poured out her soul, without pretensions and inhibitions. Her efforts were noticed and appreciated by the guests whom she interviewed, and by readers. In short time the local events attracted a global audience. It did not matter that she concentrated on goings on around town, because the town was London, and the news portal was the second most visited on the World Wide Web. Her guests were icons from the lively arts community, often peppered with politicians eager to rejuvenate their image. The local events scene was read in London and Wisconsin, in Brisbane and Jaipur, yet the popularity never hit her on the head. She remained a humble, if ever inquisitive a journalist, though never of the shock variety. She had the ability to make her guests comfortable and open as only friends can. She became sought after, she built a devoted audience, and became, at last, treated to the highest professional honor — that of espousing jealousy among her colleagues. Yet, she was not satisfied. She wanted more. She wanted challenge. She wanted to go out there, to fight for a story instead having it land on her lap, as it had become of late when celebrities began to call to be interviewed be her. She was too smart to be satisfied when her vanity was tickled. She eagerly awaited new opportunities, as she once awaited a chance to leap from internship to editorial. It had finally come. She recognized it in the editor's voice. A special assignment was in the offing. And she was ready for it.

The editor invited her to sit down, but she remained standing, the energy keeping her on her toes — it was the only sign of her excited anticipation.

"You have a keen ear for the current affairs," the editor went on.

"I like to keep it in the context of larger issues," she replied eagerly. "More transcendental, all encompassing, and above all — human."

"Quite."

"What is current time but a fleeting moment, eh?"

"Right you are. Nonetheless. We're a news organization, which, by definition, sets us firmly afoot in the present. Timely, accurate, and honest reporting as our trademark. Our readers appreciate it."

The editor never took such a roundabout way to come to the point, and it made her the more hungry for the story, for it meant that it would not be an easy task.

The editor continued, satisfied in having peaked his reporter's interest. "Being true to ourselves and to our readers means that we cannot publish just about any story that builds at the tips of our reporter's tongues. We don't do that sort of thing, which is what sets us apart from many of the outlets out there, in the Internet age. We don't allow ourselves to be swept by the overwhelming, if fleeting — as you put it — euphoria of the moment. Our facts are always verified, and thoroughly researched. Of course, the nature of the business is such that in order to provide timely coverage we must find ways to streamline this process. Sources that proved reliable and trustworthy are sometimes, and in the interest of expediency, given preferential treatment, sort of a blank check. This has recently happened when we were faced with the biggest story of the day, a week, a year, perhaps even a decade. We reported it timely, accurately, and honestly. You are, of course, aware of what I am referring to."

She was aware, or at least she suspected what it was about, her suddenly pale face the confirmation.

The editor continued, "Our uncompromising professionalism was rewarded when we were one of a handful of news media organizations selected by the document leaking website, the whistleblower portal, to view and publish some of the most sensitive documents to ever see the light of day. It has worked well for us, for our readers, and for the public at large for a number of years now. Our partnership with the whistleblower portal has changed everything in the way news is being obtained and reported. It's a win-win situation for all, consumers and providers, even for the governments who had allowed themselves to be swept by unwarranted secrecy. Recently, however, a shadow has been cast over our partnership. I am of course talking about the whistleblower portal and the talk of the day, the online court. We've all watched the proceedings, many of us agreed with the verdicts. Yet, the outcome, the killings in the name of justice, or rather — WikiJustice — as they refer to it now, has gone too far. I'm not suggesting that the people who were killed did or did not deserve to be punished for their proven crimes, and I use this word carefully for they were proven guilty by the leaked documents. Unfortunately, justice was served wrongly, and, however unwittingly, we are in part to blame for it, for we reported both — on the leaked documents and on the results of the online poll's outcome. Then people died—"

"I don't see how it should have anything to do with us." The words poured out through her dry lips; she said it only for the sake of opening her mouth for she was afraid that her teeth would start to chatter.

"It doesn't, unless..." The editor-in-chief looked into her yes, and watched her face very closely. "Unless there exists a connection between our partner — the whistleblower portal — and the online court, and the killings."

This time she blushed, a deep crimson flush covered her face, poured down her slender neck and dripped into the cleavage.

Thy editor pressed while the iron was hot, "See, we don't know who stands behind the document-leaking portal, though we suspect that it's a cooperative effort of various journalists, and activists. Who they were was never important, as long as the documents they acquired were genuine. They were, and they continue to be genuine, and the issue is not about the documents per se. It's about our association with the whistleblower site, and whether or not, it is a front for WikiJustice, and by extension to the lynching." He ended with his eyes set firmly on her face.

She said nothing. It became clear that she was not picked for the job for her skills. It pained her, and more than she wanted to admit even before herself. Asking questions, volunteering answers, or in any way engaging her boss on the subject would amount to admitting that she was not fit for the job as a journalist, that she accepted that she was chosen for it for an altogether different reason. She still wanted the assignment, perhaps now more than ever, if only to prove that she was worthy of the most important story of the decade, and not just because of her personal connection. She was a good journalist. She believed herself to be, and her audience and guests agreed. She could do it. She would, despite being personally involved, as despite her heart trembling at the prospect of meeting with the man who was at the center of the assignment.

She waited for the editor to spell out the request. It was all she could do to show him that she was first and foremost a journalist in this affair.

He said at last, "I want you, Amanda, to establish, or disprove the connection. I want you to go out there, to talk to your father, and find out whether he, Damian Allende, has anything to do with the whistleblower portal, and the killings."

5

"You're flying out tomorrow?" the man asked with surprise in his voice, and alertness in his eyes. His left brow arched like a rainbow, the colorful effect was the result of the flickering candlelight reflecting from the wineglass.

"I'm sorry, Andrew." Amanda said absentmindedly, as though only her body was still present at the table. She suggested the restaurant, feeling guilty for having to leave so abruptly, without a prior warning. Although she was not flying before the next day, her mind has already departed.

"Tomorrow is the day!" he said with well feigned reproach, his mind already probing possible reasons for her sudden decision.

Something in his voice struck a chord. The feeling of guilt returned, multiplied. Her drifting eyes focused on his face, glazed over his auburn hair, as though stroking it. She knew how much he was looking forward to this weekend. She was too, by extension; least of all for the chance for the two of them to spend this time together, after a period of hectic job deadlines that kept them apart. She reached over the table, where her fingers embraced his hand, and gently caressed it.

"Something's come up at work, and I have to go," she said, and her words pricked up his ears.

He probed for further details, "A story? But you do local events. Stories come to you."

"You know that I too have been looking forward to this weekend."

She really did. While many girlfriends would attend the hackers' convention only to appease their boyfriends, Amanda had added her name to the list of attendees for two reasons: personal, and professional — and not necessarily in that order. Her professional curiosity drew her to the parallel sub-conference dedicated to technologies and techniques developed to circumvent the existing news-publishing model, whereas her personal reasons were split between the chance to spend the weekend with Andrew, and to attend the video conference with the key speaker — her estranged father, Damian Allende — the much-celebrated journalist, whose innovative work has revolutionized the industry.

"It's *the* day." Andrew feigned hurt feelings, though his voice lacked persuasion. "It's the quintessence of months of solitary work. Getting together, exchanging ideas, networking, and putting faces to nicknames you only know from chatrooms — it's the equivalent to the Oscars, but better, without all the weirdos."

"We'll go together to the next one, in Berlin. We'll fly to Vegas, too. I promise. This, however, I can't help. I must take the assignment. It's im— " She checked herself. She did not want to suggest that her work was more important. "It's a big story. I want to take it. I need to."

Andrew sighed, but said nothing. How he hated himself for having to play this double game. He raised his wineglass and sipped slowly, to cover his eyes, lest they reveal his thoughts. Continuing to turn the glass in his hand, he said, "Of course, my darling. I'm sorry I came at you so harshly. It's just that your announcement took me by surprise. We've been apart so much lately. You, with you exploding career, and I, with the new bank infrastructure."

She smiled with her sad eyes. In the past weeks they have been spending more time apart than together. She appreciated him mentioning his work as the culprit, since it was mostly hers that was responsible. The job was taking over her life, claiming exclusivity. Not only has her column grown from month to month, encompassing an ever increasing number of subjects, but she had recently signed on to host a series of podcasts, and videocasts. For the past several weeks she has been recording shows for the upcoming launch. It was a new and satisfying adventure, but it left little time for private life. To be true, she hardly noticed that her personal life had shrunk to the smallest denominator — the weekly, or twice-weekly, at most, dinners with Andrew. She blamed mostly herself, though Andrew was busy, too. His bank has been upgrading its infrastructure, whatever that meant, requiring Andrew to work long days, nights, even weekends. The convention, planned and anticipated for weeks, was an opportunity for them to spend time together. Now they were going to lose even this rare break.

"You know that I love you," Amanda said.

"And I you," he reciprocated.

Their fingers embraced on the red table cloth.

"We're going to get through this, you'll see. Time flies. Christmas and New Year's will be here before we know it. We'll go away. Just the two of us, and the Alps."

"I look forward to that," he replied.

It was not really the missed convention that bothered him. He too was concerned about the shrinking amount of time they shared together. If it was up to him they would have moved in together already. Shared space would automatically afford them more time in each other's company. But Amanda was not ready for it. The short time they had known one another was an understandable reason, and Andrew did not press. Not very strongly, at any point, but he made several overtures toward the subject, and was turned down each time. They dated whenever their respectful schedules permitted. It had gone on for several months now. A man less assured of himself might not have been this patient, but Andrew had a good reason to wait, and, more to the point — he understood how important the personal space were for a woman whose work demanded so much public exposure. He did not want to bring her to the point where she would have to chose between work and the relationship. He knew how difficult a decision it would be, for he too had found himself in similar circumstances.

Five years her senior, Andrew was a good and understanding man by nature. Mature for his age, philosophical at heart, he was cast into a cold world that expected of him quantifiable results. He treaded carefully, and balanced well between the necessities of his work, and the desires of his heart. He did well until he met Amanda, when the world he thought he had in his grip suddenly trembled in its foundations. Andrew fell in love. It was not unheard of, of course, to fall for the target. It happened to more experienced agents, whom one would expect to be immune from the affairs of the heart, if only by virtue of knowing all the traps. He too should have known the dangers, but his youthful impressionism took precedence over training. His humanistic interests, which he carefully withheld from his employer (after all, everyone has the right to some privacy — as he justified to himself — if only privacy of thought, especially in a service that dissects all private life for reasons of security) helped him to retain his belief in the purity of soul in the face of less than morally justifiable actions that he was expected to perform in the line of duty. Andrew was an artist at heart, though job requirements forced him to keep his creative expression under lock. Some day, he was convinced of it, he would open the lock. Andrew loved to read, and he devoured classics of literature whenever he could steal the time. It was the literature that spoiled his mind — as his employer would argue, if found out. Andrew learned through the works of the great humanists that what his recruiters sold as an exciting life set on changing the world was not only folly, since he participated in prolonging the status quo, but that what he was doing was also plain wrong. Still, and philosophical that he was, Andrew came to realize that no profession was without its shady sides. Life and human condition sometimes placed one in situations that called for less than honorable or ethical undertaking, and nowhere was this truer than in the security services, with the obvious primacy belonging to the military. There was, however, one distinguishing aspect of the work of a clandestine agent that had allowed him to function and hold onto his senses in the world of institutional depravity: It was the deprived world, and the absolute conviction that no evil reaction can repair the effects of like action. To combat evil, the great writers taught him, one must arm its arsenal with the weapons of good. His paymaster had offered him a host of such weapons, with the general promise of spreading democracy being among the most potent. Andrew might have been an idealist, but he was not naïve, and he soon realized, as did many of his predecessors, that his vision of his role in the world differed quite dramatically from that which he was cast into by his employer. Though he joined the agency tempted by the promise of an exciting life — and what young man does not dream of becoming a spy — he gradually became disillusioned. He knew for some time now that his days in the employ of the agency were numbered. He was ready to part even before he received the commission to get close to the only daughter of Damian Allende. And then he fell in love with her.

Amanda's voice roused him from his daydream.

She said, "If we get tired of snow we'll just drive down to soak up some of that Mediterranean sun. And who knows," she added with a wink, "we may even grow tired of each other."

"That could not happen, I assure you. I miss you more every day. I can't bear the thought of us parting." Here, at least, he was telling the truth, and it showed in his eyes, was evident in his voice.

"We'll be together again, soon."

"Can I—" Andrew bit his tongue. *If only we could go together*, he finished in his thoughts. He could not say it, though. He could not contradict the lies that he already used to justify inviting her to the convention. In the end she agreed to join him without much ado. His bosses were pleased, because it meant that he might, at last, meet the man whose life he was sent to infiltrate. Even after Damian Allende announced that he would video-conference, the agency found it promising, for Andrew would be able to bring up the subject of Amanda's father, something she closely guarded thus far. Andrew awaited that day with impatience for two reasons: for the chance to meet, even if only via a video-link, the man whom he was beginning to admire, and for the 48 hours he would spend with the woman he loved. Now these plans lay in ruins.

"Can I contact you?" he asked.

"Of course, silly. I'm not a spy on a secret mission."

He froze momentarily.

"I'll have my mobile," she added.

Andrew forced a smile. Although her words were meant as a joke, they threw him off balance. They reminded him of his dual role. He hated himself for it. Having resolved some weeks ago to come clean, he seemed to delve deeper into the lies. He could not bring himself to explain his role. How could he say that he sought her friendship on false pretenses, and then fell in love? Yet it had to be done. He awaited just the right moment, gradually setting up the conditions for the big announcement. It had to be delivered thoughtfully and gently. He could not bear the prospect of losing her because of the true reasons that crossed their paths, or because of what he represented. He was better than his job pegged him. Now and then he mentioned the books he read; he talked about the effect they had on his mind, of the ideas they seeded in his head. He refrained from mentioning her father, having, officially, no prior knowledge of the relationship between them.

He waited for Amanda to mention it first — it would make it easier for him to come clean. But she never did. He found out through the agency about her assignment, a last minute decision made only this morning. He knew she was going to meet her father. He so wanted to join her, convinced that her father would understand. He felt that he had a lot in common with Damian Allende — enough to gain a sympathetic ear, and an ally in convincing the woman that he was honest. Alas this would have required yet another lie, and Andrew was through with lies.

6

There was a time when Amanda considered her father a role model. Though from a distance, she saw Damian Allende as the epitome of an independent journalist: a thorough researcher, uncompromising, honest, objective, and a precursor in the industry searching for its place in the digital world. She admired his boldness in embracing of new media. His contribution to the creation of online journals that rivaled established traditional publications was the work of a rebel breaking all the rules, going against the grain. She was proud of her father as only a fourteen year old girl could. Even now as she sat on the plane en route to see the father she had not seen in years, and after all that they, as a family, had been through, she thought of these times with a tinge of nostalgia. Those were the good times. And then things started to change, when, emboldened by his successes in revolutionizing of the industry, Damian set out to change the world. His new quest marked the beginning of his gradual distancing and isolation from the family. Damian was spending more and more time with organizations devoted to governmental transparency and accountability, in expense of time spent with his family.

Amanda cringed and pressed her forehead against the cold aircraft window as the memories of these times returned. To this day the years of Damian's crusade had a bad connotation in her mind, though objectively speaking — and Amanda was able to distance herself from her emotions to see it clearly — they proved the most successful years in her father's career, for they led to the creation of the online court, the most talked-about venture in citizen-activism in decades. Unlike the scores of his supporters, who saw only the end result, Amanda knew the heavy price Damian had paid to arrive at this point. She knew the sacrifices he made, and the pain it caused his wife and daughter. She knew it intimately for she was the recipient of Damian's ups and downs as his independent journalism gave way to ardent activism. Though at the time resentful, from the perspective of years she grew to understand that he had no choice. Faced with cold, hypocritical, and unwilling to change power structures, Damian had only two roads to take: retreat, or clash head on with the old world that he so wanted to change. He chose the latter. Years of work on his projects were marked by the loss of his wife, the distancing and virtual loss of contact with his daughter, and the ultimate success of his online justice project. No longer on speaking terms, blaming him for the death of her mother, Amanda followed her father's endeavors, whether she wanted to or not. Damian Allende's name became a household name after the first edition of his online court. It overshadowed the news of the whistleblower portal, without which his project would not have been possible. The last year, a year of the outcome of the poll taken among hundreds of thousands of citizens from around the world, was a time to reconnect with her father. Her old sentiments, the image of a lone rebel, returned on the wind of the overwhelming attacks launched by the corporate media. Amanda found herself feeling certain sympathy for Damian. Although she never forgave him for abandoning his wife and daughter, she was proud of his accomplishments. It was not enough to seek contact with him, nonetheless it allowed her to look at her father in a different light, and perhaps, in time, as she often thought, it might help her reestablish a connection.

Amanda looked down into the vast space between the aircraft and the black ocean underneath, and thought, "Could the distance between us be repaired?" Those years spent apart were in her young life as vast as the water beneath, stretching as far as the eye could see, its shores only visible in imagination. The image of the father she knew as a young girl was dominated by a man who abandoned her mother, and let her to die alone. For years she did not think she could forgive him. Yet over the last year a new picture began to pervade its way into her mind, set chiefly by the events associated with Damian's online court — that of a warrior for openness and accountability, and Amanda was yet again stricken by her father's dedication to his work, something she could not help but admire. She found similarities in herself. It was not just that she followed in his footsteps, and became a journalist, but that she was just as devoted to her work. She reflected on her relationship with Andrew and conceded that it did not go beyond the initial stages of dating solely because interest in work took precedence over her private life. She realized that she was her father's daughter, for better or for worse, and it did not alarm her at first when the news of the killings had reached her. Not for a moment did she believe them attributable to her father. She knew him well enough, despite the years of absence, for she now judged him through her own eyes, to know that he could not have done or advocated for the murders for the simple fact that such acts would have taken away from the greater achievement — the creation of his online court. It was the participation of such great number of people, from so many different places and backgrounds, that was the ultimate realization of Damian's dreams.

Amanda deplaned in Reykjavik disheveled and tired. Troubling thoughts tormented her throughout the flight and did not leave after touchdown. With her body tired, and her mind tense, she spent the taxi ride going over ways in which she would start the conversation. Regrets? Accusations? Pity? What was the point going over things that were done and over? She came here to do her job, not to feel sorry for herself, or to blame her father for having taken away her chance of having a happy family. What was done was done. No point regretting the past; one only regrets things one has not done. She did not want to look back at her life some day and think of the years she spent feeling sorry for herself. Amanda believed in going forward.

The house was not what she expected, not that she knew what to expect, having in her mind the image of the family apartment in Buenos Aires, and the picture of a vagabond man who left it and never settled down. She knew, of course, that Damian had recently moved to this North Atlantic island for the protection of the freedom of expression this small nation offered to journalists. She knew about the house donated by his supporters. But it was not the house she imagined her father in. A man who lived for years without a fixed address did not fit in a small, single-story structure with a white picket fence, surrounded by a wooded lot, and with an unobstructed, if distant view of the ocean.

7

"I did not think you'd come."

Damian's first words to his daughter, delivered face-to-face, after so many years, felt awkward to both of them. It reminded them of the call he placed to her the other day, out of the blue. It was short, with neither saying much, and ended with Damian inviting Amanda to his new home.

"How could I turn down the invitation to see the man the entire world would like to meet." She tried to sound humorous, her eyes pointing to the living room that was crammed with people. It turned out still more awkward. The smile vanished from her lips, and she looked into his eyes, the expression of pain in hers. She added quickly, to cover her unease, "I was appalled by how the media treated you. I don't know why, since it's so typical of them."

"As long as people see through their game — they are only giving me free publicity."

They were standing in the doorway, with people passing them on their way in or out of the house. One particularly large man required the entire entryway to pass, making it necessary for the two to move. It broke the spell that constrained them, albeit not entirely, which was evident by the embrace, delivered as though from a distance, their cheeks barely brushing.

In the end Damian could not let go; he pulled his daughter closer, and held her tightly in his arms. He said with her hands in his, "I'm sorry we won't be able to sit down to chat today, but, as you can see—" He nodded toward the living room. "I am so glad that you came, though. We have much to talk about—" He bit his tongue; it sounded wrong, as though he was trying to put pressure on her, whereas he meant to put the past behind them, and to concentrate on now. He added quickly, "I'd like to hear about your podcasts. It sounds so exciting."

She looked at him with puzzled eyes. How did he know about the podcasts? It was not yet announced, a company secret. It occurred to her that her father was not as removed from her life as she thought him to be, that he followed her progress as she did his. It made her feel vulnerable. The façade she was wearing was beginning to crumble. Suddenly she was just a little girl in her father's embrace. How she wanted to be close to him, right now!

Amanda said, "How can I help? May as well be useful."

"Think nothing of it. In fact I'm a little embarrassed for being treated as sort of celebrity. It is merely enough for me to wish 'Little table, cover thyself', and voilà — it is set."

"You deserve it. What you do is groundbreaking."

He looked deep into her eyes, searching for reasons that made her say it. Encouraged by what he found in them, he said, "Tomorrow we shall have all to ourselves. And I hope the day after tomorrow, and the day after that. Tonight you must forgive me. I owe myself to these folks. Without them much of what I accomplished would not be possible."

She saw the emotional strain on his face and it made her feel better and stronger, for it proved that her father was a human being underneath the very public and almost superhuman persona that she knew from his portrayal in the media. She breezed through the crowd without making eye contact, too drained to stop for a chat, or even to grab any of the hors d'œuvres that filled trays on the dining table. She emerged outside, in the large backyard flanked by trees. The air was damp and cold, and the quiet of the dark night was broken only by the rhythmic sound of distant waves washing the shore. Soon Amanda's mind joined the rhythm of the nature. She allowed herself to be swept away. Nothing existed but the sea, the moist earth at her feet, and the salty black veil over her head. Everything that occupied her mind, that kept it in a tight grip, was suddenly gone, and it felt as Schiller had said, that when one leaves everything behind, the only thing left is solitude. It was the solitude in which some find the mother of all anxieties, or the great healer and the source of strength. Amanda was a strong person by nature and conviction. Obstacles for her were nothing but temporary challenges to overcome — mere hurdles in a race of life; they were a sport.

Amanda did not know how long she was out for. She felt it in her bones, and she could tell by the expanse between the beach and the lights of the house, that she covered a fair distance. Yet, despite the physical fatigue, she felt stronger than when she arrived on the island. She emerged unscathed from what might have overwhelmed a weaker mind — the dreaded, and the anticipated meeting with her father. It told her that, whatever the reasons that separated them, not all was lost. They had another chance. They both were afraid to spoil by a wrong word, or gesture, but the important thing was that they both wanted it. They were ready to try it, to fight for it. They had to. They only had each other in the whole world.

Amanda returned to the house with regained inner peace. The crowd grew during the time she was away, threatening to burst the house in the seams, spilling into the front and back yards. She observed her father for a time. Surrounded by suits and casual slacks, he mingled in this mixed crowd with confidence, as though belonging to both. Amanda felt a certain closeness to him, feeling what he must have felt right now, ready to take on the world. They were truly alike, and the realization of it filled her with strength. She smiled, and went upstairs, to a guest bedroom where she found her suitcase. She put her head down on the pillow.

Amanda woke up to a clamor and laughter that penetrated that walls. It was a happy sound that pushed aside any dark thoughts that might have lingered at the back of her mind. She did not rush. She showered, slipped into fresh clothes, and thus refreshed she descended the staircase.

The ground floor was brightly lit. The party showed no signs of easing. The people lingered about, with appetizers and drinks in their hands. Amanda could not tell how many were squeezed into the house. *Apparently too many*, she thought as she observed that some took turns by walking out, and coming back when the chill of the night drove them in. She wandered about until she found herself in the kitchen, driven to it by the smells of the bake oven. She picked up a small plate, topped it with unknown fruits of the sea, and proceeded to observe the guests. As she had observed previously — it was a mixed crowd, where tailored suits rubbed elbows with tracksuits. Most were young, not much older than she was, with the top age matching her father's. Some had the unmistakable aura of computer programmers, others could not be mistaken for anyone but journalists, and then there were the career civil servants, with a few lawyers thrown in to spice it all up. As mixed as the crowd was everyone exuded a sense of belonging, the expensive suits and the crumpled up sweatshirts alike. In the middle of them all was Damian Allende, the one unifying element in this otherwise unlikely gathering. Amanda realized that with such a wide assortment of supporters her father was set to achieve whatever he set out for. He was a natural, able to multitask with everyone, whoever came up to him, speaking to each on an equal footing, giving each his time, answering and talking to with the same concentration and dedication.

Despite the open windows and the damp breeze pouring in from the sea, the house became overheated by the overall excitement and the sheer number of people. Amanda pushed on through and went outside for a breath of air. The night felt much warmer now, too warm for this time of year in this part of the world. The volcanoes, the hot geysers, and the effects of the Gulf Stream were a welcome surprise. She remained outside, eager to breathe in the fresh iodized air, so refreshing after the stifling London smog. Someone came by with a plate of snacks. She grabbed a small canapé, followed it with a glass of wine, and contemplated her next move when she spotted something in the darkness surrounding the trees that formed the perimeter of the property. The sensation was so extraordinary that the hand raising the snack froze in place before it reached the mouth. Out there, not more that twenty paces away, Amanda saw her father facing a young man. They exchanged some words that she could not hear, and began to walk away into the dark void. The unmistakably firm, spring-like gait of her father's companion made Amanda exclaim a sound of disbelief and bewilderment. The young man was her boyfriend, Andrew Walker, and he was disappearing with her father into the darkness of the barren island.

8

The young man introduced himself. "My name is Andrew Walker, and I flew across the ocean to warn you."

Damian Allende has heard it all before, which was why he did not turn the man down, despite being approached when he took a short break away from the crowd, to seek moment's solitude in the darkest corner of the backyard. He assumed it was one of the many well-wishers, often believers and perpetuators of conspiracy theories, who predicted that his efforts would draw punishment from the mighty and powerful whom he set his sights at. He continued to listen, finding certain humor in the stranger's dire predictions.

The young man went on. "I think the Company wants to assassinate you." Seeing as the announcement had no effect, he added, "I think they plan for me to do the wet job."

The words grabbed Damian's attention. With his eyes penetrating the darkness he tried to focus on the face that was within a striking distance. The patio lights cast shadows that highlighted the crease between the eyes, and on the square jaws. The eyes that seemed to shine their own light told him that it was no conspiracy theory, that it was the real deal. The man who called himself Andrew Walker slipped his hand under Damian's elbow, and lead him past the trees, into complete darkness. He followed, suddenly feeling devoid of his free will. They stopped abruptly and Damian looked up into the firmament of a cloudless sky. If he had to die now he wanted the stars to bear witness that he was dying with clear conscience. He tried to make the world a better place, and even if he did not succeed, he at least paved the way. Damian kept his chin up, refusing to look down at the killer — it was not the image he wanted to part the world with.

A time passed, yet nothing happened. A shot was not fired. A blade was not inserted into his ribcage. Damian's curiosity won. He concentrated his eyes on the dark shadow that stood between him and the house. He could no longer make out facial features, but saw the mist that rose with every breath. The frequency with which it rose told Damian that perhaps not all was lost.

The visitor confirmed Damian's conjectures.

"I won't do it."

A more recreant man would have, perhaps, seized the opportunity to flee, but Damian was used to receiving threats. He quickly recovered his senses.

He asked threateningly, "What do you want, then?"

"I had to tell you this, and then some."

Damian waited. He could now hear the fast breaths, and concluded that the man required encouragement.

He asked, "Are you new at... this sort of thing?"

"Yes— No! I mean, I have never before—" The man lost his train of thought, apparently overwhelmed by the disclosure. "However," he added, "I had to tell you this, so you'd know that if I don't do it, then someone else will."

"And this is why you came all the way here? To tell me to look out for someone who wants to kill me? Someone like you, who will emerge from the darkness, but will not bother with the introduction."

"Actually, I came for two reasons — to warn you, and to meet you."

"You certainly know how to make an entry... with a bang."

"I thought it best if there were no secrets between us. It wouldn't be a good start. I learned that the hard way."

"A start? Young man, if you wanted to intrigue me then you've succeeded."

"But now that I got this far I don't know how to proceed."

"Just shoot."

Andrew Walker appreciated the humor. His voice was visibly relaxed when he said, "I want to join you."

Damian did not reply immediately. His thoughts were dominated by surprise mixed with suspicion. Was this all a ruse? Surely the world's most powerful spy agency would not come up with such blatantly poor scheme to infiltrate his life and work.

The visitor sensed his doubts. He continued, "It's true. Or half of it, anyway. About a year ago, after your first online trial, I was ordered to keep an eye on you. I paid close attention to your work, at first as part of the assignment, and gradually out of rising interest. What I've learned turned into fascination. I won't exaggerate when I say that I admire your work. It was ingenious to combine the material available from the whistleblower portal with your online court. It literally opened the eyes of the world, mine including. All those leaked documents, ignored or downplayed by all who were mentioned in them, at last had to be confronted. This in turn, the universal vilification directed at you, was the admittance to all charges, and it made me question my orders. You see, among those mentioned in the leaked documents were some of my bosses. This was the last straw. When I had the proof in front of my eyes, when I learned what I have been a party to, I wanted out. I wrote a letter of resignation. Ultimately though, I did not send it. I couldn't, because It would've meant that I'd be away from... you... and..." Andrew stumbled.

Damian was moved by the impassioned speech but did not show it. He heard praise in so many ways, and in so many languages already, that he did not give in. He said coldly, without concern, "You know that distance is a relative term in the digital age. You can access the whistleblower portal from anywhere. You can take part in the online court wherever you are. You don't have to be physically close to me to participate in my work."

"It isn't that! I didn't hand in the resignation so as to remain close to you, but because I fell in love with your daughter."

Damian inhaled deeply. Used to taking on life with a grain of salt, he was not easily impressed. This Andrew Walker, however, had astonished him three times in the space of a quarter of an hour. It made Damian wary. He was not the sort of man who liked surprises. Surprises, in his vocabulary, were the result of recklessness. Damian Allende could not afford to be reckless. He learned it more than two decades ago that careful preparation and meticulous execution of a job were the best guarantors of a life with few, if any, surprises. Had he been better prepared and followed basic precautions instead giving in to emotions he would not have been caught hacking into the government servers. Without this record that lingered with him, his life would have been easier. He was careful ever since. Clear strategy, careful planning, and thorough implementation of laid out plans, led to his current successes. That he has allowed himself to be surprised by this young fellow told Damian to tread carefully.

He said, "I did not realize that you came with Amanda."

"I didn't. Amanda does not know that I'm here," Andrew replied emphatically. Upon consideration he added, "She doesn't know what I *really* do."

Damian exhaled a whistle. "You used her to get to me, then!"

"There's more. She doesn't know that I know about you. She never mentioned you, and, as she kept her mother's maiden name, I could not bring myself to inquire about you. I could not afford to break my cover."

His voice sounded sincere, and his words were passionate, even exalted. Damian could not tell whether the man was a good actor, or whether he was telling the truth.

"You speak of honesty. You say that you are in love with my daughter. Yet, you are lying to her."

"My whole life is a lie. My job is based on deception, it's the only way it can be done. Sometimes I don't even know what's real, and what isn't, anymore. I lied in order to get close to your daughter. When I realized my feelings for her it was too late to tell the truth."

"If the whistleblower portal taught us anything it is that the truth cannot be contained; it will leak out one way or another."

Andrew sighed. "How could I tell her in the same breath that I love her, but the only way to meet her was to spy on her father?"

Oh, how much he would like to see the young man's face! Was the tearful admission sincere?

"Tell me. Have you watched the last online court?"

Andrew was taken aback by the question. "Not all of it."

"No, I wouldn't expect it. It was one of the longest indictments in history. It took hours just to read out the names of the accused, two full days to read the charges laid out against them. Those were the most trying days in my life. To name some of the crimes committed was hard enough, to imagine them unbearable. Yet it was a learning experience, a good insight to human empathy. You see, I've been accused of running a witch-hunt, as though the outcome of the poll could be predicted. The results proved otherwise — many of the accused were let off the hook. Know why? It wasn't that evidence was not supportive of their crimes, but because they admitted their guilt, and repented before the poll took place."

Damian wished again that he could see the young man's face. However, what was not evident to the eye he could detect through other senses. The silence was the most telling.

"You will have to tell her, you know. It's the only way if you hope for any kind of future together."

"Of course," Andrew said at last, his voice stretched, faltering. "She deserves and must know the truth."

"Why, then, do I sense hesitation?"

"No hesitation. Amanda must know the truth if I am to stand a chance that she'll keep me. But, Amanda and I are only one part of the equation."

"Oh?"

"Just as Amy can't be expected to love a liar, I am not sure that I can accept that her father abets murder."

9

Damian Allende raised his eyebrows.

Andrew could not see the reaction. From the silence that followed he concluded that he hit the spot. He pressed on, "Your online trials have resulted in murders. Copycats from all over the world are promising to deliver justice, vigilante-style."

Damian suddenly felt cold. He suggested at the sound of the chatter of his own teeth, "Shall we take a turn around the meadow?"

They strode in the deep grass. The rhythmic sound of waves grew as they neared the sea. They came to a stop on a beach covered with large pebbles. It was brighter here, the harbor across the bay providing enough illumination to make out facial contours.

Damian picked up a pebble, and cast it into the ocean. He said, "So, you are blaming me for rekindling people's desire for justice."

"The desire for justice never wanes. It's the form of justice that worries me."

"Was it just when the paramilitary forces raided a village, and killed those banana farmers who refused to sell their land to transnational corporations?"

Andrew shot back, "Was it just when a mob lynched the commander of the unit that killed the farmers and burned the village?"

"The tone of your voice suggests that you'd rather they went after the president of the corporation that wanted the farmers' land."

Andrew sneered before replying. "Don't turn it into a farce."

"Is it a farce when millions of people have access to classified information documenting crimes that corporations and governments want hidden? Is it farce when millions who are afraid to do so in the face of evil, can safely voice their opinion online?"

No reply followed, and Damian continued, "You say I inspired murder. I say I facilitated a vessel for the people to speak up and to be heard. For many of them the ability to voice their grievances is the only justice they'll ever see."

"Inciting murder is not a way to commit justice."

"I take it that you are not from Texas, or some other jurisdiction where capital punishment is observed?"

"I'm not arguing with you about state-sponsored murder. That's a whole other can of worms."

Damian took a turn around the beach. He picked up a pebble and cast it into the sea. He repeated it several times. At last he wiped his hands on his trousers, and said, "What is done with the results of the polls is not for me to decide. It is telling, however, that despite the evidence available on the whistleblower portal, and despite the results of the votes cast by millions of people, not one of those who were brought to face the court of the people was brought to justice in the traditional sense. To the contrary. While all jurisdictions ignored the documents published by the document-leaking portal, and all ignored the results of my polls, they had at the same time the audacity to lash out against me and the people who participated in the online court. What's more some of your politicians have publicly called for my assassination, and have even, apparently, put a plan of action."

Andrew took a step toward Damian, as though to ensure that sincerity in his voice would not be missed. "It would be disingenuous of me to defend a system that condones death penalty, let alone extrajudicial killing. It is wrong. Do you know how I came to understand that it is wrong? Thanks to you. Your project helped me open my eyes, it made me question the order of things. I realize that our justice system is flawed, perhaps even unjust. I don't know how, or if ever, it can be fixed. But of one thing I am certain — my future with Amanda has very poor prospects when she finds out that I do not respect her father, whether she approves of his work or not."

Damian was taken aback. These were the first words that stung his heart, that truly hurt. He was used to all kinds of vile attacks. He was prepared for criticism from the start. He was ready to absorb the attacks for the storm he helped to unleash. He drew the strength from the masses that participated in his online court, thus encouraging the continuation of his project. But among those millions of voices one was conspicuously missing — Amanda's. What did his daughter think of his work? Did she come to Reykjavik to offer her support, or to condemn? After all those years of separation Damian could not doubt that his daughter's visit little to do with his out-of-the-blue invitation, and was somehow related to his work. Perhaps some of the attacks launched against him had trickled down to his daughter? It was not inconceivable that with the kind of attention he was receiving, sooner or later someone would discover his only living relative, and everything he does or has done would come crashing down on her. Despite his best efforts to insulate her — and that was how Damian understood the life apart — he had unleashed a storm over his daughter's life.

"That's a blow below the belt," Damian said with sadness. "You've put me in the corner. I sense, though, that you have something else on your mind. What is it?"

This time Andrew took his turn around the beach. He strolled back and forth kicking pebbles from underneath his feet. He picked up one, and cast it into the sea. Damian watched him closely, his eyes following the silhouette that paced nervously in front of him.

"Had I received orders to assassinate you I would have, perhaps, done it. But I was ordered to infiltrate your life first. What I learned about you had opened my eyes. I owe you for saving me from becoming just like those people you put on trial. I admire your work. I know that the results of the polls are beyond your control. On the other hand I cannot respect you if there's a shred of truth in what they say about you."

"Is there?"

"My employers have built a believable case against you. They claim that you are the founder of the whistleblower portal, that you created it in order to collect the classified documents to build a case against government officials, and then created the online court to justify your vigilante justice."

"And you believe this?"

"Call me indoctrinated, but I've been with the Company long enough to know that everything it does is carefully prepared. There is no room for emotional reaction, which suggests that there is some grain of truth in the rumors that you've been slated for assassination. Perhaps it's because of the avalanche you unleashed. You've inspired people to take justice into their own hands. Whether you are, somehow, behind the killings, or whether these killings are committed without your direct support, doesn't matter. The bottom line is that you've done nothing to condemn them. This makes you guilty."

"Do you think all Germans guilty because they did not stop Hitler? Do you think all your compatriots guilty because they did not stop your president from waging wars of terror? What about capital punishment? Are we all guilty when our justice system kills in the name of the law?"

"Everyone has to answer this question for himself. I would tell the president what I think of him if I was given the chance. Who knows, some day I may have that opportunity. The fact of the matter is that right now I'm standing here, before you."

They faced one another. Standing three paces apart their eyes saw nothing but the contours of the other's face. Damian did not have to see Andrew's eyes to understand the gravity of the moment.

"I sense that you've come to make a proposition."

Andrew replied without ado, "Here's how I see the way for us to get through it: I want you to place yourself on trial. I want you to gather all the supporting documentation: the evidence of you organizing the online court, the way it is conducted, with the classified files, the resulting convictions, and the killings they spawned. Let the people decide whether you are guilty, or not."

Damian exhaled. He thought about something to that effect when he first conceived of the online court, whereby a campaign would have been launched to determine whether his idea would be met with approval. In the end the mass-participation proved to be the green light. He had all the support he needed to know that his work mattered.

He said so, and added, "Why do I get the feeling that you've already condemned me, and in your eyes I am guilty? It seems to me that the trial, whichever way it turned out, would only absolve your conscience. You believe me responsible for those killings, do you not?"

"Responsible? Maybe. I can assure you, though, that I shall do everything I can to verify whether the allegations raised by my employers are true, or not. Guilty? I don't know. Place yourself on trial, let the people answer that question."

They stood still, facing one another. Not a word was said for a long time, only steam of their breaths reminding that they were alive.

"What do you say, Mr. Allende?" Andrew asked at last, pressing expectancy in his voice.

"Whether it is blackmail, or barter, it seems that my daughter's happiness depends on how I proceed."

It was easy to imagine that Andrew's face blushed when his breathing increased, and he replied hurriedly, "I'm a new man. I've changed because of your work. I have a past I want to bury behind. I want to shelter Amy from the world I was a part of, and I don't want her cast into it when it turns out that all those accusations my agency directs against you are true. Is it blackmail? Barter? Maybe it's one man's concern for the girl he loves? Pick whatever you like, but know that the happiness of two hearts is in your hands."

"I love my daughter more than anything," Damian said emphatically. "And I would do anything to win her back."

"Do you agree to place yourself on trial?"

"I certainly don't want Amy to think of her father as a monster. But, this is not the same as admitting to doubt my moral integrity and the validity of the project I started."

"Do you agree?"

"I agree. What do you propose?"

Andrew sighed. From the long time it took him to come up with a reply it was evident that he has not thought it through. "I admit I only thought about it in the last half hour. It seems clear, though, that you must stand trial before subjecting anyone else to the same."

"How much time do you give me?"

"Naturally I'd like it to be done and over as soon as possible, however, it is only fair that you should have sufficient time to prepare your case carefully. I too shall require time to verify, or disprove, the link my agency alleges between you, the whistleblower portal, and the assassinations. Shall we say... three months?"

"Truth needs not defend itself for it is absolute. Remember the words of your fellow-countryman, Thomas Paine: *Such is the irresistible nature of truth, that all it asks, and all it wants, is the liberty of appearing.* I do not need to prove myself, as light needs no special defense to distinguish itself from darkness. I am ready to appear even tomorrow. It is you who needs the time."

"Do not denounce me, for it is you, of all people, who should know that to accept the absolute truth one must first doubt it."

"You impress me. Call it prejudice, if you wish, but I did not expect such formed opinions from someone of your profession."

"What's thinking got to do with my profession?"

"Do they not teach you to kill? Tell me, Andrew, can an independent-minded person follow orders that insult all notions of justice and morality? I think not. You know it too, and what's more you have come to realize it all on your own. It impresses especially that you were able to step beyond the boyhood dream of becoming a spy, or a soldier, that highest level of subjugation, and chose to decide for yourself what is right and what is wrong. At the risk of sounding cocky, let me add how impressed I am that you came to realize it at such an early age, not too late to put it behind you and start anew, before the baggage becomes too heavy. This is why I agree to your terms. Not because I doubt my own moral right, or my project's just principles, but because I am proud that you love and care for my daughter. I shall prove, if that's what it takes, that I am worthy of your love for each other."

It was clear that Damian's words moved the young man. Andrew turned his head so as not to show emotion, but his breathing was the giveaway.

"There is one aspect of your proposition that worries me, though," Damian continued. "What will happen to you, should you receive orders to kill me?"

The question acted like a bucket of cold water on a hot head.

"It is a consideration I haven't given much thought. Besides, the possibility of your assassination is only a rumor."

"It's beyond rumor when your policymakers talk about it openly, in public. What will you do, Andrew, when you receive orders to kill me?"

"I'm not the man I was when I started working for the agency—"

Damian cut him off, "Will you disobey orders? What will happen to you, then? What will happen to you and Amy when you're disgraced, perhaps jailed?"

Andrew considered his answer before replying. "While the Company does plenty of killing these days, it often goes with the need for plausible deniability. I suppose I can stall, even abort the hit, if I deem the circumstances unfavorable. It will give you time. The trouble is, though, that if I don't do it then someone else will."

"Then I may not have the three months we've agreed on."

"Our agreement stands. Three months from today you shall stand trial."

"Dead or alive?"

"I will see to it that you face your jury alive."

"Is it even possible?" Damian asked with sheer curiosity, his voice devoid of irony that his words suggested. "Popular culture leads one to believe, and documents found in the whistleblower portal lend some evidence to it, that once the most powerful intelligence agency sets its sights on someone—"

"You'd be surprised how many blunders are committed, and how many successes can be attributed to sheer coincidence," Andrew cut him off. "Besides, I am your best shield. I know how the killers would operate. I know how to outwit their tactics, and dodge their weapons."

"For how long?"

Andrew shrugged. It was good that Damian did not see the gesture for it did not speak well of the young man's conviction.

"Enough to see your trial go through."

"And then?" Damian was relentless.

When no reply followed, he added, "I am not prying out of concern for my own safety. I am used to threats. I've lived with them long before the first online trial. It's one of the reasons I haven't had a fixed address, until this island nation extended its invitation along with guarantees of security. It is for the same reason I've had limited contact with Amy. I was hoping that over the years it would become forgotten that I have a daughter. It is my only week spot, my Achilles heel, if you wish. So you see, I am asking you because I worry about her: What then?"

"Amanda is more dear to me than my own life," was the reply.

"That is in no way reassuring."

"Let's just say that this job has taught me that in the world of treachery and backstabbing, where you are as reckoned with as last year's snow, it pays to keep an ace up your sleeve."

10

Damian was intrigued. It was not often that one was approached by a spy who had a heart set on one's daughter. He was impressed with the young man's moral concerns, not least because of his employment background, but because of an overall state of youth desensitized by violence, corruption, and lies permeating from all areas of life. He was bemused when Andrew insisted that Amy ought to know nothing of the arrangement, and in particular on his spy employment, but the feeling lasted a fleeting moment, until the boy insisted that he should come clean on his own.

They returned to the house without saying a word. Nothing more could be said. Actions, and only actions, would speak for them.

The party had reached this stage when the guests were enthused enough about their varied drinking companions to not have noticed their host's absence. The only one awaiting his return with impatience and trepidation was Amanda. She did disbelieve her eyes — as is so often used in literature — and knew that the man who disappeared with her father into the darkness of the night was none other but Andrew, her boyfriend. It was thus that she showed no surprise at seeing the two of them emerge into the lit backyard.

"You are spared the social necessity of introducing us, my darling, for we have already met," Damian opened upon seeing his daughter.

Amanda watched the two of them without a word.

Andrew approached, kissed her on the cheek.

She did not return the affection.

Someone passed by, a glass of amber-colored liquor in his hand; he turned abruptly at seeing the host, approached him, and began an excited, if pointless conversation.

"We shall talk at length tomorrow," Damian said to the young couple, and strode away with his guest.

Amanda thought that he winked to Andrew before taking off. It was too much for her. She turned on her heels and trotted towards dense coniferous trees that offered excellent shelter from the damp chilly wind from the sea, and from prying ears of the intoxicated crowd. Faint contours of a structure appeared in the darkness; she led the way, and found it to be a small gazebo. Low-powered string lights hang from underneath the ceiling, providing romantic illumination, but romance was the last thing on Amanda's mind. Once inside the gazebo, she turned to face Andrew.

"Explain to me," she said, "how is it that my father scarcely has two minutes to talk to me, whereas he can disappear with you into the darkness for two hours."

He knew better than to come up with excuses at such a time.

"What I had to talk to your father about could not wait."

He saw the woman's eyes squint, making her brows arch, and realized that it was not the right thing to say, however well meant.

"I see that I've asked the wrong question. What I should've said was: How do you know that my father is my father?"

He answered with sincerity, "Oh, Amy, I have known it for some time, but given your father's circumstance I waited for you to bring it up."

"And you went around my back when I didn't."

"No, it isn't like that—"

"How is it, Andrew? You're supposed to be at a conference in London, yet you're under the Arctic Circle. If that wasn't enough, you talk to my father before even seeing me."

"I tried reaching you on the phone," he said in a week voice, as one usually does when the excuse is meek. "But, it was off."

It happened to be true. Amanda forgot to switch on her mobile after she landed in Iceland. She said in no less vehement voice, "It doesn't explain why you're here."

"It does!" he protested, desperate to stop the rift from getting bigger. "In a way it does. When I found out who your father was I followed his work. I found it quite fascinating, controversial to be sure, but what groundbreaking work is not controversial? Your father did, he had the guts to do, what many of us in the IT world dream of, but seldom have the foresight and the nose to execute. He turned the world upside-down."

"And it fascinated you because?" she asked less vehemently.

He noticed. His hopes up, he said with passion, "Well, it's a sort of sense of camaraderie. The programmers, much as the hacking community, are an extended family, you know. Those were my initial feelings. Then, of course, the rest kicked in. There is no greater satisfaction for a hacker to know that one can deliver a giant, if virtual, kick in the establishment's butt. From there on it was only a step to realize that your father was doing more than that. He started revolution of openness and accountability. When, at last, I became aware of the scope of his work, when I realized that he was not only aiming his work at exposing the corporations and their grip on the governments, but was actually in the process of changing the world, I could not wait to meet him. I can't tell you how much I wanted it, yet I respected your privacy. I waited."

She thrust a long deep look into his eyes. They were sincere, sparkling with enthusiasm. She said in a voice that was warmer, "Until today."

"Yes, until today. It could not be put off any longer."

"Need I even ask why?"

"Amy," he started gently. He did not want to alarm her, but the way he said her name, the affection he put into this single word, would have been enough to reawaken Madame Bovary's passion. Amanda did not lack passion for Andrew, or for her life, but she did, nonetheless, look at him with a softer eye. She listened to him intently, her eyes darting from his lips to his eyes so as not to miss a single word and its meaning. Andrew continued in the same tone, "Your father's work stubbed at some very powerful interests. What he accomplished is nothing short of revolutionary. He single-handedly inspired, armed, and gave hope to a large number of people, while collecting many enemies along the way. I don't need to remind you of the many commentators and politicians who called for your father's assassination, as I am certain you know these all too well, what with your newspaper being the recipient of many such op-eds. What you might not know is that there is a cyber war being launched to stop your father from conducting his work. To survive, and to continue on, your father will need all the help he can get. I came here to offer myself to him."

Silence fell between them. Only the distant sound of the waves, dangerous in their might, and the murmur of the wind in the grasses, like the whisper of the dead, could be heard. An occasional burst of laughter reached them from the house, reminding that they were not alone, not abandoned in a dark and inhospitable world.

"As you can see," Amanda nodded to the brightly lit house, "my father has some influential friends of his own."

"I've noticed. I recognized some of the faces, even though I hardly watch television. But, Amy, those who set their sights on your father are more powerful, for they are invisible, faceless, operating through proxies, often in the dark."

She trembled, but said bravely, if too briskly to conceal the fact the his words sent shivers down her spine, "They have names if they can be identified, and their identities lift the veil off the faceless and invisible power that they, supposedly, wield."

"The people toasting your father right now may be well known figures, good for PR purposes, but they cannot stop those who wish him evil. To stop evil one must use same weapons and tactics."

"Can you?"

"I can," he confirmed vehemently. "Not alone, perhaps, but I have friends in the community who can lend their talent."

She shivered again, and Andrew thought he heard her utter something to the effect of 'some talent you have', but it could have been the wind. She cast a quick look into his eyes, and shivered again. Was it something she saw in them, or was it only the chilly wind that made her stand up and start for the house. She felt surer of herself when she neared the house and the happy clamor of clinking glass and careless laughs.

She turned to Andrew, who followed her closely, and said, "And is that the only reason you came here? To warn my father and offer him your help?"

He came closer, so close they could feel each other's breath.

"No," he said. "I came here for yet another reason, one that keeps me awake at night, and makes me weak in my knees."

She waited for his answer, with her eyes firmly set on his.

"When the attacks against your father are launched, perhaps tomorrow, maybe in a week, or a month, your father shall be a very busy man. And so shall I, because he accepted my offer of help. You and I— We may not see much of each other for a long time, not in a way I'd like to spend the time together. That is why I followed you here. I cannot, and do not want to put it off any longer. I am in love with you, and I want to marry you."

11

Damian Allende stood in the yard, outside of the circle of light cast by the porch lanterns, breathing in the refreshing, damp air. The party had ended, and the last of the guests departed. He had every reason to be satisfied — several members of parliament offered to fast track his application for residency; benefactors raised funds; and volunteers donated their time. Damian's immediate future was secured, and his project's lifeline extended. Yet, instead of a happy face, Damian's brows were crossed. Troubling thoughts occupied his mind. Some two dozen steps away his daughter and the young man sat in the gazebo, wrapped in a blanket, chirping like a pair of night owls. He watched them from the distance, curious to see the effect Andrew's confession sparked in Amanda. The couple seemed close, engrossed in one another. It was not surprising given the boy's persuasiveness and passion; after all it was the passion, followed by his arresting honesty, that convinced Damian to agree to Andrew's ultimatum. He reasoned too that by working with the young man he would get to see more of his daughter. They hardly saw each other since the passing of Amy's mother. He was aware that it was largely his own doing. His near-complete devotion to his work, and the ensuing life on the road, did not help the troubled marriage. Over time he found it comforting to think that the early onset of threats led to his absence, making it safer for his two closest souls. There was substance to it when several countries officially designated him an unwanted visitor, and various groups sent in threatening messages. It legitimized his work, gave it a meaning, and reaffirmed the path he had taken. The arrest warrants issued by numerous tyrannical regimes at last showed, not only to the world, but above all to his family, that Damian was working to make a positive difference in the world. Amy's mother forgave him on her premature deathbed, but the daughter, too young to fully grasp the inner workings of the world of adults, with their backstabbing, treachery, and lies, saw him as the culprit of family breakup. So many times was he stricken by doubts and stinging regrets over her silent reproaches for having chosen the path that distanced him from the family; so many times he considered dropping everything to be with Amy, but the death threats were real, and he reasoned that by staying away he sheltered her from danger. As time went by reunification became increasingly less likely. Amanda kept her mother's name, blamed Damian for her death. Though she never dressed it in those words, Damian felt it was so. Her mother's maiden name, the returned unread letters, and unanswered telephone calls, were all telling it too well that their relationship had died along with the only person that bound them together. Of course it was not true, not entirely, but how does one explain to a preteen that pharmacological treatment could not prevent or halt the deadly disease? Following his wife's death, and with Amy becoming more distant and hostile, he was ready to give up his activism. He could not bear the prospect of losing his daughter, something that became a painful possibility when she refused to accept money for tuition, wanting nothing to do with him. A lawyer-friend came to the rescue by explaining to the girl that an alimony was not an act of pity, far from it, it was a form of punishment, often most severe, for it led to a complete emotional separation, as financial troubles often do. The girl accepted. The payments were their only connection over the next years. Damian watched his daughter from the distance. He waited, convincing himself that the right age would straighten things out. What was the right age? Was there even such thing? He did not know. As time went by it became more difficult to turn back the clock. The aunt who took Amy to London seemed to foster the girl's hatred for her father.

Years went by without direct contact between the two. Secretly they followed the other's progress, though. The Internet made it possible and unavoidable as both their names cropped up — Amanda's, as she grew in popularity, and Damian's as he gained notoriety. In time they learned to appreciate the old wisdom — becoming convinced that time truly does have the ability to, if not heal, than certainly to patch wounds. Damian discovered that hard work on a project that wholly occupied his mind was an excellent remedy for many sorrows, whereas Amanda found that intellectual challenges combined with the demands of fame pushed all squabbles into distant perspective.

Damian recalled the first open meeting with his daughter. It was two years ago, at the aunt's funeral. The trepidation of the expectancy of the meeting still made his hands glisten with sweat. That meeting marked the end of the vitriolic aversion, and the beginning of a new, though still distant relationship. They stayed in cordial, though very sporadic, touch. Damian understood what caused the shift in his daughter's attitude — the death of the last living relative, combined with the increasing attacks against her father, at last prompted Amanda to seek reconciliation. Alas the same threats that he faced from numerous sources around the world were a cause for Damian to worry ever more for his daughter's safety. He did not exaggerate when he said to Andrew that she was his Achilles heel, and those who wished him evil knew it all too well. Upon realization of this scary prospect, it was Damian who, to great pain, sought to distance himself from his daughter. He avoided her every call to meet, always finding excuses. Until last week, when he called her out-of-the-blue, and the daughter he loved above all else, had come to him. He was overwhelmed. It was not true that he could not find time away from his guests to talk to her at length. He feared the conversation that had been brewing in each of them all those years. It took him much of the evening to calm, and to realize that at last fate had brought them together. It was time to patch the rift, to mend the break that no one — and each of them, caused. It was time to talk about all that which was bottled up for such a long time.

But as he watched his daughter being embraced by her loving boyfriend, smiling, kissing, and happy, Damian was stricken with doubts. Why dig out the old ghosts? Why bring all the pain back? Would Amanda not take his explanations as admission of guilt, of which she accused him for so many years? Why tempt the fate that had at last brought them together? Why rekindle that which split them in the first place, now that it was slowly becoming forgotten? Did he even have the right to bring it all out to life again? What did he know about the young woman, about the amends she made with herself, that allowed her to come here? What did he know about the pain that caused her to seek to distance herself in the first place? That it was painful Damian did not doubt. He had kept discreet watch over his daughter all this time. Whenever he flew to London — and his visits became more frequent as his work demanded and his heart required — he made sure that he found time to watch her as she grew up, from a preteen, to a buoyant teen, and finally into a blossoming young woman. He watched her progress in school. He noticed the lack of friends, the solitude she kept. Was it not pain that led her to seek such a life? Could he, or more importantly — should he bring back the dark shadow that covered her past, now that a bright light shone its young rays? The smiling face that he now observed, and the happy chatter that he heard, himself unseen under the roof of the verandah, convinced Damian that he had no right to spoil it.

It is a chronicler's duty as well as common courtesy towards the reader to note that just as his genuine desire not to break his daughter's happiness drove the father to come to the conclusions and decisions that had been germinating in his mind and came to fruition at seeing Amanda in the embrace of her loving boyfriend, it was also his weakness and fear for the consequences of rekindling the long-buried pain of his own that prompted Damian to quietly turn on his heels, to return to the house, and to slowly climb the staircase to his room, to open the closet and draw out the dusty backpack that traveled so many paths with him, on four continents; it made him cast a tired look around the room, pull out the drawer where he kept writing paper and utensils, and sat down at his desk to write in quick and passionate words. He wrote two pages, and read them afterwards. For a minute he struggled with his thoughts and crumpled the sheets; he placed them in the small urn that he used for pins and other small items, and lit it on fire. Watching the paper burn he picked up a fresh sheet and wrote two words. When finished he folded the page in three, and pressed long on the creases before slipping it into an envelope. He licked the glue, sealed the envelope, and placed it in his pocket. He approached the window, and looked out onto the gazebo, where the two lovers still kept a tight embrace. He picked up the packed backpack and descended to the ground level.

12

"I wonder what he usually has for breakfast? Or what he drinks, for that matter? Juice? Tea? Coffee? Black? Sugar?"

Amanda was rummaging through kitchen cabinets, thinking out loud. Having found nothing in the — still mostly unused — cabinets, she gave up. Wearing slacks, her hair in disarray, she yawned time and again. It was a long night, even for her young body, the emotional anxiety multiplied by jet lag. She approached the panoramic window and gazed outside. It was a steel-grey day; every blade of grass, every twig on the trees, and every leaf on the ground, looked as though it was sprayed with lead. It's one of those places that fair better at night, she thought, and left for the adjoining room.

"There's enough here to feed a hungry ZOO," said Andrew, his nose in the fridge. "What's good about hosting a party. It's the remnants." With a grin of satisfaction on his face he approached the kitchen table with a plate of cold cuts. He went back to the fridge, where he spotted a bag of Arabica beans. While searching for a grinder, his eyes caught the white envelope set against the percolator, his name handwritten in hurried writing. Andrew had a bad feeling. He opened the envelope with a pairing knife, drew out a single sheet folded in three. Two words were written in the middle of the page. He stared at them until his initial bewilderment changed to helpless anger. Amanda called out to him, but he did not move; he needed time to suppress his emotions.

Andrew found the woman in the living room. She stood in front of the wall decorated with awards and recognitions from a wide range of organizations, groups, and professional associations. Printed, or placated, the trophies praised Damian Allende for such accomplishments as fostering free speech, and campaigning for human rights.

"Look at these," she said. "I had no idea."

Smokescreen, Andrew thought to himself.

He said, "Let's eat."

"Maybe we should wait for him?" Amanda replied over her shoulder, not looking.

"I'm starving," he said and returned to the kitchen.

She joined him. "No coffee?"

"No grinder."

She smiled, picked up a small object that stood by the percolator. "He hasn't changed. I remember how he always drove mom crazy. Always liked to keep his hands busy. You'd find him with sunflower seeds, cracking the shells with his teeth, and dropping them all over the place. If it wasn't sunflower then it was pumpkin seeds, hazelnuts, or something equally messy, but providing occupation for his hands. We never had a food mixer. Father prepared every meal from scratch, the old-fashioned way. One day he refused to buy ground meat, and came home with a manual grinder. It was perhaps the most advanced machine in the kitchen. He did all the work in the kitchen, including coffee grinding, meat grinding, dough mixing, and the like." She raised the item she was holding in her hand. "He roasted and then crushed the coffee in a pill crusher, bean by bean. Mom was happy, she said it kept his fingers busy, away from the keyboard."

"Ultimately, though, it did not." Andrew commented and reached for the pill crusher. He considered using it, his eyes darting from the small item to the large coffee bag.

"No, but who knows where he would've ended up if he spent more time on the keyboard. I think he understood it, too, after he got away a bit too easily from the first hacking conviction."

Amanda filled the kettle, and put it on the range. She came to the table, and sat down; she yawned.

"I'm not hungry," she said. "Need to wake up first. I think I'll wait for him. But you should go ahead," she added when she saw the quick look he gave her.

Andrew swallowed some potato salad, washed it down with milk, and said without raising his eyes from the plate, "You may have to wait a while."

A wide yawn was the woman's only response.

They sat in silence for a time, the only sounds being Andrew's clinking cutlery, and his masticating lips.

"I thought that London was dreary," Amanda said lazily, her eyes on the sky outside.

"It is nearly the Arctic Circle. And at this time of year we're lucky there's any light."

She was not listening, thinking out loud, "What would possess him to move here? Freedom of the press, I suppose."

He swallowed another bite, and asked, "Do you consider him a journalist?"

The question caught her off guard. She nodded towards the room with the trophies. "Many do. Quite impressive, considering that he never actually received a diploma in journalism."

"What is a diploma but official confirmation of entry into the world of yes-men. True talent needs no institutionalized recognition. In any case, in the age of the Internet, and blogging, that sort of confirmation becomes irrelevant."

She cast a long look at him.

"Have you turned into one of those blind followers of Damian Allende?"

He buttered a slice of bread, and dipped his fork into a jar of marinated squid. "I do admire his guts. He's a trailblazer. He's done a lot of good work, this much is clear. It's enough to look at the awards, to see what price he paid to receive them."

"Why did you join him, Andy?"

"I told you. I admire what he does. That, and the fact that he's your father."

She watched him closely.

"You know what he's accused of?"

He nodded.

"Does it not bother you?"

He rinsed his mouth with the last of the milk, swallowed.

"Until there's proof of it, I'm willing to give him the benefit of the doubt." His words hung in the air like a cushion for what followed. "Do you?"

She could not bring herself to look at him when she said, "I'm here on a job. It's a big story, perhaps the biggest. I came to find out if there's any truth to the allegations. Do I think he's guilty? I'm a journalist. I'm not here to judge. He is, and will remain my father, regardless of the outcome."

"If you doubt him, and if others doubt him, then he is already condemned. As are the hopes of the millions who participated in his online court."

She looked at him, her face expressionless.

"I don't think the story alone brought you here, Amy. I think you wanted to be close to your father at the time of need. So, the question is: Do you believe your father guilty? Do you believe there's any truth to him using the whistleblower portal, and his online court, to justify the lynching?"

She thought about the father she remembered. The ever busy-handed man whose nose was always stuck in the computer screen. Too busy for his sick wife, absent, and in his absence responsible for her death. Was it the man capable of turning his computer skills into work of evil, as his accusers suggest? The profile fits — a loner who abandoned his wife and child, and spent the next decade on the road. Yet, it was the same man whose gentle fingers caressed her when she was a little girl. She could almost feel his hand stroking her hair, she could see him turn the pages of the books he read to her at bedtime, every night. Was this the man capable of planning and carrying out cold-blooded murders?

She muttered something in response.

"I didn't hear you."

"No. I don't think he is guilty of these allegations. That's not what he devoted his life to. That's not what he gave up his family for."

Andrew reached over the table, and put his hand over hers.

"Good. Because your father needs your trust."

With his other hand he retrieved the envelope, removed the single sheet of paper and slipped it across the table.

She read the two words.

"Three months?" She looked at him. "What does it mean?"

He told her about the trial her father agreed to place himself on, and finished, "I think— I think he couldn't face facing you before the results are in."

13

Amanda stared at him, speechless, not comprehending.

"I'm sorry, Amy. I know what it looks like, but you shouldn't give up on him."

"What do you mean — you know what it looks like?" She asked with sudden hostility.

This time Andrew looked at her with puzzled eyes. How could she not understand?

He said, "Whether the allegations are true, or not, the sad fact remains that your father's work has led to the killings. He's done nothing to condemn them, which may be read as endorsement. Now he wants to present his case to the same audience that convicted the villains, and let them decide if he should continue."

"I don't accept it. That he is, or may be guilty!"

"Nonetheless, he could not face you and fled. After so much mud had been thrown at him over the years, he wants to appear crystal clear in your eyes. Placing himself on trial may achieve just that."

Amanda stood up without a word, and left the kitchen in a hurry. She stormed from room to room, but soon slowed down when she realized, with resignation, that her father was not in the house. He was gone. Emotions ranging from anger to sheer puzzlement shot through her mind. How could he leave without a word? Could Andrew be right: Could father want to clear his name before the first confrontation with the daughter he hadn't seen in a long time? It could not be! Damian believed in what he did, he was proud of his work. Amanda was convinced of it. They might have spent a decade apart, but they were daughter and father, and they were very much alike. They always had been. Before mom got sick they preferred each other's company. She was Damian's favorite, just as he was her favorite parent. They always understood each other well. Despite the long separation, and under the conditions that forced the rift, Amanda still understood her father enough to know what really prevented him from facing her. It was the same reason that kept her from seeking contact years after the pain subsided. She dreaded the long and painful conversation that awaited them. Much had to be cleared. About mom. About them. Who knows if the meeting would have taken place at all if not for the assignment she received from her editor? Suddenly, Amanda scolded herself. Did she come here solely because of the job? Of course not! It was a compound of events that brought her here, at the heart of it her desire to settle things with father. The assignment was only the trigger. She gathered her courage and flew to meet him. *Where is your courage, father?* she thought.

Amanda returned to the kitchen. Andrew was still at the table, putting his mobile phone in his short pocket, and clumsily trying to hide the fact that he was using it. She noticed that his face turned white. She wanted to confront him, to release her anger. She pulled the chair sharply, and barely sat down when her face lit up, her alert eyes on the doorway.

"See!" she said triumphantly. "You were wrong. I knew he wouldn't leave without a word."

She started for the door.

Andrew heard it too — the sound of a lock being turned, or rather someone trying to turn the lock. Has Damian changed his mind? Puzzled, he followed the woman.

Andrew realized what was happening when passing through the dining room he caught, with the corner of his eye, a movement outside the windows. A blurry figure rushed stooped toward the back of the house. With someone else tampering with the lock it could only mean one thing.

He caught Amanda's arm just as she was reaching for the door handle. With his hand over her mouth he pulled her close, and whispered to her ear, "It's not your father."

She was stunned, too surprised to offer resistance.

From here on things happened fast. The door opened quietly, a notch. Andrew realized that it was too late to flee. When a hit squad covers the exits, the only recourse left is to take charge of the situation.

He felt the woman become tense in his arms, and he saw the reason —
a glove-clad hand pushing through the crack in the opened doors.
Andrew judged the height of the assailant by the level at which he held
the door and with one swift move of his torso his leg shot up. He hit
the man on the face just as it appeared from around the door.

Although the surprise was absolute, and the kick precise, the
assailant forced his way in.

Andrew was ready. As his foot was making contact with the
assailant's nose his hand grabbed the wrist, lowering it while
simultaneously pulling closer to deliver a knee blow in the groin. This
did the trick. With the man writhing at his feet, Andrew struck him
behind the ear. Without watching the effect, for he knew the outcome
of the blow, Andrew raised his finger to his lips.

Amanda did not need a special reminder to remain quiet; she was
sufficiently stunned to be at a lack for words. Stupefied, and with her
eyes on the body stretched at her feet, she allowed herself to be
ushered to the adjoining room — a small windowless pantry. Entirely
passive, she watched as the door closed behind Andrew, and she was
left in the room all alone.

Andrew did not have the time to return to the body of the first
assailant, to seize the weapon the man undoubtedly carried on him. He
could have used a firearm to deal with the second one, alas, strategically
speaking, it was more important to act fast. He would improvise,
remembering from his training that a typical house can be a regular
armory. He rushed to the kitchen, where he found the second man,
doubtless drawn to it by the smell of freshly toasted bread. Andrew
approached the kitchen from Damian's trophy room, just as the
assailant peeked around the corner into the hallway; his body language
told that he had noticed his comrade stretched on the floor.

"Do not move!" Andrew warned in a cold and determined voice.

The man froze.

Andrew waited, knowing that in situations such as this men often
make the gravest mistakes.

Whether a newbie, or underestimating the opponent, the assailant
muttered under his nose, "*Yob tvoyu mat!*" At the same time his muscles
flexed.

"Don't make me shoot you like a dog!" Andrew noticed the tensing of the muscles, and he warned in the man's native tongue, "Drop your gun, very slowly, and stand against the wall."

A split second later the man spun around while ducking simultaneously. Before the hand that held the pistol made the circle, before the muzzle had time to align with the target, Andrew tossed the meat chopper that he picked up from a magnetic holder attached to the cabinet. He watched the utensil's sharp edge strike the man's hand, wedging in deeply, pinning it into the doorframe. He saw his eyes cross, and roll back as the man struggled to contain a cry of pain. Before he could utter a sound, Andrew was already onto him, using another kitchen tool to deliver a blow behind the ear.

Andrew stood frozen in place for some time, unable to move, his eyes on the hand with a protruding chopper, barely bleeding. The assailant carried no weapon. Attached to his wrist, and dangling freely, was a small stun gun. A stun gun!

He came to at the sound of a cry.

Amanda was standing at his side, her eyes fixed on a grotesque figure of a man lying on the floor, unconscious, his hand pinned to the doorframe. She slowly turned to Andrew, her eyes drawn to a wooden meat tenderizer in his hand. At last she looked up, and focused on her boyfriend's face.

She took a step back, and uttered through her trembling lips, "Who are you?"

14

Whatever explanations Andrew may have offered, they had to wait. The two assailants were following orders, and when these were not followed through, more may show up at the doorstep. It was, thus, imperative to act swiftly. His firm and uncompromising stance, coupled with the evidence in the form of two bodies was all that was necessary to convince Amanda to refrain from asking further questions. Andrew proceeded to tie up the men, while Amanda watched him, bewildered by the side of him she did not know.

With their bags largely untouched, gathering belongings was a snap. Within minutes they were on the way to the airport. As grey buildings whizzed by the side of the road, Andrew noticed that every minute of their parting with the scene of the ghastly events added to the woman's tension, and his explanation of the events at Damian's house could not be postponed indefinitely. In order to successfully pass through the airport security Amanda had to be brought in to the dark world of the truth surrounding Damian Allende.

"Your father has stepped on the toes of some very mean people," Andrew started cautiously. "It's part of the reason he had to leave in a hurry." He was inventing, but not entirely. Damian did get under the skin of some bad characters, and sooner or later would end up on the run. In fact, Andrew thought, Damian was in effect on the run for years, and his life on the road was the result of his work that predated the creation of the online court. The events of today were a natural culmination.

"I know who my father is, but who are you?" Amanda was still shaken by the image of the two tied-up men in her father's house.

He took his eyes off the road to face her. The rental swerved momentarily, sparing him from the uncomfortable necessity to meet her eyes as he countered to regain control.

"I'm your father's new partner. I told you."

"Does it explain what happened there? What you did there... These men stood no chance."

"It was self-defense, Amy."

"I'm not sure I could do it, self-defense or otherwise. Not like that."

"You'd be surprised what you're capable of when the situation calls for it."

"Yet I was frozen. You, on the other hand— You acted with precision of a pro."

"It's Tae-kwon-do. I trained fifteen years. You know it. A kick like that is nothing. It's basics."

"Really? Is that where you learned to use a meat chopper? I saw how you handled it. It's as though it belonged in your hand, like a computer keyboard in my father's. I saw how you brought these men down, with a precise strike that does not kill, but incapacitates."

He attempted to shrug it off. "Every boy knows how to handle pistols, and knives, and the like. That's what we play with as soon as we can grasp more that a pacifier. Cowboys and Indians. Cops and gangsters. Good guys and bad guys. Short guns and long guns. It's in our blood."

She watched him closely for a while. He could sense that she was not convinced when she asked, "What was it all about?"

"I told you: Your father upset some very bad and powerful people."

"They did not look upset. They were determined."

"What happened in the house was only a prelude to what's coming. These men were hitmen, Amy. Russians, judging by their tongue—"

"Russians?" she repeated doubtfully.

"Several powerful Russians were tried in your father's online court. All were found guilty of one thing or another. Add to it the recent lynching of men whom your father put on trial, and you have the answer."

"What is the answer? Retaliation?"

"Retaliation. Self-defense. Does it matter? Others simply don't want it to happen to them. They don't want to be killed. It's animal instinct. Kill, or be killed."

"My father is not a killer!"

"It doesn't really matter. His work serves as the catalyst for lynching. Those who feel threatened by his work see only one way to stop him."

She turned her head to face him. "And you? What does it mean for you now that you joined him?"

"I don't know," he replied truthfully. "Your father has a large network of volunteers helping him do the work. Far as I know none of them are in danger. I don't think I'm in danger; harassed — yes, but that's the fate of any journalist, or an activist who does not bow to the powers that be. That's why he and I have a verbal agreement. No one knows we work together. No one will." His last words hung on an unfinished note.

Amanda noticed. She asked, "But?"

He should not add oil to fire, but it had to be said. Too many drastic events lay ahead to keep her sheltered from finding out. In any case she deserved to know.

"I don't think I have to worry. Your father's enemies don't know about me. You, on the other hand, must take precautions."

"I?" She was puzzled.

"The longer your father remains elusive, while threatening to go ahead with the next installment of his online court, the more those fingered by him will want to stop him. Those two hitmen were a sign of things to come. We lucked out in there, but your father will be hunted down until he is stopped. If he keeps eluding his captors you will be used as bait."

Amanda did not react the way he might have expected. She said with sudden defiance spiced with a tinge of bitterness, "They're in for quite the surprise, then! It proves how little they know about Damian Allende. They don't know how important his work is to him. They don't know that it is more important than anything and anyone. Even if they find out, which I doubt, that he has a daughter, they're in for a surprise if they expect to persuade him to stop his work on account of my safety."

"You're wrong, Amy! Your father loves you. A lot!"

"Thank you for saying it, Andy. But as things are, he has scarcely seen me in the last ten years."

"You're wrong," he repeated forcefully. "Your father has seen you. He watched you from the day your ways had parted. He's paid your alimony not because of court orders, as you were led to believe, but because he is your father, and he loves and cares about you. He used the money to trace your whereabouts. He cared about you to have traveled to London several times a year just for a chance to take a glimpse at you as you walked to and from school. He followed you on the street, not daring to approach for all the resentment you held for him."

It was not his place to say all this. Yet, it was done. It could not be avoided. He needed Amanda on his side. He glanced at her. Her eyes glistened. He tried to reach for her hand but the traffic nearing the airport was too busy to divert his attention.

Amanda turned her head in order not show the tears in her eyes.

They did not speak the rest of the way.

With the rental car returned, they hurried to the departures hall.

"Where to?" Amanda asked, struggling to keep her calm.

He should have thought better of it before replying. He did not think it suspicious that he should know with such conviction where Damian Allende was headed. He could not tell her that, while she searched the house for her father, he received a coded message from his superior officer, confirming that Damian Allende boarded a plane. Improvising at a time such as this, when the woman's nerves were stretched to their limits, would have saved them from plenty of unnecessary hurdles ahead. Alas, he loved her too much, and believed to be loved in return, to consider that what happened this morning made her doubt his intentions and identity.

Andrew said with conviction, as though he purchased the tickets himself, "After Damian. To London."

15

Dick Verso was the London station chief. He was an experienced officer, who learned his craft in the Cold War, when the Company concentrated on intelligence, rather than assassinations. He was an old bird whose wings were being clipped by the new brass. His extensive contacts, dating to his early days in the field, were the only reason that he still had the overseas job. He tried to make good use of his position, teaching his officers the tested espionage ways of the increasingly more distant past, so readily dismissed by the hawks, who displayed their bravado for targeted killings, using drones, and other techno-toys, that kept them out of danger, while pleasing the more and more extremist White House administration. Dick Verso was an anachronism in the world of 21st Century espionage, but he was delivering results, and had to be reckoned with by his superiors. His strict insistence on following intelligence values based on the use of the brains, rather than guns, had earned him the nickname drawn from a literal translation of his name. All but one of his officers believed the nickname deserved. The two met only hours after the jetliner touched down on the English soil. They were sitting on a bench on the bank of river Thames, with the white noise of the heavy traffic behind their backs.

Dick Verso opened the conversation.

"We've lost Allende. The man has the uncanny ability to slip through the tightest net."

Andrew Walker's face flushed ever so faintly that an untrained eye would construe it a flicker of the setting sun reflecting off the dark water. He was glad that the chief's eyes were elsewhere, for the sun was nowhere to be seen this evening. He said nothing, afraid his voice might betray the relief the news had brought.

The station chief continued, "Our Reykjavik team went to Allende's home. The two men you roughed up were Russian agents."

"I had no choice."

"Of course. Merely stating the obvious."

"They know who did it to them?"

"No proof yet, but they'll figure it out, which means we are running against time. What about the girl?"

The answer was slow in coming as Andrew gathered his thoughts. "She's worried."

"I meant — has she any idea where her father might be?"

"No."

"Apply pressure. The media's contacts are as extensive as any intelligence agency's. The newspaper may be able to locate Allende, what with their insight into the world of independent journalists and bloggers; someone out there must know where he's hiding." He watched Andrew closely and added, "We must hurry, for we now have additional competition. A Brit was killed yesterday; an oil tycoon who was tried and convicted in Allende's court. He had highly placed friends, and now the MI5 wants our man."

"Kill?"

"Worse. They want him arrested."

Andrew shot his boss an uncomprehending gaze.

Dick Verso explained, "It goes against Langley's current position regarding Damian Allende."

"Which is…?"

"The CIA will not interfere with the running of his online court."

Andrew turned to face his boss, wide eyed. "Forgive me, chief, but this is too much to absorb. You have to backtrack a bit for me. What's going on?"

The chief evidently misconstrued Andrew's confusion. "I'm with you, Andrew. Allende's responsible for the killing of Americans. He should pay the price. His hit list includes—"

"His… what?"

"His latest kangaroo court has convicted dozens of our policy makers, politicians, as well as corporate execs on government contracts. He ought to be stopped before more of our citizens are lynched. It ought to act as a signal to his comrades and copycats."

"What made the headquarters change its position?" Andrew asked throatily.

The chief looked at him with a peculiar spark in his eye. The spark faded before he replied, "Sorry, Andrew, that information is above your paygrade. Your new orders are to locate Allende, and keep him from getting into the British, the Russian, or any other hands."

"This may not be possible. The MI5 are resourceful. We can't compete on their soil."

"No. But, we have one asset, which they do not."

Andrew knew what the chief had in mind. He feigned interest in a barge treading the water, so as not to show the expression of apprehension in his eyes.

The chief said, "The daughter. Use her to draw Allende." He reached into his coat pocket. He passed a folded newspaper to Andrew. "You can't use our safe houses. The Brits know most of them, and if they do then so do the Russians. Use the money to disappear from their radar. Do not contact the station, unless absolutely necessary."

"For how long?"

"As long as you need to, but keep in mind that time is running out. Work on the girl; she's your girlfriend for Chrissakes. Make her understand that it's in Allende's best interest if we find him first."

Four weeks had passed. Four men convicted in Damian's online court were lynched during this time. At least four hit squads prowled London in search of the man now universally acknowledged as the instigator behind what the media dubbed as mob justice. Andrew Walker spent four restless weeks trying to trace the whereabouts of Damian Allende — the world's most wanted man. Despite the support of his intelligence service his efforts were unsuccessful. As time went by Andrew became increasingly more worried, and it did not help to consider that Damian's ability to disappear was a good sign — it proved that the fugitive was resourceful and could take care of himself. With the Russians, the British, and the Israelis using their best hounds to track Allende, it was indeed, as the station chief had said, a race against time. The chief's hopes to use Amanda did not materialize, and it was indeed surprising that Damian did not make attempts to inquire about her, but in this, at least, Andrew found encouragement, as it was testament of regard for his ability to protect Damian's daughter.

Indeed, Andrew's primary concern was Amanda's safety. Following the event in Reykjavik she developed a certain esteem for Andrew that he, at first, construed as reverence for his strength and ability to take charge in challenging circumstances. It took him time to realize that something else was present in Amanda's attitude toward him. He could not quite place it at first, and realized with consternation, that his inability to read her true feelings, was the result of her making every effort to conceal them; he began to sense it gradually, finding confirmation in her demeanor, in the ways she embraced him, kissed him, and shared her thoughts with him — all with a discernible distance. Had it been any other circumstances, he would have found explanation for it in mere fatigue caused by frequent change of locales, constant life on the road, of never fully unpacked suitcases, but with the circumstances being what they were, with adrenaline running high, with the risk that should unite them ever stronger, he had to concede that his actions in Reykjavik were responsible for the change. Amanda did not trust him.

16

During those first four weeks in hiding Amanda fell behind on her work for the newspaper. Because of concerns for their safety, Andrew insisted that contact with the editor-in-chief must be postponed at least until he received a word from the station chief that it was safe. The newspaper was forced to turn to a reserve of interviews conducted earlier, and for a number of reasons not yet published. But even those had run out, and the newspaper hired a temporary replacement, while keeping Amanda employed on a premise of special assignment. The editor-in-chief had not given up on the exclusive scoop on Damian Allende, and was prepared to go a long way to accommodate his reporter, but Amanda expected that his patience would run out eventually. She could not help it. She could not work, and not merely out of concern for herself, but because her mind was elsewhere. Her every thought was split between her father, and the man whom she thought she knew and loved.

The events of the four weeks that were initiated in Reykjavik, caused her to see Andrew in a whole new light. Frequent lodging changes were inconvenient, but the necessity to swap SIM cards, even entire handsets, combined with the overall ease of living under an assumed identity, was suspicious. Amanda grew wary of Andrew's resources, not so much the financial, as the organizational ones. She did not ask questions but was curious about the source of the excellently forged documents he used to register both them in the various locales. Her journalistic sense led her to keep a close eye on Andrew, the supposed IT security officer at one of London's chief commercial banks. While the inquiry yielded positive results, the ease with which she acquired it strengthened her doubts that set seed that morning in Iceland.

Andrew's resourcefulness shown that fateful day served as fertilizer for her doubts. Four weeks after the Odyssey through bed and breakfasts, hotels and dingy flats, had began, she became convinced that her boyfriend was not whom he purported to be. Her conviction became firm one morning with a conversation she overheard while in the shower. The bathroom window in one of the flats they rented overlooked a tiny balcony. As was her custom Amanda liked to lathe her hair away from the stream of water. She stepped out of the stall and it was then that the peculiar words reached her via the window left ajar to let the steam out of the bathroom.

Andrew stayed in sporadic, but necessary, contact with Dick Verso. The station chief used an unregistered mobile phone to appraise Andrew on the Company's progress in locating Damian Allende. That morning he telephoned to pass on the news that a Russian oligarch, the darling of the Moscow regime, a personal friend of the president, a powerful energy magnate, and one of the most powerful men in Russia, was killed. Convicted in the online court of environmental pollution in the pristine regions of Siberia, and of embezzling billions in public funds that he funneled to the state-owned corporation that he chaired, the oligarch was assassinated by unknown assailants; the killing was clean and swift — a professional job. It followed to reason that the Russian intelligence service would step up their efforts to catch the instigator, yet the information from sources close to the Kremlin was puzzling: The Russians did, indeed, increase their presence in the United Kingdom, but, despite the loss of their prominent citizen, they had no intention of killing Damian Allende. Quite to the contrary — the word on the street had it that the fugitive was to be offered protection from competing services. As puzzling as it were, the news was good for Damian, in accordance with the old saying: Where two dogs fight, a rabbit gets away.

Andrew was on the balcony, not three feet away from Amanda, separated by a wall and small vent-window, speaking to his mobile handset, too absorbed in the conversation to notice the prying ears, convinced of privacy by the sound of running water.

"Sooner or later they will catch on to us. ... I'm not worried about the small fish, but now the Brits, the Russians, the Chinese, the French, and the Israelis are closing in! ... How long can we elude them? ... No, I don't want protection. It may spook her even more. ... She's made no contact. ... I'd know, I assure you. ... He must be in London. Where else could he disappear so completely? ..."

Three or four minutes later he walked in to the bathroom, and announced, "We have to move."

Amanda had heard it too often to bother asking, "Again?" Instead she unplugged the hairdryer, wrapped a towel around her head, and went to the bedroom to gather her belongings. There was not much, and the packing was brief. She was quite used to living out of her suitcase, with only the bare necessities taken out; it reminded her of the summer she spent backpacking, only this time it was much more inconvenient. She was no longer a teenager. She refrained from asking questions for as long as her heightened curiosity allowed. It was not long. With the suitcase packed, dressed to leave, she cast a long look around the flat. "How long do we have to go on like this?"

"Until we're safe," Andrew replied.

"Are we ever going to be safe?"

"Darling, I told you. I won't let anything happen to you."

"Yes, you said that. But Andrew, as much as you worry about me, I worry about you. I'm worried about the weight you're putting on your shoulders. How long can you carry it on? How long can you elude these... people?"

Something in her voice made him stop what he was doing — the last sweep under the bed and in the nooks and crannies. He stood up straight, approached her, and embraced.

"We're not alone. I have friends. We can stay ahead of the pursuers as long as necessary."

"But that's the point: How long is necessary? Look at this," she pointed to the suitcases, cast a sweeping look around the dingy flat, the only type that allowed the weekly rentals, without a credit check, or the use of credit cards. She looked into his eyes. "How long can we live like this, Andrew?"

They had had similar conversations before, but Andrew sensed that this time she would not be brushed off with the same tale of the necessity to keep low profile. Besides, it was wearing on him too. He loosened the embrace, and approached his suitcase to zip it. He said over his shoulder, "You know it isn't about you or me. It is about your father. We have to do this for him. We have no choice but to live this way, to avoid the bad guys, until your father's situation is resolved."

"Would it not be better if we called the police?"

He turned to face her. "Your father wouldn't want that."

"Perhaps he would if he knew what his daughter has to go through."

"He knows that you are in safe hands, that nothing will happen to you as long as we're together."

"Does he? How does he know this?"

Andrew realized that he said too much. He repeated, "I won't let anything happen to you."

"You sound persuasive, Andrew, but were does your confidence come from? We can't use our phones for more than a day. We can hardly stay in one place for more than three nights. We're living off a single small suitcase each. We carry our own cutlery and mugs—"

"It's all temporary. It will change."

"When?"

He was spared the uncomfortable conversation by a sound at the door. At first it was a quiet brush, as though someone pressed an ear against the surface. It was followed by a vigorous knock.

"Come quick!" He grabbed her hand, and pulled her gently, but firmly, toward the balcony.

Andrew congratulated himself for the doorstopper — an adjustable steel bar that he carried from flat to flat, and from hotel to hotel; it would buy them several minutes. The flat's location was part of the consideration, too. Each was carefully chosen with means of escape in mind. A successful escape was not only a matter of multiple exits. At least one had to be inaccessible to the assailants. It was the only way to ensure Amanda's safety. The current place, while described by the woman as dingy, had the advantage over more flashy locations. Of the three possible access routes, only one was available to the enemy. The narrow balcony that spanned the length of the tenement building had no fire escapes; rather it simply led from one flat to another, with simple plastic barriers separating balconies. Andrew banked on either entering one of the neighboring flats, or using the next available route. The apartment complex had a large inner courtyard that could only be accessed through one of two gates, with a key; one of the gates led to the neighboring building, and thus to safety. Standing on the balcony Andrew considered his options. It was the suitcase in Amy's hand that helped him decide. He should have really insisted on smaller luggage size, but gave up after one of early arguments. Now, the heavy object limited their choices.

Andrew proceeded along the balcony line, with Amanda following. The plastic semi-transparent barriers separating balconies were there for privacy only. They were the administration's response to the fire department's requirements. Each barrier slid-open, allowing tenants to flee in case of emergency. Such an emergency arose, and Andrew and Amanda pushed on through until they found an open apartment door. They breezed through the flat — no inhabitants in sight — and into the staircase. Moments later they emerged on the street.

The ground was burning under their feet. Andrew led the way, walking briskly, but not running, so as not to raise unwanted attention. It was a close call. The third one in a row. Next time they may not be as lucky. Being left to his own devices — and that really was what it amounted to, despite the infrequent contact with Dick Verso — was becoming too heavy for Andrew's lone shoulders. Some day they may not slip through the net set up by the pursuers. Perhaps, as the station chief suggested, Andrew should step up pressure on Amanda in order to use her employer's contacts to help trace Damian. Reunited, they could join forces, come up with a strategy.

Andrew was so deeply entrenched in thought that he scarcely paid attention to the surroundings. Believing in a fail-proof escape route, he pushed on without any additional precautions. He neglected to follow the basic rules of escape and evasion. Whether out of thoughtful reverie, or arrogance, he allowed himself to become accosted by three men, only steps away from the entrance to the Underground.

17

Before they were shoved into a non-descript van, their heads were covered with dark sacs of breathable material. Judging by the length of the trip, and increasing traffic along the way, Andrew surmised that they were driven to central London. Their hoods were not taken off until they climbed five flights of stairs of a building that was under complete renovation. The floor was littered with building material — concrete rubble, rubberized rugs, and lots of cements bags. The cement bags were piled in several locations, in what resembled a child's idea of a fort, reminding Andrew of snow forts he made in his childhood. The fort protected a desk topped with computer screens and other electronic equipment. The entire floor was divided into sections by plastic splash covers — as used by painters and construction companies — and through them Andrew could make out the rooftops of the surrounding buildings; the view was largely obscured by scaffolds and tarps, and telling him that they were on the top floor. He realized that the building and the renovation were a pretext for utilizing the location for reasons other than envisioned by city planners: Two cubes of metal mesh, resembling mosquito window screen, stood in the middle of the floor, complete with cots and chairs. Evidently it was a jail of sorts; that it was not raised specifically for Andrew and Amanda was clear from the sloppy cleaning job — several blotches of what seemed like dried blood on the concrete floor suggested that the cubes were used before, and for reasons that sent shivers down the captives' spines. Andrew shuddered and hoped that Amanda did not notice the blood, hoping that, if she did, she may consider it an industrial spill — oil, or paint. He did not want her spirit to wane. Their situation was bad, of course, but not terminal. The cubes, as the hoods over their heads, despite the ominous message they sent, were actually a promising sign. They meant that he and Amanda were only prisoners. Who were their captors? Andrew could not yet tell, for the three men who brought them here refused to answer his questions. He had some ideas, of course, with the station chief's warning foremost on his mind. The building being under construction was a clue, as well: Although the boom was over, the construction industry was still largely staffed and managed by Eastern European companies. The confirmation came in the form of a meticulously dressed man in his late fifties, or early sixties, who was accompanied by several burly men. He was approached by one of the three guards who brought Andrew and Amanda. From the way the guard addressed the newcomer it was evident that the man was the top figure in the power structure that bound these men. He listened to the report with his eyes on the captives. At last he approached the cubes, scanning the faces of the locked woman and man.

He stopped in front of the woman, and addressed her in accented English, "Your father has done truly formidable work."

Amanda did not react.

Good, Andrew thought. Suppressing emotion, especially anger or fear, was the correct response, as these would be seized upon. He tried to lend her support with his expressive gaze, but Amanda did not return his look. Her eyes were set on the foreigner.

The man continued, "Your father has shown that sort of talent, determination, and some decency — call it social conscience — which can, almost overnight, crush years of systematic efforts to limit, or censor, the flow of information. His use of social networking, or crowdsourcing, was ingenious. Going beyond nationhood, religion, or race, he took the best the Internet has to offer. It would be a terrible waste if his work could not continue."

Amanda remained silent, but a miniscule twitch in the corner of her eye showed that she was intrigued by the last, and least expected, comment.

This sort of cheap reverse psychology won't work, Andrew thought with satisfaction. He knew that Amanda was too sharp to fall for it.

The newcomer in a tailored suit turned to one of the guards. He flicked his finger and a chair was brought to him. He sat down facing the woman. He leaned back, and said, "I'm acquainted with your work, too. My daughter is one of your most ardent followers."

Another cheap trick, Andrew thought, while trying to send a mental message to Amanda.

The man went on, "You're probably wondering why such drastic measures to deliver a few compliments." He cast a wide look around the cube and past it — to the barren floor with building material scattered here and there. "However deserving your, and your father's work, may be, compliments are not the reason for you being here. Though happy I am to meet you, your presence here isn't really the main objective. It is the means. I am confident that it will, at last, procure a chance of my meeting your father."

Amanda exhaled a short loud breath, something resembling a sneer.

"I know, I know! Why should the man desired by every media outlet in the world consent to meet me. You are thinking that I should line up like everybody else. Perhaps it would, in time, offer me a chance to chat with Damian Allende. But I am not everybody else. I am not accustomed to waiting, and I've waited for this opportunity far too long already. My patience has run out. I've brought you here in hope that you may persuade your father to see me, face-to-face. It is very important that he does."

Amanda said nothing.

"Naturally you are not inclined to oblige. I can understand it. The circumstances of our meeting are not exactly trust-evoking. Perhaps, though, your reservations can be set aside in exchanged for the greater good—"

"I'm not an animal!" Amanda cut him off.

The man appeared confused at first. Then he understood. "Of course not, and I assure you that you are not in a ZOO cage. You're in... well, you're in the cube for your own protection."

The young woman sneered again, her face expressing utter contempt.

The man said, "The cube is not locked. You can come out at any time—" He stood up just as she did, and added hurriedly, with his arm raised, "However! I hope you will reconsider."

Something in his voice spelled urgency. Amanda hesitated before reaching for the mesh door.

The foreigner continued, "It's not a cage, and you are not a prisoner. The cube serves a special purpose."

With his eyes on the woman he flicked his fingers. The guard approached, exchanged several quick words with the boss, and proceeded towards the second cage where Andrew was held. He stopped in front of it, reached under his jacket and drew out a pistol.

Andrew was standing with his arms crossed, watching the unfolding events with bemusements that masked concern. At the sight of the weapon his eyes narrowed, but he contained his anxiety so as not to show weakness.

The guard stood not more than five feet away. With only a mesh wall between them he raised the pistol, aimed, and fired.

Andrew closed his eyes. Before the shot resounded in the vast concrete space, he could hear another sound. It was the sound of Amanda's cry.

18

Andrew opened his eyes. The guard stood across the mesh wall, his pistol now holstered. His face pale grey, resembling the hue of the metal mesh, Andrew examined his own body. He was unhurt. Apparently the wire mesh was bulletproof. He shifted his puzzled gaze to the man in the fancy suit.

The man addressed Amanda, "As I said — the cube is for your protection. Combined with my men, and reinforced by other security measures, it is currently the safest place in all of London."

She was too shaken to take his calm demeanor lightly, or to even understand the meaning of his words. Looking at Andrew, her tear-filled eyes were asking: Are you alright?

Andrew did not have time to process what had just occurred. He was not shot, which counted for something, but what about psychological wounds? To his surprise, the initial horror wore off almost as quickly as it appeared, thanks chiefly to the swiftness with which the unexpected event took place. It was clear that it was staged for the performance's sake, with Andrew's participation being reduced to an unwitting actor. He knew, however, that the play had a deeper meaning from that of being purely visual.

Amanda turned to the stranger, her pale face turning red. Too upset to use her voice, her eyes expressed what she could not dress into words.

The mysterious foreigner continued, "Your father has found himself in the most precarious circumstances, and while he might've lit the fire himself, it does not follow that he should burn in it. Let us meet, and I can help him."

"Help?" she forced herself to repeat.

"I can protect him."

She sneered, and glanced to Andrew. "Really?"

The sarcasm in her voice, combined with the peculiar look she cast to Andrew was all too telling. The stranger understood. "I take it that similar promises have already been made to you."

Amanda's cold shoulder was the only answer. She turned her eyes from Andrew, and sat on the aluminum chair, her elbows on the table, her head embraced by her hands.

Andrew's eyes desperately sought Amanda's. He realized what the foreigner was up to, and wanted to counter the inevitable with silent pleas, and a message of love on his face. Alas, she did not return his look. Andrew's face paled. It was more painful to realize that she knew, or suspected, what he wanted to reveal to her so many times already. He wished he had done it.

the stranger went on, "Naturally you are quite right to be cautious about choosing your friends. If only you were cautious when you allowed this distinction to include Mr. Goodman—"

She raised her eyes, but checked herself before prying for explanations.

"He didn't even have the courtesy to tell you his real name?"

Andrew's eyes were on her face, pleading.

The foreigner pushed on, his eyes lacking the expression of satisfaction, even showing some compassion, as though it gave him no pleasure to bring up such painful news. "I can imagine the pretenses that allowed this man to get close to you, Amanda. I understand how difficult it must be to find that you were deceived by this man, day after day, for so many months. I do not envy how you must wonder what is more dear to him — your affection, or his allegiance to his employer?"

She brought herself to ask, "What are you hoping to achieve with this?"

"I am hoping that this disclosure will let you see who your friends really are."

She said nothing. Instead, she cast him a grave look.

The stranger objected, "You mustn't blame the messenger."

Amanda's reaction was not what Andrew expected in the circumstances.

She said, "Why does it surprise you that a woman might prefer the evil she is familiar with, from one whose name she doesn't even know?"

The stranger's face showed disappointment. "My mistake. I assumed that you would have recognized me. After all, we are in the same line of business, so to speak. Please forgive my manners. My name is, of course, Kalgun. Soba Kalgun."

Of course, Amanda thought. She was familiar with the name Soba Kalgun, as anyone in the news media would be. But it was the other name... what was it — Goodman? — that had the more profound effect on her, and was responsible for her self-assurance, so carefully maintained up to this point, to suddenly deflate. Andrew's supposedly real name, combined with the natural simplicity it was delivered by the slick foreigner, marked the extent of her resourcefulness. She could no longer play blasé when what she really wanted was — cry.

Andrew saw the brave face she put on, and noticed the effort it took her to hold back the tears that sparkled in the corners of her eyes.

The man named Kalgun, whether oblivious of the torment he was causing, or doing it with premeditation, pressed on, his every word a sharp point driving deep into Amanda's body. "I won't pretend that I'm your friend. To tell the truth I care for you only inasmuch as it benefits my chances of meeting your father. At least in this respect my intentions are worlds removed from this man's." He pointed his chin to Andrew. "Unlike this impostor, I wish your father no ill. And I sincerely hope that your presence here will facilitate my meeting him. It may be the only way for Damian Allende to avoid meeting the fate bestowed upon him by the like of this Mr. Walker, or Goodman."

Soba Kalgun paused, intrigued by the deeply emotional, if silent, theater developing between the captives. The emotions that traveled between the two were as clear as if they were written in permanent ink. It was a combination of disenchantment, broken hopes, and the birth of hatred.

Kalgun went on, "Your father, dear Amanda, is a hunted man. The Americans and Israelis, the Chinese and the Pakistanis, the French and the British — everyone wants to dispose of him as quickly as possible, before he strikes any more of their government officials, or business leaders—"

"My father is not a killer!" Amanda cut him off, her eyes still on Andrew.

"He is worse. He is seen as the instigator, or the brains behind the killings. His online court is the true thorn in everybody's eye, and the only solution everyone sees is to remove it."

"He is not an instigator of these crimes, either!" Amanda said in no less vehement tone.

"Perhaps not intentionally. Not at first. What started as an interesting sociological project, what with the Third World dictators placed on trial in front of the very people they oppress, has turned into a travesty that hit too close to home. Need I remind you that your father was the darling of the Western world as long he concentrated on the distant and exotic dictators? He became a leper when turned against our own. Did he expect to be petted on the head when he brought the misdeeds of our leaders into the spotlight? No, no, do not be offended. I'm not here to judge him. Nor is it my intention to commend him. Your father is the tailor of his own destiny. The rest of us are only spectators. He has put on a good show, to be sure. He has demonstrated that there is not a single government on the face of this wretched planet that does not have dirty hands. Furthermore, he has shown the corruptness of the corporate media, its systematic failure to report on the crimes and excesses of the governments. In the process he has made enemies among the mighty, and those who serve them, the media not excluding. Everyone wants him stopped. Everyone, save for the people who have, at last, found a white knight to avenge the corruption and crimes that they watched year after year, month after month, day after day, in utter helplessness."

She hissed through her teeth, "And you? What do you want?"

Soba Kalgun took a deep breath before replying. "I want Damian Allende to continue doing what he's started."

19

"Of course you do!" Andrew Walker decided that it was time to halt Kalgun's destructive rant.

To his surprise it was Amanda who objected to his sarcastic snarl.

"If you don't mind, Andrew! I'd like to hear it."

Andrew knew that it was his own fault. He should have come clean before things went out of hand. He knew her enough to know that she cared little for the man who kidnapped her, and she gave him the time of day only to get back at the boyfriend who hurt her so badly.

Andrew tried to appeal to her, "Come now, Amy! Can you believe a man who kidnapped you?"

She shot back, bitingly, "Should I trust a man who befriended me, only to sneak closer to my father?"

"It's not like that, Amy." Andrew protested, his voice lacking conviction. He added quietly, "Not entirely."

"Your credibility leaves much to be desired, Mr. Walker, or Goodman." Soba Kalgun took advantage to further sow mistrust between the two, his words intended for the woman.

Andrew did not give up. "It says something about a man who puts a black hood over your eyes." He added, with his eyes on Amanda's, "Can you ever be sure that he isn't deceiving you?"

Amanda sighed.

Kalgun's only reply was a grin of pity.

The silence lasted whole two minutes. Everyone's attention was centered on the woman, who, following Andrew's words, turned her back to both men. Her shoulders rose in quiet sobbing. They heard nothing until she turned again to face them, an expression of determination in her eyes.

With her voice quiet, harboring latent warning, she said to Andrew, "Is any of it true?"

He replied hurriedly, sensing a decisive moment in their relationship, "Yes, and no. I do work for the intelligence, but I do not intend to harm your father. You must believe me!"

"Ha!" Soba Kalgun exhaled.

Amanda was not convinced, either, and it showed on her face.

Andrew was losing ground.

"Amy," he pleaded. "I can't tell you how often I wanted to come clean. How I wanted to tell you the truth—"

"You should have!" She cut him off, icily.

"Amy—"

"Enough, Andrew! You lied to me for months, every day, even during the most intimate moments. You came close to me under false pretenses. How can I believe anything you say?" She turned to Kalgun. "And you, mister, don't flatter yourself thinking that you've convinced me as to your intentions. You're not that different from one another — one tried to get close to my father through my heart, the other by force."

Kalgun took no offence. "I can understand your apprehension. The circumstances of our meeting are most unfortunate, but necessary. The hood, the dark van, the cube — these are all precautionary measures used for your protection."

"Ha-ha!" Andrew burst out with sarcasm.

Kalgun continued with his eyes on Amanda's, "I have no reason to deceive you. I shall achieve what I want with or without your help. Although, I admit, it'd be infinitely easier and better for all involved if you'd consider helping."

"It was very considerate of you to offer your protection, however differently it may seem," she said with derision.

"I wish we could've met in better circumstances, alas, with your father being the most wanted man, with the best-skilled and ill-intentioned pursuers on his tail, you have become part of the game. The players are ruthless, playing hard, and the response must be likewise. My men picked you up off the street—"

"Snatched." She corrected.

Kalgun did not object. He continued, "And they covered your head so as to protect your identity should someone peek into the van. These men," he pointed to the guards, "are here to offer protection, nothing more."

"Then they won't mind if I leave the cage?"

Amanda did not wait for a reply. She opened the mesh door and stepped outside of the cube.

Kalgun sighed. "I wish you'd reconsider. There are men, out there, who are determined to do you harm."

"Why would anyone want to harm me?" Amanda asked, her eyes blinking innocently.

"You are pursued by killers who want to use you to get close to your father. That's the gist of it. Therefore the sooner your father and I meet face to face, the sooner we'll be able to discard these crude precautionary measures."

"Why does it sound like blackmail?"

"It is mere urgency."

His pleading voice made her consider her words before plying. "How do you see it work?"

"Convince your father to come here. I can offer him protection."

"Amy!" Andrew warned.

She did not even grace him with a look when she said to Kalgun, "Why not do it yourself?"

"Your father is on the run; he doesn't know a friend from a foe; he would sooner trust you."

The logic of the statement and its conclusion were inescapable.

"That's the key, isn't it? My father won't trust you, yet you expect it of me."

Kalgun nodded.

"Give me a reason why I should," she said angrily.

"You are out of the cube. And you are free to leave the building."

"No one will stop me?"

"No one."

"No one will follow me?"

"Not my men."

Amanda started for the nearest exit, an opening in the concrete wall.

"I said — not my men. I can't vouch for your father's enemies, though."

She paused.

"At least consider some protection," Kalgun said with well feigned resignation.

He flicked his fingers and one of the guards reached in to something on the table behind the bags of cement. He approached the woman, and handed the object to her.

She looked at it, then at Kalgun. "A bullet-proof vest?"

"You will need it."

She glanced at Andrew. Something in his eyes, a sign of desperate plea, or feelings for her, made her realize the impossible situation she found herself in. Pointing her head to the vest, and then to the cubes, she said, "It's mere theatrics. If you want my help you have to do better to convince me of your intentions. Start by explaining who you are."

Kalgun said with the expression of injured pride, "I would've thought that my name said it all."

Amanda did know about Kalgun, as much as any journalist would, but she reasoned that Andrew did not, and that by confronting the two men she might learn more of both of the their intentions.

She said, "You flatter yourself."

"Ha! One learns something new every day. Alright. My name is Soba Kalgun, and I am the owner of your newspaper's biggest competitor. I own many newspapers and magazines."

"So, you're that Kalgun!" Andrew said from his cube. He added, "Oligarch. KGB."

Unexpectedly for Andrew, Amanda took his side, her big eyes on the Russian's, "Andrew has a point."

"My past is not a secret."

"But it sure places you in a whole new light!" Andrew felt he was gaining points.

Kalgun shrugged. "Let's not veer off the main objective."

"On the contrary," Andrew clung on to the idea. "It's worth asking why the KGB wants to lay its hands on the most wanted man in the world!"

Kalgun lost his patience, "You're putting too much weight on the past. KGB no longer exists. It's time you and your wizards accepted the facts instead of perpetuating the old tales of the bogeyman. Perhaps then, instead of getting stuck in the mud of the days gone by, your agency would have been able to avoid the blunders it made, and continues to make."

Despite the harsh criticism Andrew had reason to triumph. Regardless of what the Russian said in his own defense, he could not escape the past, and of the two of them no one's past was darker than that of the former KGB officer. Amanda might reconsider placing her thrust in such a man after all, Andrew hoped.

Kalgun wanted the topic to end. "We'll chat about the past some other time. Today let us concentrate on things that matter here and now."

"We can't escape that tiny, insignificant issue of trust," Amanda said. "Right now your associations, past and present, do not bode well. For instance: What does a media mogul, with ties to the KGB and the Kremlin, want from the man who set out to expose and bring to justice both institutions?"

"It isn't as sinister as you paint it. You'd see through it if only you'd put aside my KGB past, and consider who I am today. I am Soba Kalgun, the owner of a growing media conglomerate, and I want Damian Allende to continue his work. I want him to offer my newspapers and television networks the exclusive access to the leaked documents that he procures through his whistleblower portal."

The surprise was absolute in its preposterousness. Amanda was speechless, unable to reply.

Andrew seized upon Kalgun's words, aware of the implications of Damian Allende being tied to classified document-publishing service, which, if proven, would make a legal case for his prosecution. He demanded, "Do you have any proof of it? What are your sources?"

"Suffice it to say that they are well-informed sources." At seeing a sneering expression on Andrew's face, Kalgun added, "You may refer to my past for the general idea."

Amanda was flustered. She too understood the implications of her father being behind the document-leaking site, an allegation that had been circling newswires since the first online trial. If proved true it would place her father at terrible odds with most jurisdictions, and would lend fuel to his ill-wishers. A case could be built to shatter the image of a pioneering champion of online free speech, and turn him into a law-breaking fugitive from justice.

Andrew tried to console her with a soothing expression, but Amanda avoided his eyes. Kalgun's assertion was indeed bad. For months now the American administration considered invoking the

Espionage Act against the founders of the whistleblower portal, all such attempts failing for a variety of reasons, least of all for the lack of clear ownership. If established, such persons would be tried for any number of offenses, including possession and distribution of classified government material, and persecuted to the full extent of the law. In essence, it would mean, almost certainly, the end of these services in favor of the need to concentrate on legal defense. Andrew was far from ready to accept Kalgun's words at face value, but saw no reason why the man should invent the accusation. But, was it the same as telling the truth? Did it even matter? He glanced at Kalgun, and then at Amanda, not seeing what they grasped instantly — the power of the pervasive propaganda network that was the mass media. He thought: Would it really be so bad if Damian was involved with, or even founded the whistleblower portal? Would it make him less of the hero that people saw in him? Let the powers that be pursue Damian, with all the resources at their disposal, for it would only reinforce the image of the knight in the white armor!

Kalgun seemed to read Andrew's mind when he said to Amanda, "Damian Allende's work is truly groundbreaking. It completely shakes the traditional media model of today. He had highlighted the complacency of the corporate media, its subservience toward the elites. Personally, as an interested party with stakes in the business, I may add that it's a contributing factor in the woes of the publishing industry. This leads me to answer the question you are undoubtedly wanting to ask: What drives me to seek cooperation with your father, the destructor of the industry? The answer is in the above and... in my big ego. And it is big. Having exclusive access to the whistleblower material would elevate my media holdings to the top."

"Greed," Andrew summarized.

Kalgun bowed slightly, with pride. With his eyes on Amanda, he said, "Your father's crusade would benefit too. I have the means to provide his safety, and to pay the legal bills that will undoubtedly pile up if he continues his work."

20

"Greed and power," Andrew thought out loud. On the face of it Kalgun's reasoning was not out of bounds with what the man represented. If capitalism was expressed in greed then its Russian oligarchic incarnation was its purest form. If Kalgun was telling the truth, and Damian Allende was the founder of the whistleblower portal — the world's largest database of leaked classified military, industrial, and diplomatic cables — then early and exclusive access to it, if not outright possession of this vast treasure trove, would be tempting indeed, as it would provide an unquestionable advantage for someone in Kalgun's position. For Andrew, greed itself was not as evil as it was often painted. It was its possession and the intent that raised the brow. Andrew, being the son of the most gluttonous of cultures, was not opposed to the idea of greed, and had Kalgun been a compatriot, he would, perhaps, think nothing of his goals, for in his mind it was perfectly reasonable to want to consolidate more power in one hand. With Kalgun being a Russian, and a former KGB officer with active ties to the Kremlin, Andrew instantly sensed deception. He set out to expose it.

"There is some truth to the old saying that one can have too much of a good thing," Andrew said.

Kalgun shot back a questioning gaze.

Andrew explained. "Amanda's father is hunted precisely because of the information that you want to possess."

"It is not the possession itself that has many governments up in arms. Who owns it, and what they do with the information, is the key. Information is power, to be sure, but used unwisely it can have the opposite effect — it can destroy its bearer. Had Damian Allende simply allowed whistleblowers to upload files to his portal it would, perhaps, never have escalated to the point where death threats were issued against him. Releasing the documents, combined with their use in his online court, has led to his near-demise."

"And you? Are you not concerned that same fate awaits you?"

"A man like me has means that are not available to mere mortals—"

"A man like you?" Andrew was amused by the pompousness.

"A man in my profession."

"Which of your professions are you referring to?"

Kalgun ignored the sarcasm. "I own enough media outlets to be reckoned with. Recognized journalism has many advantages over activist journalism. Your policymakers would not dare call so openly for the assassination of a journalist who did what Allende did as a private citizen. Though one must doubt whether any journalist would dare do what he set out to achieve. Damian Allende has challenged the authority. In the process he has amassed a powerful weapon. The information he has gathered through the whistleblower portal can effect profound changes."

"Is this what you're after? The power to effect change? Is this what the media is for?"

"I understand what you're getting at. You're thinking: What does an ex-KGB officer want from the most sensitive information to come out of the deepest vaults of his country's old adversary? Am I right?"

"Isn't it true?"

"The truth is that you are blinded by your professional prejudice, and of the worst kind. You see only the past, what I was, not what I am. Once a spy always a spy sort of mentality."

"Do you blame me for being concerned about you vying for this sensitive information?"

Kalgun realized that he would not get through to this young man. Glancing at the woman, he was beginning to worry that the ranting man might impact her decision. As though she had a choice, he thought. He looked closer at the girl. She seemed to listen intently to the exchange of words. Something told him, however — and Kalgun was a good observer of people and their emotions — that as keenly as she observed their verbal sparring, Amanda's concerns for her father were filtered through her feelings for Andrew. It was clear in the way she gazed at him, blushed and paled at the sound of his voice, that his treachery and dishonesty had not erased her love for him. It gave Kalgun an idea. He might yet succeed.

Kalgun said to Andrew, "You don't have to rely solely upon my word. Join me. Become the agent of change."

Andrew was taken aback by the offer. He wanted to object, but found himself able to utter only two words. "The what?"

"Do it for whatever reasons motivate you. Do it to redeem yourself in the eyes of this young lady."

Kalgun knew he hit the spot. He saw in the two sets of eyes. He saw it in the timid look Andrew shot to Amanda, and he saw it in the woman's blushed face. He pressed, "I know about the private agreement you made with Damian Allende. I know about the trial Allende wants to subject himself to. I know about your voluntary mission to join him in refining of his portal. I am guessing the reasons that motivate you. I am guessing that you are not quite satisfied with the role you play in the world affairs. So, I am offering you a chance to help change the world. Join me. Help turn the media into the force of good."

Andrew was flustered. Kalgun's words were not something he expected, but what surprised him even more was the effect the unexpected offer had on Amanda. Her eyes hung on his lips as though the future of the world depended upon his answer. Yet Andrew was short for words, a most unusual occurrence for a man with a sharp mind, and who was trained, as well as naturally predisposed to be a step ahead of his adversary. When he could not outwit his opponents he made the appearance of it, for Andrew's life was based on deception, it was a part of his job, it became a part of his life. This time, for the first time, he allowed himself to be taken off guard.

Amanda was puzzled by Andrew's silence. She shot a look to Kalgun, and saw the answer on his face. It made her angry. She did not like being used as a pawn. She said, "You are ignoring one crucial aspect. My father has nothing to do with the whistleblower portal, at least not in any significantly different way from anybody else. Everyone can access the leaked documents, and do whatever the heck they want with them. That does not make everyone a potential founder of the portal, does it. My father's only guilt, in his persecutors' eyes, is in the way he used the information stored on the whistleblower portal. Granted, and only from the perspective of time, and the events that preceded it, that the online court might not have been the most fortunate expression of his disagreement with the status quo, but it did reverberate with the people. That's what is at the core of the hysteria. The assassinations that are attributed to my father are only the expression of universal frustration with corrupt governance and judicial systems. He provided a vessel to voice this frustration, but to blame him for the assassinations is ludicrous. He cannot be held responsible for the actions of those who view the results of his online court."

"As a newspaperman I wholeheartedly agree with you. Your father, like any journalist, is only the messenger, not responsible for the actions of consumers of his news. Unfortunately for him, your father has gone further. By founding the whistleblower portal, and actively commissioning the leaking of classified documents, he has placed himself in a judiciary limbo, open to interpretation and abuse."

"No one has made a compelling case of providing proof that he is involved with the whistleblower portal."

"Oh, but he is! Your father is the chief driving force behind the WikiJustice—"

"Come again? Wiki... what?"

"It's what they call it. It's a collaborative effort. Accurately speaking it is crowdsourcing, but it's quite the mouthful for many who are not proficient in the English language; hence — WikiJustice. From the collection of leaked documents via the whistleblower portal, to utilizing them to convict the offenders in the online court, to delivering punishment — it's all done through mass participation of like-minded people."

Andrew awakened from his momentary stupor. He repeated the Russian's words, "Delivering punishment?"

"Murder. Justice. Punishment. The definition depends on the point of view. It is, however, an undeniable fact, that the assassinations have taken place. They are the final stage in a string of events that originated with the leaked documents."

"Ha-ha!" Amanda projected a nervous laugh.

"And just who carries out those assassination?" Andrew asked.

"Clearly not Damian Allende himself," Kalgun replied.

"Stop this." Amanda said in a weak voice.

Andrew appeared not to hear her plea, or, perhaps, wanted to make up for his previous loss of tongue. He prowled on, "There is no proof of Allende having anything to do with the assassinations."

Kalgun replied, "It does not change my offer, whether he does or not."

"I see. From the standpoint of a news media owner you win either way. If Allende agrees to work with you you'll get the inside scoop from the whistleblower portal, and your stock will go up even higher should it turn out that your source is also the assassin. Only why do I get the feeling that you aren't telling us quite the full story? Why do I feel that there is something else that tempts you even more?"

"Stop it!" Amanda raised her voice. "I won't listen to it anymore. My father may be many things but he is not a killer!" She faced Kalgun, and accused him, "All you do is disseminate lies. As a newspaperman you should know better than to rely on rumors—"

She paused abruptly at seeing the Russian make a sudden gesture.

Kalgun flicked his fingers and one of the guards approached him with something in his hand. Kalgun took it and handed it over to the woman. It was a single sheet of paper.

She glanced at it. Her eyes devoured it top to bottom.

Andrew watched as her face turned as white as the sheet in her hand.

"What is it, Amy?"

She did not react.

"Talk to me!" Andrew persisted.

Kalgun signaled his man, who approached the woman, took the sheet out of her hand, and walked over to the cube. He slid the paper through a narrow crack between the mesh door and its frame.

Andrew recognized the seal of the Central Intelligence Agency. He read the document hungrily. Then he read it again, slowly. It was an internal circular recognizing an organization dubbed WikiJustice, and listing several names of its founders. The organization's mandate was summarized in a motto: "To remove the social ill — the individuals, organizations, and corporations — whose actions are detrimental to the wellbeing of society." The document appeared genuine, similar in every respect to the countless ones Andrew had seen in the course of his work.

"Amy!" he started. He could not find the right words. What could he say? Instead he turned to Kalgun.

The Russian understood the silent question. "I suppose you're wondering where this document came from? Ha-ha! Damian Allende would appreciate the irony. You see, whistleblowers are not a new invention. They predate the Internet age. In the news circles we refer to them as sources."

"You have sources inside the CIA?"

Kalgun nodded ever so slightly that it could be construed as the result of a deep breath intake.

"Are those your journalistic sources, or the KGB's?"

"Does it make any difference?"

Andrew gnawed his teeth. He said angrily, "This could be a fabrication."

"I considered this option. But the fabrication could only come from the CIA, which raises a question: What's in it for the notorious spy agency?"

Andrew had no answer.

Kalgun went on, "Whatever the case may be, I am of the firm opinion that nobody's crimes are irreversible, some may even be considered justifiable. Damian Allende, directly or indirectly, is involved in the murders that were sparked by his online court. It is not my place to judge him. Personally, I hold considerable sympathy for his work. The world is better off for the loss of the perpetrators of crimes that he had the guts to expose. Professionally, though, I want to get to the bottom it. I want the scoop. I want to tear it apart and look inside to the intestines of the beast!" He ended with a spark in his eyes.

Andrew watched him closely. So much for the rhetoric about building the media as the source of good, he thought. Aloud he said, "What do you propose?"

"I want to reach Damian Allende. I want to provide a safe working environment for his project. Together we can build true alternative media, we'll form a powerful Fifth Estate, one able to stand up to the corporate media and its puppet master — the government elites."

"Ha-ha!" Andrew burst out. "That's very ambitious, if suicidal for a corporate media mogul."

"Do not rush to conclusions. I am a businessman. It is true that with hard work, and some luck, I managed to build one of the largest media holdings in Europe. One of. That's what it will ever be. And it is not good enough. I am motivated by new challenges. With the world's media being held by a narrowing group of what the liberal press refers to as the media barons, I can, at best, be counted as one of them. I am one of them. Today I control an X number of outlets. Tomorrow I'll have an X plus one. The next day I may lose one to my competition. And so it'll turn. I've reached the pinnacle of my... greed, if you want to call it as such. We all, the media moguls, are playing with a stick, like a bunch of dogs in the park, pulling it out of each other's teeth. Some gains, some losses. The stick keeps changing hands, but it remains the same stick. I want a new toy. But, where do I get it from in this limited world? My counterparts satisfy their hunger for a new stick by eavesdropping on citizens and public figures' mobile phones, or by running for office, funding political parties, building sweatshops, or by sinking their profits into a myriad of other ventures. None of them make significant inroads into the world of the media. I know. I've been at it. I've reached that stage where I know I cannot grow, not in a way to satisfy me. What do I have left? Become a politician? What for? I own politicians. Make more money by buying up industries? I already have more money than I can ever spend. Here comes Damian Allende, a man who opened my eyes to a whole new world, a world that's already out there. It is fractured, disorganized, lacking financing and organization, but high on spirit. It's the independent press, the blogs, and the ad hoc lone gunmen who suddenly see the light; they print community alerts, they blog about corruption on local and broad level; some of them go all the way out, far out, and take on the world cabal of the New Order. One thing that unites them all is the Internet crackpot stigma, often successfully raised and sustained by those who stand to lose from this grassroots journalism. What if this were to change? What if all these crackpots were united? What if they were assured of a wide audience through many different channels?" Kalgun cast a sweeping look from Amanda to Andrew. The expression of fascination in his eyes was undeniable. The Russian was truly swept by his idea. He continued excitedly, a possessed man, "I can do it. I can build the world's largest alternative news media, in opposition to the corporate outlets, and keeping checks on the governments and the corporations that fund the corporate, the corrupt model. I can form the true Fifth Estate, a power in itself."

Kalgun's passionate rant had this profound effect on Amanda, that only two alike minds share when swept by the same idea. She was, however, in possession of a sharp mind, one not easily affected by shear passion. She saw the apparent flaw in Kalgun's reasoning. She asked, "How can you justify the stakes you have in the, as you called it — the corrupt corporate media — with that of the alternative?"

Kalgun replied without much ado, an image of mischievous satisfaction on his face, "It's perfectly simple, and Andrew has already nailed it down. I am driven by the most powerful desire of all — I want it all. I want to eat the bread from both baskets."

21

The same mentality that might have convinced torturers of the validity of information extracted under pain, had convinced the Russian that his captives believed the sincerity of his grandiose plans. It did not occur to him that an offer accepted under duress might be neither sincere nor binding. While he banked on finding a keen ear, he expected it as being the effect of his own performance more than anything. He has made his case, an impassioned plea that he so often utilized to great success in dealing with dilettantes to shore up investment for his early business deals. He found then that showing a human face along with promise of great rewards worked better than concentrating solely on the latter. Many years spent in the position of nearly feudal authority as head of his media empire had stripped him of the basic ability to read and understand the desires motivating the common folk. Had he himself suffered hardships of the heart in his life, he would have, perhaps, understood that the couple who were in his grip would agree to anything that offered them a chance to better their current condition.

Amanda's motivations to accept Kalgun's words at face value were expertly hidden. The countless interviews she conducted with, often intimidating, celebrities, allowed her to put on the face required to show the Russian that his reasoning had convinced her to accept his offer. She was less successful at the second challenge, that of avoiding the pleading eyes of the man whom she loved and who betrayed her so badly.

Andrew was indeed desperately trying to catch Amanda's eyes. He was devastated by the turn of events. To be caught by the Russian was one thing, but to lose the trust of the woman he loved was something else. Cursing himself for not coming clean with her, he found himself in the unenviable position to come up with a plan to regain the upper hand in dealing with their captor, and to assure Amanda of the sincerity of his unswerving affection and intentions. He understood that the latter would be the hard part. What could he say that would not resemble a desperate attempt at excuses of the vilest of villains? Did he not seek her friendship under false pretenses? Did he not accept the commission to infiltrate her father's life? Those were undeniable facts exposed by the Russian. No amount of pleading and explaining could change what was done. To say now that he had experienced a change of heart, that he had fallen in love with her, and was swept by her father's work, would only be taken for an excuse of a cornered liar. Seeing her, as she avoided his eyes, Andrew realized that only one avenue was left to him. To regain the trust and affection of the woman he loved he must prove his worth by action, not by words. And it appeared to him, that the only way to reach her, was through that, which was dear to her — Damian Allende.

Andrew asked the Russian, feigned amicability in his voice, "How do you plan to find Damian?"

Kalgun smiled. "I already have. This was the easy part."

Amanda raised her deep blue eyes to the Russian. While she said nothing her eyes expressed alarm mixed with hope.

Andrew asked quickly, not able to conceal his anxiety, "Then what do you need Amy for?"

"I expressed it very clearly."

"Allende will not come to you, so you must lure him in."

"A brute's choice of words, but they accurately describe the idea."

"Allende doesn't trust you. Do you think he'll change his mind when he finds out you kidnapped his daughter?"

"There goes your antagonism again. I hope," Kalgun turned to Amanda, "that you don't think me all that bad. Contrary to what Mr. Walker, or Goodman, says — you were not kidnapped. You were brought here, in haste, to be offered protection. Your father needs protection too, and urgently—"

"Mr. Walker," she cut him off, taking special care to pronounce the name with ice-cold intonation, "raised a good point earlier on. Trust is not something that can be flicked on with a switch. It must be earned."

"Did I not prove it by letting you out of the cube, despite the advice of my security chief? Did I not prove it by sharing with you my plans?"

Andrew reminded, "I am still in the cage!"

Kalgun turned to him, "The fact that you are here at all is due to the transcript of your conversation conducted with Damian Allende that night in Reykjavik. I read it with interest. You seemed convincingly sincere—"

Andrew recalled the two men with stun guns. Kalgun had the place bugged. He found hope in it. "I thought it was a private conversation," he said.

Amanda could not help it. She glanced at Andrew.

Andrew hoped that she would ask for the transcript; it would go a long way in reasserting his sincerity.

Instead, Kalgun replied, "I'm glad you felt that way. It only proves that you were sincere, not putting on a show. And it is the reason you are here. You're in the cube for your own protection. And for mine, too."

"Do you think I might lash out at you?"

"Nothing of the sort. Your friends, however, might try. I'm certain they are somewhere in the neighborhood, looking for you. They would've found you already if not for the cube. It's a sort of a Faraday cube — it blocks electromagnetic waves, making eavesdropping useless. Essentially it prevents mobile scanners from detecting your RFID chip. Step out of the cube and pretty soon we'll have half the world's spies on our hands, all looking for you."

"The RFID chip? You've tapped into the CIA personnel files of our covert operatives!"

"As did the intelligence services of several countries, not all of whom are particularly fond of America."

"The other services be damned. I'm talking about you! You've found my chip's ID, and the frequencies to scan."

"Don't sound so shocked. One does what one can to overcome obstacles."

"But you've unearthed information that you're not supposed to, that no one is supposed to."

"Should it bother you?"

"Should it bother me? You can track our agents, monitor their every move!"

"I suppose it would be no use saying that I cared to track only one? One that does not identify with the agency, anymore?"

"What you did does not impact the agency alone — it's an attack against America. You bet your ass it bothers me!"

Kalgun chewed on the statement before replying, his eyes shooting telling looks at the woman. "Let us not lose focus," he said.

Andrew could not argue with the logic, least of all because he was struck with a sudden thought. Kalgun was right — Amanda was his first priority. He looked at the woman, but asked the Russian, "Do you have the transcript of my conversation with Damian Allende?"

Kalgun followed his gaze and understood. He flicked his fingers and one of his guards began to type something on the computer.

Amanda realized what motivated Andrew to bring up the transcript. Yet, recent events taught her that what people say did not necessarily match their intentions. She would not fall for any more careless whispers.

She asked sharply, "Where is my father?"

Kalgun replied without any signs of malice or duplicity, "Staying at a friend's mansion outside of London."

"Where?"

He gave the location. "While it served him well those past weeks, the place cannot be considered safe any longer. Your father must be persuaded to leave the mansion and to come here. The urgency must not be underestimated. If I found him then so can his enemies."

The woman caught the accent he placed on the last word. It amused her. The Russian tried to make a distinction between himself and the other parties who were in pursuit of Damian Allende. That was rich! She was not buying it. She might have been young, born after the Cold War, but even she understood that no one who carried a high rank in the former KGB, and whose fortune was tied to the ruling elites of a corruption-ridden country, could be trusted. The same sentiment included Andrew. It made no difference to her whether one served the KGB or the CIA. Where deception was the modus operandi one could not take anything at face value.

Andrew interrupted her thoughts. He asked the Russian, "Where do I fit in it?"

Kalgun glanced at Amanda before replying. In this, perhaps involuntary, gesture was all the reply necessary. It was clear that

Andrew was here only in consideration of the woman. The Russian's words made no such claims however. "You can make good on the promises you made to Damian Allende."

"You expect me to perform like a ZOO animal, locked in a cage?"

"Certainly not. And it's not a cage—"

"A cube. Sure."

"It's a temporary measure. You shall leave it as soon as we're ready."

"Meaning?"

Kalgun glanced at Amanda again. She understood that Andrew's fate was in her hands. Yet she made no gesture, and said no words that would help Kalgun determine how she felt about the man who betrayed her so badly. Evidently coming to the conclusion that she would have objected to the idea of Andrew working with her father if it was abhorrent to her, Kalgun took her silence for an agreement.

"Amanda will record the message for her father. You will encode it according with the encryption you agreed upon in Reykjavik."

Andrew had other questions when the guard approached. He handed his boss a tablet computer. Kalgun passed it on to Amanda. "The transcript. It should put Mr. Walker in a somewhat more favorable light."

She did not look at the portable device, and did not extend her hand. Instead, she asked, "Might I be shown to the ladies' room first?"

Perhaps it was something in her voice that caused Kalgun to hesitate for a moment. Recalling his claims about mutual trust he replied quickly, "Misha will show you the way."

Amanda noticed the hesitation. The Russian was consumed by doubt. The realization reaffirmed her own misgivings about him. Doubt is contagious and persistent, sometimes for a good reason, she thought. It keeps one's head straight when one is confronted with demagogues and ideologues. Doubt was driving her to do what she was about to do. She followed the guard through a maze of building rubble and dusty material, all dumped by laborers that were nowhere to be found. The building was undergoing a major renovation, the rooms stripped to bare concrete — a clear sign that the project was a lengthy one. Three portable toilet stalls were installed in a room similar to every other — it was a concrete cube, with gashes where doors and windows were once present, now blocked off with cinder blocks and lumber.

The guard withdrew outside, to the corridor.

Amanda had to act fast. She looked at the shabby devices that smelled as though they had not been emptied in quite some time, but nothing came to mind. The room was a trap. Bare concrete walls housed nothing but the portable toilets. Having no plan, driven by a single desire to flee, she began to panic. She opened the door to one of the toilets, taking care to make enough noise to convince the guard that she was in fact using it. As she opened the door and glanced inside she was struck with an idea. It was a long shot, but she had a chance. One in three. Not much, but she had to try anyway.

Some minutes had passed. The guard was alarmed by the prolonged silence. He came in to the cold grey room, and listened intently. He said in his guttural, heavily accented voice, "Miss?" He repeated it several times. When no answer followed, he approached the row of potties. He knocked on one. Not hearing a reply he yanked the door.

At that moment the toilet swallowed him up; it fell upon him, knocking him down and constricting his moves, not unlike a coffin. The initial shock was his undoing. Had he reacted immediately, he would have succeeded in propping up the potty. The seconds of astonished inactivity were Amanda's gain. She wasted no time. After having overturned the toilet, she pushed the neighboring one on top of it. It did not cover the former but it pinned it down, providing additional weight. The third toilet made it nearly impossible for any man, no matter how strong, to free himself from the constrained space. Enraged at last, the guard roared, his voice muted underneath the pile pinning him down.

Amanda did not wait to hear the foreign execrations. She hurried away, searching for the fastest way out. She made a mental note of the staircase they passed on the way to the bathroom and headed in what she thought was the route to escape, but in the excitement she lost her orientation. It was a pure chance that she reached the stairs. She covered them skipping three and four at once, as she used to do in the old days, when she lived with her aunt on the top floor of an apartment building.

Outside, on the street, she hesitated a split second. Which way? Did it matter? She turned right. Several blocks later she spotted a familiar sign. The Underground.

22

Run, Amy, run! Andrew commended Amanda in his mind. She would have been out of the building by now, on the street, away, and free, and none of the hollering could do to change it. He watched the Russians — as they spread out, in panic, trying to catch up with her — and smiled; he was confident that they would not succeed; he knew Amy was resourceful enough to outrun them, given the headway. The ten minutes that passed since she left the floor would have been a plenty, as long as she did not procrastinate on doubt, or the like. He heard no doubt in her harsh voice when she addressed him, and saw none of it in her eyes, where deep resentment reigned. Oh, no, Amy would be stricken with no doubt about having left him behind. It was a bitter-sweet realization, and he had only himself to blame for it, for not having come clean; Amy being gone created a situation where he could think about his own safety, and act accordingly.

A half an hour passed before the Russians realized that the woman had outwitted them, and got away. Kalgun appeared to take the news in his stride, given all the hope he placed on her. In his eyes, Andrew noticed, could be seen a severe reprimand that would be forthcoming toward the agent who, so amateurishly, allowed the girl to slip away.

"She should consider herself lucky if she survives a day," he said to Andrew. "Half the world's intelligence services are looking for her, to say nothing of the various guns-for-hire."

"If you're fishing for my cooperation then you're way off." Andrew said. "You saw how she took the news of my being with the CIA — she wants nothing to do with me."

"Women!" Kalgun said. "Who knows what will offend them. The real question is whether you want her to fall prey to predators who want nothing more than to lay their hands on her?" He knew how to reach to someone's conscience.

"I don't know where she might be," Andrew replied, struggling to remain indifferent.

Kalgun watched him closely for a minute, or so. Apparently convinced of the young man's sincerity, he said, "Alright. I believe that you did not put her up to it, that you care enough about her, regardless of what feelings she might have for you at the moment, to not jeopardize her life." Kalgun saw that he hit the weak spot.

That son-of-a-bitch! Andrew thought. He knew, of course, that the oligarch was right — Amanda was no safer out there, on the street, than she was here, in the cage. Here, at least, she faced evil that did not overtly threaten to take her life, one that, for whatever his true intentions, offered protection from the other, the unknown, and thus infinitely more menacing evil. He knew that, as much as he wanted Amanda to get away, she had nowhere to go, and that Kalgun's cage was the only place to seek shelter in.

The Russian saw that the young man was sufficiently prepped for what he had to say next.

"It's in her own interest that she come back."

"We both know where she'd gone," Andrew said.

"Indeed. There's only one place she could go."

Andrew raised his browse, his confusion unfeigned. "What's holding you back, then? Why not pick her up?"

"You don't know why?"

Andrew's puzzled look was the only reply.

"Your station chief has men watching the mansion where your father is hiding."

He did not know. All communications with the chief suggested that Damian's whereabouts were unknown.

Kalgun continued, "If we move in we'll risk a confrontation that no one wants."

"Let them be, then."

Kalgun shook his head. "It's bad news for both of them."

"How is that?"

Kalgun shot him a bemused look. "I would've thought you'd understand why Amanda must not fall into the CIA's hands."

He played along. "Enlighten me."

"Come now. You must know what's at stake."

"I did not buy your alternative media empire mumbo-jumbo, if that's what you mean."

"That's not what I meant, and we both know it. Surely, Andrew, you must be wondering what the CIA is hatching by not doing anything to stop Allende from carrying on with the next online trial?"

The thought had crossed his mind, but he had come up with no sensible answer.

Kalgun presses on, mercilessly, "You must've wondered why the CIA is offering protection to a man who had been called a traitor, who had been accused of running witch hunts against members of the American administration, even of providing justification for their assassinations?"

Andrew did not know what had prompted the decision. He had attempted to extract the answer from Dick Verso, but was always brushed off with the 'need-to-know', or 'it's above your paygrade' formula. Andrew was angry, and not because this arrogant former-spy of a hostile service knew the things that he should not, but rather because Andrew did not.

"Fuck you!" he said for the lack of other words.

Kalgun was not offended. He said simply, "You've been deceived."

"You purport to know things that you shouldn't." Andrew replied after a long time — time he used to rethink what he had learned today, what he had suspected for some time.

"We are living in the age of information. It's know, or die."

"What else do you know?" Andrew asked, almost resignedly.

"It's what I don't know that matters."

"Go on."

"Why does the CIA protect Damian Allende?"

"Why does it matter? And, more importantly, why does it matter so much to you?"

Kalgun studied Andrew's face. Could this young man be oblivious to everything that has happened?

He said, "I'm a nosy newspaperman. The CIA's unnatural interest in the man who should be slated for assassination, intrigues me. As it should you, and quite personally, I should think."

"I've been told it's above my paygrade to ask such questions."

"Asking questions is never a matter of a paygrade. The answer, though, may, and too often is."

"What is to be done, then?"

"In time, I would suggest looking in to the whistleblower portal. But for the lack of it — and I assure you that my people already checked it thoroughly — you have to turn into other ways."

"Such as?"

Kalgun explained at length.

Work with Kalgun to get around the CIA? Andrew was near to rejecting the idea, when he was stricken by second thoughts. He should at least hear what the Russian had to offer.

"What you propose amounts to treachery," Andrew replied cautiously. "Going behind the station's back, and all."

"We all have to make hard choices — that's what life is all about. Sometimes these are right choices, sometimes wrong, and we either rejoice, or mourn. This is one such moment — you must chose between saving Amanda, and her father, and… doing nothing. What will it be, Andrew?"

"Perhaps it's the best of the bad situation if they should fall into American hands. They could be assured certain safety—"

Kalgun watched him closely when he said, "Can you trust your employer's unknown intentions? Whatever the CIA's plans for Damian may be today, a day will come when he shall become a liability. It's always been this way — one day a friend, the next a burden. Is this what you want for them, when this mysterious interest in Allende's work wanes, and assuming that he doesn't simply vanish — being dragged through the courts, for years, with almost certain conviction down the road?" Seeing doubt on the American's face, he added eagerly, "I can arrange so that they will never have to confront any courts. My lawyers will use every trick to keep them out of it. But, if you have something against lawyers, then I can go a different route. I can offer them new identities. They can disappear off the radar."

The offer, as tempting as it was, could not be taken as sincere, given the man whose lips it was uttered from. Andrew was conscious of it, and not for a minute ready to fall for Kalgun's promises. All the same, something in the Russian's words gave him hope. It was the opportunity to do something, anything. It was hell of a lot more than sitting in despair.

Andrew dropped all pretenses, and asked, "How do you see it done?"

"I would provide intelligence data from the CIA operation. You would analyze it, make sense of it, and hopefully, together, we could extract the Allendes before the CIA makes a move against them."

"Why do you need me at all, if you have access to our— to the CIA's active op communication?"

"You know the codes. You can decipher them quicker than my men. We can act faster."

"You couldn't be more blunt — I'm just a tool for you to get close to Allende."

"We all play our roles in the game of life."

What was his role? Nothing to show, nothing to be proud of. If anything, he felt guilty about what he had done, not about his parting with the CIA — his mind was made up on this point, and based on thorough reasoning — but guilty for disappointing the man who had been his mentor, and who, for some unknown reasons, took him under his wing, showed him the ropes, and had high hopes for his growth within the agency. Kalgun's offer to bypass the chief was tempting. It alarmed Andrew that Kalgun would be able to use the CIA resources — it was all but a confirmation of the oligarch's active role within the Russian intelligence — yet it was not entirely surprising, for it was well known that many Russian oligarchs built their fortunes, and conducted their business dealings, with the aid of the notorious spy agency.

"I won't do anything that could harm my country," Andrew said.

"I would not place you in such a position," Kalgun replied readily.

23

"Amy?" Damian Allende was stunned.

With a golf club in his hand, he stood frozen in place, for a moment musing that the woman was a fairy emerging out of misty air. It was the cold metal in his hand that at last convinced him that he was not day dreaming. If he expressed his daughter's name in the form of a question it was not because he doubted his eyes, but because he had been thinking about her, and standing now before him was the embodiment of his thoughts. Damian was one of those people who believed in ESP, yet remained surprised at each occurrence, as though ready to shout to the skeptical world: "See, I'm not a crackpot." His daughter had traversed the sphere of dreams and materialized from moist air. She differed from the image stored in his mind, however. Gone was the self-assured, successful journalist, a coveted host to celebrities. The drenched and sorrowful looking creature was the epitome of misery.

Damian was not a golfer. He carried the club only to satisfy the itch in his hands. Amanda understood it, recalling his busy hands. It was comical, though, to see a man dressed in heavy overcoat, thick boots, and that expression of summer — a golf club — in his hand. The image made her smile. It was the first smile in a long time. How long? Too long. She could not remember when she last smiled this carelessly. The smile lifted the heavy weight off her shoulders, it smoothed the crease between her brows. At the same time the suddenly vanished tension made her feel light. So light. The last thing she saw were a pair of strong hands reaching to stop the world from spinning.

When she came to she was in an airy bedroom of a large home. It was the delicious smell that woke her. Some minutes later, bathed and dressed in clean dry clothes that fit her casually, she looked more herself again. She found Damian in the kitchen, seated at the utility table, engaged in conversation with an elderly woman.

"Ah, there you are!" Damian stood up and embraced his daughter. He turned to the elderly, "Mrs. Hall, allow me to introduce my daughter, Amanda."

The tall, elderly lady with a long white ponytail looked younger than her seventy-five years would have it. The carefree country life served her well. Apolitical life away from the conniving and corrupting influence of a big city had its good points.

"Oh, the young lady does not look anything like her pictures." The woman pointed to the stack of newspapers piled on the chair by the fireplace.

Damian introduced cheerfully, evidently excited by the presence of his daughter, "This is Mrs. Hall, the mother of a dear friend of mine who graciously let me bunk here for the time being." To the elder lady, "Clothes change a man, as they do to a woman, Mrs. Hall. In any event, the photo is two years old."

Clothes certainly can change a man, Amanda thought. Her father's appearance was equally surprising to her, as hers was to him. Damian Allende abandoned his trademark chivalric white shirts with wide cuffs, in favor of a sporty tweed jacket with large leather patches on the elbows, a quintessential country squire's outfit. His hair was different too, although this change was the least surprising, for Amanda was used to her father's eccentric hairdos. Every time his image appeared in the news Damian sported a new haircut. His critics pointed to it as evidence of his guilty conscience, and a trick of a fugitive from justice, but his true reasons were quite innocent. It was part of his image. Damian's face appearing from television and computer screens was not that of a founder of the online court. The different haircuts of varying length and color represented the everyman, the average judge in the online court. Overtime, however, the changing hairdo became a necessity known to every celebrity — the media had elevated him to a household name, he was recognizable on the street. It made Damian angry; he always maintained that it was the opposite to what he set out to achieve — the focus should not be placed on him, but on those whom he brought to trial.

The lady of the house interrupted Amanda's thoughts, "Pray tell me how you arrived here at Edgewood Hall. Your father tells a most extraordinary, and nearly unbelievable story."

Amanda glanced at her father. She longed to talk to him, but obliged the old lady. "On foot," she replied simply.

"On foot! Three miles in this weather!"

"Ordinarily I'd say what is three miles, when I'm used to jogging longer distance every morning, but to tell the truth it felt much further, perhaps because of the weather."

Her father smiled, and said, "It was further." To the host, "Amanda did not come from London on the bus. She took the train."

"Oh, no you didn't!" The lady pushed back in her chair, her disbelieving eyes devouring the young woman head to toe. "No wonder you needed a rest. The train station is upwards of five miles!"

They chatted in this light manner until the supper was finished. They dined together at the utility kitchen table, in the only room kept warm all day. Mrs. Hall's old and frank demeanor allowed Amanda to push aside her worries, if only for an hour, during which she entertained the host with some of the more memorable encounters with the rich and famous, the guest stars of her column.

"I wish my son and daughter-in-law were here," Mrs. Hall said when the supper was over. "They would have loved to meet such a charming young lady."

"Does she not know who you are?" Amanda asked some time after dinner.

They were walking along the gravel road that encircled the property along its perimeter. One side of the road was lined with trees that provided privacy from the carriageway, and on the other were open fields, dotted with trees; the rooftop of the mansion was visible above tree crowns that surrounded it, bathed in orange hues of the setting sun.

"She does, naturally," replied Damian Allende.

"And she doesn't mind you staying in her home?"

"Technically it isn't hers. It belongs to her son. And no — she doesn't mind. Don't think her oblivious to the outside world, though. She's an exceptionally sharp and feisty lady who stays clear of politics. That's what she considers the campaign against me. It's all politics to her. She'd know. Both — her father, and her husband, were members of parliament. Both died prematurely, because of the stress of politics, as she puts it. Life taught her two things about men — they are dogs for women and politics. There's no cure for either, so she stays clear from it, making her statement through utter and complete disregard for anything politics."

"Is it?"

"What?"

"Is it all about the politics?"

Allende sighed before replying. "Politicians are involved. Many were convicted by the people, some were cleared. The media and others, who are slated to stand trial next, are making it political. I hope, though, that you don't think this to be the reason why I created the online court. Politicians are tried not because they are politicians, but because they hold public office. They were elected to serve the people, yet they act against their interest. They act against the society and against the individual."

"The same can be said about many who do not hold any public office."

"I sincerely hope that anyone, whose acts harm society or a single person, will have their day in court. If not in my court, then perhaps some future court, when enough evidence is collected to make a case against them."

"Dad," Amanda said quietly after a period of silence.

He froze at the sound of the word. He has not heard it since she was a little girl. He felt her fingers slip under his elbow.

"Dad," she repeated. "There are people who are convinced that you punish them only out of vengeance. This is why they want to stop you."

"No, Amy, it isn't like that—"

"They are after you!" She persisted. "They will follow you wherever you go, and when they find you, they will stop you, by whatever means."

He put his hand on the fingers that embraced his sleeve. He looked into her eyes, and said, "They can harm me, but they cannot stop what I started! Not anymore. The truth, once set free, cannot be imprisoned or suppressed, it spreads like the wind, in all directions. It turns up everywhere, in every part of the world, and in every heart and mind."

Amanda looked closer at her father. His eyes were glowing. Perhaps it was the reflection of the setting sun, but the glowing fiery spark in his pupils gave Damian the look of a prophet. Amanda shivered at the comparison.

Damian noticed. He said, "We should go back. It's getting cold."

The mansion stood on some seven hundred acres of what was mostly fields, surrounded and dotted with mixed trees. The fields were crisscrossed by gravel paths. Damian picked one that was the shortest way home.

Amanda was not finished. She stalled by pulling gently, but firmly, on his arm. "They are looking for you and are getting close. They know where you're hiding."

He shot her a quick look. "Did Andrew find me?"

"No. He tried, though. He looked for you since you disappeared from Reykjavik."

Damian said nothing, awaiting the inevitable. The only sign of his uneasiness was in the suddenly flexed muscles in his arm.

Amanda carried on, "Andrew did not find you, but the Russians did. They know you're here."

Damian resumed the walk. He knew there was more. He waited for the remainder in silence, the only sound the cracking gravel under their feet.

Amanda thought about it for many hours, but now that they arrived at this juncture she did not know how to break it. On the one hand she wanted to highlight the urgency of the situation, but on the other she would rather downplay the risks to herself — she did not want to be the obstacle in her father's work. She never expressed it in those exact words, but she was proud of her father. She admired his principles, regardless of the true objectives behind his project. Her father was making a difference and she was proud to be his daughter. She wanted to cherish the feeling, and thought it indestructible until Kalgun arrived on the scene. Was her father the man behind… What did Kalgun call it? The WikiJustice? The collaborative project of collecting evidence, trying, convicting, and assassinating those whose actions he deemed harmful to society? Was her father the inspiration behind the killings?

Amanda looked into her father's eyes again. They were glowing, filled with burning flames. It was not the reflection of the setting sun. Those were actual flames she saw in his pupils. This time the image did not make her shiver. It made her hot to her spine. She looked ahead and saw what Damian's eyes were focused on.

The mansion was on fire.

24

The entire left wing of the house was ablaze. It was where the kitchen was located, and Damian's first thoughts went to Mrs. Hall. With flames oozing out of the windows, where they dined only an hour earlier, Damian's heart rose to his throat. He started fast for the house, cutting briskly across the moist grass.

"Dad!" Amanda cried, and followed. She caught up to him not a hundred steps from the house, with only a tennis court separating them from the building. The court was surrounded by dwarf cedar trees, barely the height of an adult human.

The trees saved them.

"Look!" Amanda pulled on his tweed sleeve.

Several figures stood about the property, one at every corner, their attention on the windows and doors. Their behavior left no doubt that they were observing exit points.

"It's them," Amanda said.

"Who?" Damian asked with puzzled eyes.

"The Russians, who else!"

"The Russians?"

"Come, dad, we've got to get out!"

"But, Mrs. Hall!"

"She's fine, see!" Amanda pointed to the parking lot.

Two men were approaching an SUV, the elderly woman between them. She was visibly distraught, constantly turning back to the house, while the men ushered her away. Two beagles followed the woman closely, their tails between their paws, their ears flat. Damian saw as one of the men opened the door of the vehicle, and held the woman's head, as police officers often do, before letting her in. He closed the doors after her, and found himself faced with two dogs who began to yelp. He swung his foot at the animals, but missed. He cursed. His words were English.

"The Russians?" Damian repeated doubtfully.

Moments later two men emerged from the house, one after another. They signaled their colleagues by shaking their heads. No words were exchanged, but a silent agreement was reached. The men dispersed, each moving in a predatory manner, carefully scanning the dusk.

"We must go!" Amanda tugged her father's arm. She started to retreat, the way they came from.

"I cannot leave her like this." Damian was stricken by guilt. He expected that this day may come. He was mentally prepared for any eventuality, for anything that might happen to him; he did not reconcile harm coming others' way.

"You saw it yourself — they brought her out of the house before anything could happen to her. They don't mean to do her harm."

"There are many degrees of harm," he said, but thought that Amanda was right.

"She's just another leverage that may be used against you; leave now and she's useless to them."

Damian struggled with himself for several moments, and said, "I have to pick up my gear."

"We can't go back!" Amanda would not have it. She struggled to remain in control of her trembling voice — having barely escaped, she could not face falling into the hands of the enemy, yet again.

"We're not going back," Damian reassured, and led the way across the fields and meadows towards a copse of trees.

Halfway across the field they could hear the distant sound of the wailing sirens. The sound grew fast.

They increased their pace and reached the trees breathless. Hidden behind them was a structure, not bigger than a garage, in its time serving perhaps as a garden shed. Some rusty garden tools and a decrepit wheelbarrow confirmed Amanda's guess. The structure was once a garden shed, now turned into a work space of a different sort. Inside stood a large worktable topped with two laptop computers, satellite phones, routers, and other electronic equipment whose purpose Amanda could not fathom.

The sirens were closer now, and soon numerous flashing lights could be discerned as vehicles turned off the carriageway, and entered the last stretch of the road that led to the gate. The firefighters, police, and ambulances, were all nearing the scene of the fire. It was a blessing that even such a large and remote property was not deplete of the prying eyes of its distant neighbors, who alerted the emergency services.

Damian was working fast, as someone prepared for the eventuality. In two sweeps he picked up what he needed, and shoved the items into a knapsack that was hanging on a door nail, while Amanda kept watch on the fields. He was finished in under two minutes, and led the way along the wall of the shed. Without a word, Amanda followed her father. This time it was not far. Behind the shed was a small addition. What Amanda saw in it filled her heart with hope — it was a motorbike.

Her heart grew larger over the next two hours as the wind cooled her head, and her arms clung onto her father's waist, the motorbike taking them away to safety.

"Tell me how it all came about," Damian asked nearly three hours later.

They were back in London, sitting on a hard couch, cups of hot chocolate in their hands. The furnishings were necessarily sparse. The couch and a table with two chairs were the only objects that could fit in the narrow room. The living room was no larger than either of the two bedrooms, and it doubled as a dining area. The flat was one of several fallback options secured by Damian's friends. He did not elaborate on the identity of the friends, or the conditions of use, and Amanda did not press, believing that a man, who for weeks eluded intelligence agencies, was sufficiently well connected to do so again.

"How safe are we here?" she asked only when they settled down.

"I suppose it depends on how you came to find me in the first place."

Amanda told him everything that happened since that night in Reykjavik.

Damian listened to her without interrupting, his trademark piercing eyes reading her face for what her words did not express.

"I'm so sorry, Amy," he said when she was finished. "I should've guessed they'd try to use you as leverage against me."

"It wasn't that bad. Just a little adventure, surely." She said it lightly, but something in her eyes suggested that the experience was anything but.

Seeing how much she wanted to appear stronger than she really was, Damian did not press. Instead, and knowing how much he owed someone else for keeping his daughter safe, he said, "You shouldn't judge Andrew so harshly."

"Oh, dad!" she replied angrily. Then, seeing as she could not ignore the subject, she added, "He came to me under false pretenses, only interested in getting close to you. He lied to me all those months!"

"True, but he had a change of heart. He fell in love with you, Amy."

"He told you that, did he!"

"He did."

"He told me, too, and guess what I think of it!"

"He told you? That's good."

"Too late. He's a liar, dad, and once a liar—"

"But is it really so impossible that someone should meet you, and fall in love with you so much that he'd want to change his ways?"

"Dad—" Her flushed cheeks proved that Damian's words found a fertile ground.

"Alright," he said amicably, and changed the subject. "So, what do you make of those Russians?"

She welcomed the change, but father's words were not without a lasting effect. She needed time to gather her thoughts, to shelve the persistent image of one man, and replace it with another.

"Kalgun," she started. "He's obviously lying."

To her surprise Damian said, "I don't know. Kalgun has fallen out of favor with Moscow. I forget the details, but his name appears somewhere in the whistleblower files."

"Dad, he burned the mansion trying to capture us!"

"What makes you think it was him? Did you recognize him at the scene?"

"N-no, but who else? He knew where you were staying!"

"That's just it. If he knew where I was staying then he could have nabbed me earlier. With you in his hands all he had to do was call me. I would have given myself up in exchange for your freedom."

Her eyes glistened when she said, "I would do the same for you."

Their eyes locked for a time. They spent several minutes in silence. Too much was on their minds to express it in words. Ten years apart could not be eliminated and summed up in a few sentences, however tender. That part had yet to wait.

Damian returned to the subject, "Did you hear, what I heard?"

She knew what he meant. "One doesn't have to be a native English speaker to curse in this language."

"Perhaps not, but in a situation as tense as it was, one would probably reach for the word most crude, and most expressive of one's feelings, which would likely come from one's native vocabulary. I'd say, Amy, that those men were not Russians. Judging by the drawl in that man's tongue, they were Americans."

As any person naturally predisposed to converse in multiple languages, Damian's ear was able to pick up such nuances as dialects, and accents, within languages he spoke, even if himself he pronounced words with, sometimes heavy, accents. Amanda shared this ability, and took it even further when it came to the English language, having the additional advantage of having grown up using it — she could tell the agent who uttered the curse against the dog, was from the southern states, close to the Mexican border. Her mind was telling her that her father was right, but her heart demanded that she disregard the option, for it further implicated Andrew. Amanda still loved Andrew, despite everything she learned about his treachery.

Damian broke her train of thought. "I am inclined to believe Kalgun's sincerity. He wouldn't be the first one to hope to consolidate the independent media."

She opposed angrily, the sentiment the stronger for the thoughts that still were present in her mind, "He can't be trusted, dad."

"I didn't say I trust him, but, I think, Kalgun can be useful to us."

"You will lose all credibility if you associate yourself with such a man."

"That's not what I meant. Kalgun owns a vast media empire; he's the biggest player in countries where independent media is routinely suppressed. He's carved out a real niche in many dictatorial places. In many cases his are the only alternative news outlets available. If we could reach the people in those places, you know what it would mean to them—"

"Nonetheless, there is something about him that makes me distrust him, and it isn't only due to his KGB past."

He took her hand and placed it in his. Gently caressing her palm with his thumb, he said, "Caution is a good instinct, but fear never let anyone change the world, not for the better."

"Is that what you're doing, dad? Are you making the world a better place?"

His thumb paused momentarily. Something in her voice told him that it was serious. His eyes sought hers, but, with her lips sunk in the cup of hot chocolate, he could not see them.

"It's a smear campaign. I guess it's finding fertile ground."

She said nothing at first. For ten years they were father and daughter only nominally, with little to show for it. The years spent apart, in resentment, if only one-sided, did plenty of damage. The last weeks, however, marked the most significant change in years. They found that both missed each other, that all those years were a terrible mistake, and they welcomed the chance that brought them together at last. Now, a dark cloud hung over the heads.

"Dad," Amanda started cautiously. She gently pulled her hand away. "I— I truly admire what you have set out to do. But I cannot ignore all those allegations against you. How can I shrug them off as mere smear campaign when such powerful forces were unleashed to stop you?"

"If you believe in what I do, if you sincerely believe that the world needs change, then does it not follow that such change should be brought about?"

"Certainly, but there are ways, and there ways."

"What if all ways were exhausted and only one was left?"

"There's always a better way, dad. There must be, or there would be no progress and the world would stand still."

"A better way? But how do we know what the better way is? Here and now only those most impacted, those who experience positive changes in their condition can vouch for it. So far their approval rating is nearly unanimous."

"The crowd isn't always the best judge of what is right, dad. This decision must be made within ourselves. Are you sure your way is the right way?"

This time Damian sunk his lips in the cup. He slurped, swallowed, and said, "I suppose you know about my agreement with Andrew?"

She nodded.

He went on, "In several weeks it shall all be decided. I will present my case to the world. I will list my sins and my accomplishments. The people will decide whether I am worthy of the trust they placed in me."

"What about me, dad? What about my trust?"

"Have I given you any reason not to trust me?"

"Dad!"

"Well?"

"I cannot ignore what is happening. People are dying, killed in the name of your online court judgments."

"Amy, look at me," Damian said. When their eyes met, he continued, "If we cannot find mutual trust then we have little hope for the future."

"You're asking me to trust you, a man I have not seen in over ten years, against multiple voices who cry foul!" Amanda's face turned crimson. She realized she went too far, after all the parting was mostly her own doing.

Damian did not bring it up. He replied, "I could say — what about the hundreds of thousands, the millions of voices, who lend their support, but it would not do. This is not about the others. It's about you and me. If we cannot trust one another— Amy, this is about the rest of our lives. If we don't have trust in each other, what future do we have?"

She sunk her eyes in his. The cup suddenly felt heavy in her hand. She put it down, dropped really, and reached out for his hand. She said, "Dad, I missed you so much. I want you back. I love you. I always did. But I'm afraid. I'm afraid of the monster everyone sees in you." Tears streamed down her cheeks, dripped onto the hand she pulled to her lips.

Damian moved closer, he brought her hand to kiss it. He embraced her. With Amanda's sobbing head on his shoulder, he said, "Believe in my Amy. Everything I did in my life I did for you and your mother."

25

The number and frequency of assassinations attributed to Damian Allende's online court had increased dramatically in the weeks that followed. Killers struck unexpectedly, murdering their victims with remarkable accuracy. While targeted individuals comprised different nationalities, an astoundingly large proportion, and growing, were Americans. The astonishment was the greater for most of those killed were men from the highest echelons of political power, with some corporate bosses thrown in, and most enjoyed private or state protection of skilled security agencies. Fear gripped Washington and the business world, with many Wall Street executives electing to spend their ill gains on armored vehicles and additional protection services. No one felt safe and it was beginning to look as though Damian Allende had achieved what he set out for — the talk about change had left the online community, penetrated the walls of the average home, and entered the national debate stage. But the debate was not directed at changing the ways of those who acted against the public interest, but rather on how to stop the monster who instigated the murders. It was believed that Allende had inspired an untold number of vigilantes who sprung up around the country to kill and wreak terror. A growing number of voices demanded answers from the country's security services, expressing their disgusted amazement at these services' inability to prevent Allende from striking time and again. Pressure was mounting on the Central Intelligence Agency to remove the threat once and for all.

Amanda was aware of the threats issued against her father. The entire world knew about them. Not a day went by without newscasts giving voice to those who called for Allende's urgent assassination.

Damian belittled all such calls, calling them frenzy wound up by media bosses who were named in his indictments, and were found guilty by the participants in the online court on a variety of charges, from theft of public resources, to drumming up public excitement for wars. Amanda understood that father tried to shelter her from the increasingly dire prospect for the future. Belittling the threats was intended to extinguish her worries, but the work Damian continued every day reignited the fuel that lighted her concerns for his safety.

Damian worked every day, round the clock. Something was consuming him, this much was evident — from the way he worked, with his nose close to the screen, so as not to miss the smallest pixel of text, taking seemingly erratic notes, as though working in a trance — to the way he rose up from the desk to walk about the room, murmuring something to himself. Despite her best efforts Amanda could not tell what kept her father this absorbed. He refused to discuss it, on the basis that he needed more evidence first, and she assumed that he was preparing the next edition of his online court. The unknown, combined with increased attacks on her father and his character, made her the more anxious. Amanda slept poorly, and lost her appetite. The living conditions were as responsible for her anxiety as the threat faced everyday from unknown enemies. The father and daughter were confined to the small flat and to each other. Stress was running high on both sides until Amanda found a solution. After changing her appearance with the help of scissors and some henna, she made frequent, if short trips to the local grocer and newsstand. The time outside, and out of the claustrophobic flat, helped her to cope with the situation.

Damian, as entrenched in work as only he could, was not oblivious to his daughter's hardship. In an effort to ease her anxiety, he shifted some of the work to her able hands. She was an excellent researcher, having started her career as such. She organized and prepared the material evidence against the next batch of public office holders who had abused their position. Not only did the work provide distraction for her mind, but it solidified her admiration for her father's Gargantuan undertaking. With some of the work thus shared, Damian had time to devote his efforts elsewhere. He was now spending inordinate amount of time reviewing the cases of the assassinated individuals. One day Amanda noticed that something in the work had deeply disturbed her father. He would walk about the room, muttering something under his nose, arguing with himself, and frantically returning to the material he was working on. He was beginning to lose sleep and appetite, and Amanda began to worry about her father's mental health.

One day, unable to contain her anxiety and growing suspicion, she asked in a tone that suggested she would not allow her self to be brushed off, "What has you so disturbed that it keeps you up at night?"

Damian looked up from the laptop screen. He was about to belittle her concerns with one of his standard answers when their eyes locked and he knew that it would not do, not this time.

"I was reviewing the murders," he started cautiously. "I think there's something awfully peculiar about them."

"Murder is awful and abhorrent, and such sentiment is not peculiar."

"Yes, you are right, of course." He searched for the right word and said, "I meant that all those recent murders have a peculiar connection, a common denominator, if you wish."

Amanda looked at him with reproach.

"I know what you must be thinking," Damian spoke hurriedly, before she could say anything. "Of course they have a common denominator. All those murdered were brought before the online court; all were tried and were found guilty. That much is clear and undeniable. But that is not what troubles me—"

"Are you truly not troubled by those killings? I don't believe it, dad." She was irritable and it showed in her tone of voice, and in the words she chose.

"That is a question of morality or philosophy." He tried to wave it off.

"And justice?" she added.

"Justice in its institutionalized sense is irrelevant. Those who were brought before the online court had broken the laws and corrupted the justice system that allowed them to get away with their crimes scot-free. They showed that justice can be manipulated, unleashed only on those who do not stand above it. In effect they showed the rest of us that justice is irrelevant, for it is not absolute, it is an object of manipulation."

"Just because it was abused by a few degenerates, does it follow that the justice system should be discarded as irrelevant?"

Damian looked at her closer. What he saw in her eyes made him turn his away. He could not face her when he said, "Justice, as it is preached from television, is no longer viable. It is a farce. But justice as a concept is indispensable in the functioning of society. It is needed, and now more than ever. But it must be justice of the people, not of political and corporate institutions."

"How do you see it, dad? A tooth for a tooth, and an eye for an eye?"

"Someday greater minds than mine will figure it out. I am convinced that a way to true accountability will be found. If anything, my work only highlights the urgency and the need for change. Meanwhile all kinds of charlatans usurp their right to tell us what is right, and what is wrong. Many more will interpret justice in their own way. Look at this," he pointed to the screen of his computer. "Look at all these people. Some of them were the most hardened mass-murderers of our day. Others were driven to misdeeds by greed. Yet others by ideology. They all exploited the weaker to build their personal wealth, or to satisfy their psychotic drive for exploitation and unleashing of misery. They were killed in apparent acts of justice. Did they deserve to be punished? Certainly, if evidence confirmed their guilt. Did they have to die? I don't know, but they did. Perhaps the killings were the result of frustration with the institutionalized justice that failed to prosecute the abusers? In hindsight, I suspect, some of them must have wondered if it would not be better to return their ill-gains, or to offer heart-felt apologies, and stay alive. But the fact remains that they were killed, and as a consequence of the online court I had created. Do I feel guilty about what happened? No. It is not why I am losing sleep. In a lawless world anything goes, and those who cross the line should be prepared to pay the price. The trouble starts when we don't know who sets the rules and the price."

"Are the people the correct route to deciding what is right and what is wrong?"

"People create laws for the people."

"But, who are those people?"

"That's exactly the point — who are those people?"

Silence fell. Amanda waited for the answer but it was not forthcoming. Her eyes fell on the computer where the list of the murdered individuals were arranged into a complicated graphic. Suddenly she understood.

"Are you telling me that you suspect foul play?"

"Isn't that what every murder is — a foul play?" he started with irony in his voice. "But no, Amy, it is not foul play that I am concerned about. It is worse. Much worse. These killings... there's more to them than meets the eye. I followed them from day one. At first I was shocked and outraged, like everybody else. Then I became curious."

"Curious?"

"It isn't often that our well intended actions lead to such dramatic consequences. Of course I was curious about the people who joined me, and about their motivations. Many people were clearly inspired by my work. It is evident, if only in the number of participants. Without their vote the project would be worthless. By taking part in the online court they showed that justice is important. Their participation en masse also led to an increase in material leaked to the whistleblower portal, without which none of it would be possible, since we would not have the evidence. Exposure of lies and liars, crimes and criminals who conduct their despicable business in the guise of public servants, would not be possible without those conscientious people who said — enough. However, some went further. The killings started, and they stole the world's attention from the important message. So I followed every killing with great interest. At first I only documented them, gathered as much detail about the way the killings were conducted, and about the victims. As I went along, as the killings multiplied, I was struck by certain... peculiarities. You see, with the exception of the very first few victims, and whose killers were caught, the rest, now standing at forty-six cases, all share some disturbing common factors."

"Yes, you said that," Amanda encouraged with incurable curiosity.

"Take a look at this table." Damian pointed to a spreadsheet featuring various details of the murder cases.

Amanda looked closer at the document. Names, numbers, and notes, all making no sense to her.

She said, "Explain."

"Beyond the obvious — the fact that all were tried before the online court, beyond the proven examples of lying, of breaking international law, causing environmental catastrophes, conducting economic swindles, and acting against the good of society — they all have something else in common."

"What is it?"

"I've been playing with the numbers, studying their biographies, re-examining their wrongdoing, checking and double-checking, and I always arrive at the same point."

"What is it, dad?"

"Bear with me, Amy. It's easy to cast accusations; not so easy to clear someone of them — my own example a case in point. Besides, it may be a case of subconscious numerology. Perhaps I'm only seeing what I want to see."

"Let me help. Let me study the list. See if I come to the same conclusions."

"Give me time. Let me apply one more methodology."

"You said it yourself — you checked and verified it time and again." Amanda was agitated, her curiosity desiring immediate answers.

"True, but the thing about numbers especially, is that one can always find in them what one wishes to find. It's a matter of will over facts."

"Put them through a process of elimination. Once you eliminate the impossible, whatever remains, no matter how improbable, must be the truth."

Damian raised his eyes from the screen. He looked into hers, amazement and pleasure on his face.

He asked in a soft voice, "You remember?"

She blushed. "Of course I remember. There are not many girls whose fathers read them to bed, not fairy tales about princes and princesses, but about the adventures of brilliant detectives."

He smiled. "To be fair I did read fairy tales to you, too, but we both found the stories about princesses turned into frogs a little... how shall I put it?"

"Fairy? As opposed to tales of detectives armed with only their brains, battling super-villains, and saving the world?"

They smiled, both recalling those peaceful, loving evenings.

"Are you such a detective now, dad?" Amanda asked when the image faded.

Damian did not reply.

"Sometimes even a great detective needs a sidekick in order to solve a mystery. Let me in on the secret. Let me help you break it."

"Amy," Damian started. He was at a loss for words. How could he tell his daughter that this case was more serious than any of the great detectives ever faced. It was so great that to even consider it went beyond anything he could imagine possible among the vast whistleblower archive of classified, and often dirty, material. But he knew that he could not prolong the mystery. Amanda was a part of his life. What happened around him impacted her. She deserved to be allowed in on the details, however dirty they might be. Perhaps her young, unspoiled mind, was what was required to solve the mystery? Perhaps her sharp, prying mind of a trained and determined journalist could see what his did not? Perhaps she could rest his suspicions at ease by debunking them? They would all find better sleep if she did.

Damian made up his mind. He was ready to share his thoughts with his daughter when his laptop made a sound. It was a critical warning sound. Damian turned to the screen where five words flashed, their message sending shivers down his spine: RUN! NOW! DO NOT WAIT!

26

Damian wasted no time pondering the meaning of the message. The fact that it appeared at all, was, in itself, cause for alarm — someone had hacked in to his computer.

"Your knapsack!" he called out to Amanda, while simultaneously grabbing the satellite phone and the laptop, shoving them into his daypack.

One of the disadvantages of life on the run was the necessity to confine one's entire life to the smallest denominator. While Damian was used to this sort of lifestyle — having no fixed address for the better part of the last decade — moving places with nothing more than a small backpack became increasingly more difficult for Amanda. The first weeks on the run with Andrew felt like an adventure, but as time went by she began to miss the basic creature comforts that accompany regular middleclass life, with a place to call home, and a daily routine. Andrew's insistence, while proven necessary, on keeping belongings to absolute minimum, quickly drove Amanda to long for all those things that fill a young woman's chest of drawers. Instead she had to learn to live out of a single knapsack that she could strap on and move at a moment's notice. Folding her clothes and keeping them by her bed at night in an order that they were worn became a habit. When the realization of the habit kicked in, her young mind drew a natural reaction — that of resentment for the forced lifestyle. She was not the princess that she so disliked in books of her childhood, nevertheless she missed some of that, which she was now being denied, for the simple fact that it was not of her own choosing. Despite the image of chic that she projected in her line of work, Amanda was drawn to simpler life, more casual than glitzy. She did not particularly miss the fancy, yet seldom comfortable attire, but she never did get used to the lack of things more ephemeral. It never agreed with her that she should not be able to snuggle up to bed with her favorite book, and not only because it would not fit into her small backpack, but rather because she found that she could not concentrate on reading. The lack of routine and the stress of the life on the run contributed to poor sleep. She slept poorly, ate poorly, and her mind was in a constant state of anxiety. It was not surprising, therefore, that she responded to the urgency with numbness. The shocking change from the engrossing conversation with her father to the call to flee the apartment was too great.

Damian Allende was already at the door, slipping on his moccasins, a backpack on his shoulders, when he realized that his daughter was not by his side. With one gaze at her he saw immediately that something was wrong. Amanda did not move an inch.

"Amy?" he said tenderly, concern in his voice.

Her head turned slowly, very slowly. She looked at him with eyes that saw nothing.

Damian was by her side in two quick steps. With his hand under her arm, he pulled her gently, but firmly, toward the door. He slipped on her shoes for her, and congratulated himself for choosing for her the moccasins that one did not waste time lacing. With one hand under his daughter's arm, the other grasping the knapsack, Damian led the way, away from the flat.

The tenement building was an elongated structure with seven staircases, and just as many entrances. The staircases, and balconies that spanned the building, made it a potentially ideal getaway station, unless the pursuers had enough manpower to man all exit points. Theoretically it was possible to monitor all exits from the four building corners. In practice the length of the building offered an advantage to the fugitive who could flee through the middle staircase and hope to get away by an easily maneuverable vehicle, such as a motorbike. Damian knew that his pursuers would expect exactly that. He knew that the net required to catch him would be finely woven. To slip through it one had to think ahead, and Damian liked to stay ahead of his opponents. His secret to outwitting his pursuers was in expectation of being caught. This forced him to plan for just such an eventuality. It allowed him to be in control of the situation. It had worked to his advantage for the last ten years.

Unbeknownst to him, however, someone else knew his way of thinking.

The secret to Damian's escape from the undoubtedly surrounded building was the laundry room, or rather its location in the basement. He knew about it before he chose the flat; he made it a point to study all of his potential safe houses and this one was no different. Damian knew that the basement system was connected to the neighboring building, a property belonging to the same administration. Expecting that his pursuers would man all exits, his first step was to reach the staircase furthest from his flat, where the risk of encountering the ascending party was the lowest. From there it was a breeze to descend to the basement. With his arm around Amanda's waist Damian traversed the underground corridor that joined the two buildings. They emerged from the furthest staircase, some three hundred feet from their own flat, and Damian breathed with relief. He could make out figures outside the building, none paying attention to his current location. Nonetheless, he had to consider that additional watchmen were present in vehicles the party arrived in. Caution was required during the last stage of the escape — a short walk around the corner, to the parked motorbike. Damian looked at Amanda. His daughter appeared absentminded throughout the ordeal, though she remained susceptible to external stimuli. She would follow him when led by hand.

They stepped out of the building. Damian walked casually, fighting the urge to run. They hardly made a dozen steps when he realized that they were spotted. A car parked up ahead suddenly pulled off the curb and started for them. Damian changed direction and increased pace. It would not do. Amanda was like an ill dog on a leash, putting on resistance as the pressure on his collar increased.

But Amanda did not resist. She could not. She was in a state of shock. The experiences of the past weeks, topped with the treacherous role of the man she loved, took their toll on her mind. She no longer registered the urgency of their plight and moved along only as a living ballast, slowly and laboriously. As a result they only covered several paces before the vehicle caught up with them, some twenty yards from the motorbike and the freedom.

Damian stopped. It was the end, a thought shot through his head. He lessened the grip on his daughter's arm and turned around to face his pursuers. He was met with a familiar face visible through the driver's side.

"Get in!" Andrew Walker shouted.

27

Andrew's face acted as a bucket of cold water, and Amanda jerked her arm. Damian did not let go, his grip the firmer for the anxiety. The struggle was short. Damian suffered none of the reservations that tormented his daughter. Andrew Walker was the man who spoke frankly and passionately about the woman he loved and the work he despised. Amanda failed to impress upon her father the warning and the distrust she felt for the man who used her for his own gains. Even now, with Andrew at the scene of the raid, Damian trusted his own instincts. He always thought himself a good judge of character and this time it was no different. The look in the American's eyes reassured Damian that Andrew was just as anxious to flee the scene as the rest of them.

"Ditch the satellite phone!" Andrew cried over his shoulder when the father and daughter sunk to the back seats.

"It's alright," Damian replied assuredly. "It can't be traced."

"It can. It is. Do it now!" Andrew persisted.

Damian caught the driver's eyes in the reverse mirror.

He said, "It was you. You warned us!"

The look on Andrew's face was the confirmation. Damian hesitated no longer. He tossed the phone out the window.

Amanda spoke for the first time since they left the flat, bitingly, "Don't listen to him, dad. He's a liar!"

Andrew sought her eyes in the mirror. What he found in them convinced him that no words could heal the rift in her heart.

With Andrew's proximity responsible for the rising of her anger, Amanda came out of the numbness almost as quickly as she plunged into it. She felt stronger with every minute she spent in the vehicle, the usurper directly before her, within reach of her stiffening arms. The wildest ideas came to her. She felt like screaming, and the longer she suppressed the desire, the more violent were the images unfolding before her mind. In them she saw herself lashing out at the driver, and struggling to regain control of the wheel. She saw herself plunging out of the moving vehicle, her father following. The more violent were her thoughts, the more outrageous they became, and their realization became less pressing, the satisfaction remaining in imagining the violent acts rather than performing them. All along, in the back of her mind, was the conviction that she could not do any of these things. She could not — as easy as her position behind the driver would have it — extend her arms, and to embrace the neck, and squeeze her long fingers until the body wilted. She could not do to Andrew what he did to the men who broke into the house in Reykjavik. But something had to be done, and quickly. She turned to her father, her eyes pleading — Why don't you do something?

Damian sensed the emotions that besieged his daughter, he saw it in her eyes, and in her tense body language. With her hand in his he felt the violent contractions of her wrist, the tightening grip of her fingers. Fearing an explosion of her agitated mind, he spoke to the driver, "Thank you for the warning. It came none too soon!"

"I only wish I could have warned you sooner. Couldn't. Had to wait for just the opportunity. They were onto you for a time now—"

"They?" Damian seized the opportunity to accentuate the discord. He gazed into his daughter's face to impress upon her the significance.

Andrew could not reply. With the traffic bunching up as they reached the main streets, he found it difficult enough to safely maneuver the vehicle while ensuring that they were not being followed, let alone engage in conversation. Yet, there was lots to be said. He tried to make reassuring eye contact through the mirror, but Amanda's eyes were nowhere to be found.

Amanda appeared absentminded, her eyes on the passing intersections, her jaw tightly clenched. She was at the last straw. In her agitated mind Andrew's sudden appearance became confirmation of his guilt, and the forced car ride a further exploit of her and her father's gullibility. For whatever reason father was oblivious to the scheming, and it became painfully evident that she would have to act to save them both. She began to pay attention to the surroundings. She did not know this part of London, but it did not dissuade her from making plans; it was unlikely that Andrew knew it any better, which gave her encouragement. She was ready to leave the vehicle the first opportunity she had, pulling father behind her. Where would they go? It did not matter, for it was better to try and die, if necessary, as free persons, than allow themselves to be driven to a butcher house, like a cargo of helpless hogs. Not her! She was not helpless! She scanned the view outside, then gazed ahead where the traffic lights were about to change. This was as good a place as any. She squeezed her father's hand, sending a silent signal.

The car came to a stop. Amanda jerked the door handle. With her right foot on the pavement she pulled her father.

Damian was caught unawares. Their hands separated.

"Amy, no!" he cried.

"Amy!" Andrew joined in.

Not expecting her father to let go of her hand, she lost her balance on separation, and the centrifugal force threw her backwards. She landed on the pavement but was on her feet before the men could react.

Lights changed. Drivers began to honk.

In one swift move Andrew unbuckled his seatbelt. He opened the door just as a bicycle passed between the vehicle and Amanda. The cyclist was not going fast and the impact was not strong, but it threw the cyclist the ground. The bicycle blocked the door, immobilizing Andrew as he watched with horror the unfolding events.

Two bulky men materialized out of nowhere. They approached Amanda, slipped their large hands under her arms, and, picking her off the ground, they carried her away to an SUV stopped in the opposite lane, separated by a median.

The incident lasted only seconds, but before Andrew struggled out onto the pavement, the SUV took off with the screech of tires.

Damian sat stupefied in his seat when Amanda jumped out of the car. What happened next went beyond his comprehension. They were practically free and for something like this to happen it was unconscionable. Amanda was kidnapped! Now that the realization dawned on him, it was too late. He could do nothing but to watch in helpless amazement as the SUV carrying his daughter disappeared in the traffic, going in the opposite direction.

At the same time Andrew's mind was working fast. With Amy in the hands of the thugs, painfully aware of the reasons behind the kidnapping, Andrew went back behind the wheel. He started the stalled car to the tune of the angry cyclist's curses. The centrifugal force closed the door through which Amanda left the car.

"What are you doing?" Damian cried. "They've got Amy! We have to go back, now!"

Andrew was driving on, his furious face spewing like words, "It's the last thing we're going to do."

"What are you talking about? We must go back!" Damian was shouting over his shoulder, his head turned back, desperately seeking the SUV in the traffic left behind.

Andrew did not reply. He was cursing, blaming himself for what had just happened.

"Go back now, Walker. You hear me!" Damian went on.

"Listen to me," Andrew ejaculated through his teeth. "Amy is safe as long as you are out of their hands."

"What?"

"She is not the target. You are. As long as you're out of their hands she will be safe."

"You can't know this! Goddamn-it!"

"Trust me!"

"Trust you? And who are you to be trusted? You're just a rookie spy who read too many novels, and watched too many movies. You just cost my daughter her life!"

Andrew replied forcefully, assuredly, "If they wanted her dead they would have done it right there, on the street. They didn't. It means they won't harm her. I am certain of it."

"What? What the Hell does that mean?" Damian slammed his fist on the seat in front of him.

Andrew could not allow another meltdown. He had to calm the father before his mind deteriorated, as the daughter's did, into despair. What better way to treat one shock with another? He spoke quickly, assuredly, "I know she is safe because, in a way, this was my operation."

Damian was shocked. They passed several intersections before he could bring himself to speak. "You made me believe that you were sympathetic to my work. Now you tell me that you had a hand in the kidnapping of my daughter!"

Andrew took his eyes off the busy road to look into Damian's face in the rearview mirror. He put all the sincerity he could muster into his words, "It's not like that. I was played. They must've been onto me. I sent the warning message when I realized that they were going to pick you up from the apartment. I did not lie to you."

"You're still working for the CIA."

"Yes, but you should not read into my words what is not in them. I don't like what I do. You had a hand in making me realize it. Studying your work convinced me that I was on the wrong side. I followed your work not only from professional interest, but as a conscientious human being. But I realized that it was not possible to reconcile what you teach with what is alleged about you. This was why I asked you to place yourself on trial."

"That ultimatum was an antithesis of trust."

"I work for an institution whose entire existence is based on illusion. I don't know what trust is."

"What about the facts?"

"The facts? Don't make me laugh. We manufacture the facts."

They rode in silence for a time. As traffic intensified, and forced him to sway dangerously on the congested street, Andrew concentrated on driving. The shock that initially gripped Damian now turned into anger. Had the ride been less frantic, not requiring him to grip the handlebar, and to concentrate on the surroundings, he would have, perhaps, fled the vehicle. But the time that it took to clear the congestion also allowed Damian to clear his head. Andrew's impassioned voice still ringing in his head, as well as recollections of the earlier encounter, had convinced Damian that the American was not lying. He could not have, willingly, caused harm to Amanda. He was in love with her. And now he was in the best position to save her. Andrew knew the people who kidnapped Amanda, he knew what motivated them, and how they operated, and there was no reason to doubt that he knew how do deal with the consequences.

Traffic eased a little, and Andrew continued, speaking quickly, condensing events of the past weeks, into one, small pill, "I did everything I could to protect you and Amy. Since that night in Reykjavik I stalled the investigation. Of course, the CIA station knew that you were in the U.K. Then the Russians caught up to us. Long story short —they have their own plans for you. The good thing is that it does not involve killing you. The bad is that one can never trust a Russian oligarch with active ties to the Kremlin. I accepted their help in tracking you down through the CIA. I monitored the communications, read the codes, and knew that the agency was able to tap into your computer. It was only a matter of hours before they found the apartment. I'm glad I was able to arrive before it was too late. We almost got away, and we would've, if it wasn't for the congestion in this goddamn city!" Andrew finished by slamming his fists on the steering wheel.

"And now you are a fugitive, too."

"A renegade. A traitor. A fugitive. I'm sure they are throwing a lot euphemisms around. It doesn't matter. It's not about me. It is, and always has been, about you and your work. You must go on."

"How can I?"

"Do not worry about Amy. She won't be harmed. I won't let them!"

"You have a way of reassuring by seeding more worry."

"She was taken only as leverage against you."

"They were right to do so."

"You mustn't give in!"

"I won't barter my daughter's life."

"You won't have to. It won't come to that."

"I find it difficult to accept it after everything you told me."

Andrew's persistence was arresting when he said, "I told you — it won't come to that. They will not harm Amy, as long as you give them the appearance of appeasement. This will buy us time."

"Time?"

"To get her out. I can do it. They taught me everything I need to know to save her. I know their safe houses. I know their people. I know how they work. And I have the advantage. They think I'm weak, outnumbered, broken... They don't expect me to act. They're wrong. If anything, the kidnapping made me stronger. I will get Amy out. I will!"

Damian listened to him with an incredulous expression on his face. The young man showed the kind of spirit an ordinary man could find very difficult to muster in similar circumstances.

"How— What am I supposed to do?" he asked.

Andrew took a moment before replying. He exited the main thoroughfare and turned to narrower, yet smoothly flowing streets. "You must continue what you've started."

"That's asking a lot, knowing that Amy's in their hands."

"You cannot stop your work. If you do, the world will spiral down on a path of self-destruction."

"Why should I care about the world. My daughter—"

"Do it for your daughter. Help make the world a better place for her. Were there more people like you the world would be a whole lot different already. Instead humanity remains stuck in seemingly permanent feudal era, with a tiny but powerful fraction wreaking misery for 99% of the world's population. You must send a clear signal to these self-proclaimed elites, who rule by fist, that their time is up, that they do not stand above the law, that the laws are here not only to keep the masses in shackles, but also to keep the elites from excesses. The rule of the law is common to all. Those who break it, who act against the common good, will be held responsible, regardless of who they are, where they reside, and what jurisdictions protect them. The time has come to show the world that no offense goes unpunished, and those who commit them will not be judged by history, or God, or some other ephemeral and distant being, but here and now, just as their victims suffer in the present. People have started to believe it possible. Back down now, and all you've done so far, and all their hopes, will crumble."

Damian was impressed. The boy reminded him of the days when he was that age, passionate against, and perhaps because of, the odds. While he was still largely riding on the wave of passion that started when he was younger, that passion was of a different kind now. It was not only a desire to change the world, as inspired by a spark, but a conscious labor of love for the goals he set out to achieve when he was younger.

Damian said, "You've clearly thought it through."

Andrew sneered, "I've done nothing else since I met your daughter and, by extension, you. The time has come to start doing things."

"How do you see it done, given the circumstances?"

"There is an organized campaign aimed at destroying your character. You must distinguish yourself from those who attack you. The world must clearly understand, and tell, good from evil."

"The world isn't built on white and black. There are plenty of shades in between."

"To say nothing of all the colors of the rainbow!" Andrew blasted the cliché. "True, but work for the Agency has taught me that the easiest way to affect change is to reach the people at the most basic level, in that narrowly defined sphere of good and evil. Thus it is important that the people see the difference between them, and you."

"And you don't think they see it now?"

"Your enemies have covered inroads to discredit you, and the lynching have turned plenty of people away from you. Whether you are, or aren't, responsible for the killings, of which your enemies accuse you, you must convince people that there is a difference between you and those who rob, kill, and wreak havoc as part of their sanctioned policy."

"And you believe that my trial will accomplish just that?"

"It will do more than that. It will give you the moral right to continue."

"What if— What if the people find me morally unfit to carry on?"

Andrew weighed his words before replying. "Then… May God have mercy on us all."

28

Andrew drew up to the curb on a busy downtown street. They left the vehicle, abandoned really, as Damian observed by the keys left in the ignition, and disappeared into the midday crowd. Andrew led the way on foot. They covered a maze of streets, double backing, and circling, to ensure they were not being followed. Almost half an hour later they arrived at a construction site. Andrew scanned the area before lifting the blue tarp, and disappearing behind it, Damian following.

The scaffolding and tarps wrapped around the building brought an image stored in Damian's imagination banks. It was the place described by Amanda, the safe house used by the Russians. Damian froze. He sensed before he saw that they were not alone. Almost at the same instant they were approached by two burly men. Damian's muscles tensed; he was ready to defend himself.

"Relax." Andrew offered reassurance, but the words that followed sent chills down Damian's spine, "These are our new allies."

Over the years Damian learned that support for his ideals came from all walks of life. He met those who joined him out of concern for the eroding press freedoms and the disappearing objectivism in the media, as well as those who intimated such concerns, but were interested in exploiting them for their own gains. Among the latter were ruling politicians, as well as opposition figures, both overt and covert, in countries of low as well as high democracy indexes, and who offered Damian support out of misguided or downright mischievous desire for an alternative voice, a voice that would express their ideology. Damian was used to brushing shoulders with politicians and business leaders who courted activists and their skills at organizing and affecting change; many of them tried to put pressure on him to follow their guidelines. Despite all that he had never been approached by a media mogul directly, an oligarch bent on building a new empire. He met him on the top floor of the building.

A man in a tailored suit approached the newcomers. Speaking with a Russian accent, he nonetheless used impeccable, if studied, English. "Mr. Allende. I am so sorry that you and your daughter were forcibly separated."

Damian said nothing. The small talk and insincere words did not interest him. He turned to Andrew as though to express bemusement at being paired with someone this blatantly disingenuous. To his even bigger surprise he watched Andrew walk into a mesh cage, close the door behind him, and approach a small aluminum desk with a laptop computer, where he sat down and immediately began typing on the keyboard, seemingly removed from the conversation developing between the two men.

"A necessary precaution," the Russian commented on Andrew's seemingly strange behavior. "The cube, I mean." He approached the mesh structure and said to Andrew, "Speaking of which. Now that you openly crossed the line, perhaps we should deactivate your chip altogether?"

"I'm not sure it's such a good idea," Andrew replied over his shoulder. "By deactivating my chip I will be sending a signal that I am no longer with the Company. Ambiguity, or plausible deniability, is the name of the game in espionage. No point burning that bridge."

"You have betrayed your colleagues and sabotaged an operation. I suggest that you have burned the bridge behind you," the Russian said in a peculiar tone, his eyes darting from Andrew to Damian.

"I'm not a traitor!" Andrew exploded suddenly.

"I'm afraid you will find it difficult explaining your actions otherwise," the Russian went on unperturbed.

"Let me worry about that."

"Can someone tell me what is going on?" Damian was losing patience.

The Russian turned to face him. "You've found a faithful follower, Mr. Allende." He nodded his head to Andrew. "This young man has just drawn a big question mark over his future. He went against his employer to save you from an imminent arrest, perhaps even something worse, and in the process he placed himself on the unenviable, though long, list of traitors—"

Andrew belittled the dire prediction. "Not all is done yet, and even if it were so—" He turned to Damian, "We had a deal. I said I'd keep the CIA off your back while you prepare your next online court. I did what I could. I kept them at bay all those weeks. What I did not expect, was that they had me figured out. They lied to me. They knew about your whereabouts on the farm, outside of London."

"I'm sorry. And I thank you for keeping Amy safe, all this time. Until now."

"I promise you—" Andrew realized he was repeating himself. He changed his train of thought. "I only wish she knew how I felt about her. It would be this much easier for her, now, all alone, wondering what's going to happen to her."

"You should've told her this a long time ago," Damian said coldly, without remorse.

"Should've — would've. It isn't easy to tell the woman who loves and trusts you that you got close to her based on false pretenses."

"If you love, and are loved—" Damian started pathetically.

"It always seems so easy when it isn't us, does it?" Andrew responded, all the while tapping on the keyboard.

Yes, I suppose it does, Damian thought. He said into the air, "So, now what?"

"I'll find her," Andrew said through his teeth, his eyes focused on the screen.

"Let me help."

Andrew raised his eyes. He gazed from the Russian to Damian. "Do you know where I've just logged in to?"

Damian needed two seconds to understand. He nodded his head.

Andrew continued, his eyes on Soba Kalgun, "You've got me doing what you wanted me to do all along." He turned to Damian, and said, as though excusing his actions, "I wouldn't have done it, except now, when they crossed the line, and the gloves are off. They should not have laid their hands on Amy!"

Damian approached the cube, gazed over Andrew's shoulder, to the computer screen.

Andrew said in a warning voice, "All the same, it is the last place you want to be caught poking around. Not if you want to avoid charges of espionage, and lose the remaining semblance of journalistic objectivism. It's bad enough you are accused of possessing classified material. You don't want to be found procuring it."

All bets are off indeed, now that they crossed the line, Damian thought. Nothing will stop me from doing what it takes to save my daughter, including laying myself at the sacrificial altar. He knew, however, that such talk would not do; Andrew was determined to see it all done the way he has envisioned it — he was the one who had lost the woman he loved, and he was determined to save her. Damian watched the slouched back of the man who loved his daughter. I love her, too, he thought, but said nothing; it would help nothing.

He turned to the Russian. "And you, Mr. Kalgun? It is Kalgun, right?"

"Forgive me. I should have done the introduction, for the honor is all mine. I guess you may attribute this omission to my being starstruck."

Damian disregarded his empty words. "Are you not concerned about poking into the American intelligence servers?"

"I'm sure my lawyers would make a good case proving that providing the hardware is not the same as inciting a break-in. Besides, what Mr. Walker is doing remains perfectly legal, as long as he remains in the employ of the Agency."

Andrew burst out a laughter. "I suppose it's no use telling that I am not using my own credentials?"

Kalgun showed no surprise. "Perhaps, then, we did not hear the remark." He showed Damian to a set of aluminum chairs and a like table, located across the floor.

"I'm not interested in idle talk," Damian said. "My primary concern is my daughter's safety."

"Naturally. And I want to assure you that you have my complete support."

"Your support isn't exactly without self-interest, is it."

They approached the table. Kalgun took one of the chairs. Damian hesitated a moment before deciding to sit down. He picked a chair across the table.

They settled in their seats, and the Russian said, "On the basic human level… I guess not. Of course I want to pursue my wants. But I am not without conscience, and I assure you that I want to, and I will do everything in my power to help you and your daughter."

"Why can't I shake the feeling that your conscience is entirely dictated by your wants?"

"Does it matter?"

Damian considered the answer before replying. "I suppose it depends on what those wants are."

"They are not that different from yours."

"If you mean Tsardom of the media empire—"

"Ha, ha!" Kalgun laughed. "No, I suppose not when you put it like that. On the other hand it is the empire that binds us."

"Does it."

"Certainly."

"I take an issue with the description, to begin with."

"Like it, or not, the independent media forms a formidable force. It is an empire, by sheer reach, though an empire in disarray. It's got huge army of staff. With every citizen being a potential outlet and source, and with a growing audience longing for alternatives, the independents have a potential to rival established news outlets. They cannot achieve it by remaining fractured."

"How do you plan to unite them?"

"To start — they need a leader."

"Am I to be the leader? Or you?"

Kalgun did not catch the sarcasm. He said, "We need each other."

"Isn't it a cooperation doomed to fail? With at least one of us perceived as the Demon, it would be more of a Rasputin — Nicholas union."

"You're exaggerating. Most of your followers take you for a prophet, not a crazed monk. I think that you are neither. I wouldn't offer you this cooperation otherwise. If this cooperation comes to fruition I shall expect you to challenge me, to challenge everything I know about this business, everything I learned about it—"

"Everything?"

"I don't pretend to know about the independent media. I know enough about it, though, to notice that it is a viable alternative to the established structures, and I do not intend to sit idly by as the news scene is changing."

"Are you a changed man, Mr. Kalgun?"

"You may say that. I suppose I am."

"Or are you just a jaded billionaire who doesn't know where else to sink his wealth?"

"On the contrary. I don't think I'll be sinking my money. But, I don't want you to think that my interest in the whole affair is wholly financial. I am a very passionate man, especially when it comes to new challenges."

"Is that what it is to you — a challenge?"

"We both have our reasons. Our motivations may differ, but the common goal unites us—"

"Ha, ha!" Damian laughed for some time, wiping tears from his eyes.

"Did I say something wrong?" Kalgun took no offense, his face unmoved; he was a good politician.

"You want an empire. Everything I do leads to breaking empires, whether these be geographical, ideological, political — you name it."

Kalgun commented with arresting honesty, "I won't interfere with you doing what you do."

Damian looked at him closer. The Russian's face showed no signs of deception, but it meant little. Every politician lies straight-faced.

He said, "I've heard it before. I was offered deals, whereby I would build an alternative to the established, and often — the only — media. I was told I could break them. That's not what I do. I do not break one empire to establish another."

"What if I guaranteed that I would not interfere with your vision and your work, that you could do as you see fit?"

"Under an organized umbrella."

Kalgun bowed his head ever so slightly.

"You do not understand me, Mr. Kalgun. I do not believe that the alternative media need to be organized. Organization and control led to the crises in the newsworld. The alternatives, the independents, are good as they are, precisely because of what they are, and how they operate. It's all in the independence they enjoy. They've challenged the big players, and that is why guys like you want in — to keep it under control."

"You are right. They challenged the big players. But they cannot last. You must be aware of the efforts of the corporate media to undermine the independent outlets. The more followers they have, the more customers they steal from the big players, the more they become subjects of ridicule. There can be only one outcome. The big fish always swallows the small."

Damian pushed back in his chair. "Have you ever seen piranhas at work? It's not the physical size but the teeth that count."

Kalgun countered, "I've read the tale about a small man being swallowed by a big fish."

"Then you must know that he survived in the belly of the fish."

"Will you?"

Damian did not reply immediately. He was amused by the Russian's persistence. The man must have known everything Damian ever did, he must have had his life examined to the smallest detail, he must have known that Damian would not bow, yet he tried time and again. That he tried at all was perplexing enough, and it now prevented Damian from dropping the subject. That, and an unexplained conviction that his daughter's safety was in this oligarch's hands.

He said, "Perhaps not, but what I started will go on. Others will follow in my footsteps."

"You can pave a smooth road for them."

The man's persistence was truly overwhelming. What was underneath the offer he was making?

"Are you offering me protection?"

"Protection is part of a bigger picture."

"My daughter is already in the hands of those who have their own plans in respect to my work."

"I can help turn things around."

"But only for a price?"

"Do not take me for a heartless beast only because I want to make a buck."

They studied one another from across the table. Both saw a face wary of the conversation. Both wondered how best to reach the other, how to push across their own point of view, and the reasons motivating their actions.

A voice from the cube broke the spell.

"Guys!" Andrew called out.

They stood up in unison, faster than was necessary, each happy for the opportunity to postpone the uncomfortable conversation.

Before they neared the cube, Damian knew the news was not good.

Andrew Walker was standing by the mesh wall, on his face an expression of weary bewilderment.

"Have you found her?" Damian asked.

"It's the strangest thing," Andrew said in a voice that matched the look on his face. "It's as though there never was an operation to raid the flat, or to kidnap Amy."

"A covert operation?"

Andrew's face told what he could not bring himself to express in words.

Damian did not give up. "Could this information be hidden from you, not accessible using your credentials?"

"It's not about credentials. I've looked where this sort of info should be found — communications traffic, orders, communiqués, requisitions, etc. Nothing. It's as though it never happened."

"But it did."

"It did." Andrew's eyes wandered to the Russian's and bounced off them quickly.

Damian did not notice. He said quickly, and despite the question mark, authoritatively, "What does it tell us, then?" The tone of resoluteness in his voice was contagious, not allowing gloomy thoughts.

Andrew replied on a positive tone, though his mind was leaning toward the worst. "It could be a black op."

A black op sounded better than the unknown. Damian clung to it. "Essentially it is a CIA operation. Right?"

The positive attitude surprised Andrew. He recognized a similar trait in Amy. When faced with seemingly insurmountable obstacles she became alert and ready to fight. Defeat was not an option for her. Like father, like daughter.

Andrew replied, "Essentially? Yes."

"Then somebody in the CIA must know about it."

The logic was clear.

Andrew said, "Of course."

Damian concluded, "Someone in whose jurisdiction the operation took place."

Andrew confirmed, "Almost certainly."

Damian hammered it down, "Let's kidnap him. Swap him for my daughter."

Consternation on Andrew's face was the initial reaction.

Damian went on, "We've run out of options, don't you see?"

"Y-yes, but the logistics of such an op—" Andrew stumbled.

Damian turned to the Russian who stood a step behind him, listening. "Mr. Kalgun?"

Soba Kalgun said nothing during the exchange of words. His face told what words did not.

"Are you certain?" the Russian asked.

"My daughter is more important to me than anything."

"It's only natural, but it isn't what I meant."

"If you want me to consider your offer—"

"I don't want to give an impression that I am bickering. If we are to be partners I will do anything to remove obstacles from your path. I am only asking this for your own sake. What you're thinking of will be linked to you. Your actions will act as ammunition against you."

"Can you help?" Damian persisted.

"Can I persuade the CIA station chief to divulge the whereabouts of your daughter, maybe even to release her? Certainly."

"Wait!" Andrew regained his composure. "The risk is too great—"

Damian cut him off, "I'm ready to take any risk in order to save my daughter."

"So am I!" Andrew assured him. "That's not what I meant. It isn't the risk for us, as it is for Amy, that I worry about."

"Do you see an alternative?"

"Let me talk to him first."

"I suggested nothing less and nothing more," Kalgun chimed in.

"I've heard about the type of persuasion used by the KGB."

"Not that different from the methods used by the CIA, I assure you."

"What do you suggest, Andrew?" Damian stopped the pointless exchange.

"I'll bargain. This," he pointed to the computer screen, "for Amy."

"You are burned. Why should they deal with you?"

"The station chief has always liked me—"

"Is it enough?"

"He knows how I feel about Amy. He knows I'd do anything for her."

"Even sell me out?"

"I won't let that happen!" Kalgun interjected.

"Yes," Andrew replied straight-faced.

Damian smiled. "I'm glad we think alike. I will gladly give myself up to save my daughter."

Both men exchanged understanding looks.

Damian added, "Since we're on the same level, I assume that you have not one, but at least two strong cards up your sleeve?"

"It's the key to a perfect hand."

"What is your secret card?"

"Something I picked up while browsing the CIA logs," Andrew nodded to the laptop computer.

"You're both needlessly heroic," Kalgun said hurriedly, on his lips a barely contained smirk. "If you just step aside and let my men bring the station chief over for a chat—"

They looked at him and each other.

Andrew spoke for both, "Let's keep it as an option of last resort."

29

The park was a popular place with mothers with strollers, and seniors with poodles. A green oasis in the concrete jungle, it offered the much needed break for the senses — the rustle of young leaves soothed the ears, the fresh spring greenery calmed the eyes, and the scent of flowers pleased the nostrils. The park on this warm and sunny spring day drew more aficionados of the outdoors than the plotters counted on, but it was so much the better. Mothers changed diapers, fathers played ball on the moist grass, and grandmothers combed their pooches. The presence of people, or witnesses, was more important than the shrubbery. The spies who met in the park this day did not want to meet in dark corners, yet they required a setting that allowed them to conduct an undisturbed conversation. The white noise of a busy place provided such an environment. This was the place where two men could to meet face-to-face, and be assured of mutual civility.

They occupied a bench that stood in the middle of the grassy expanse, between a playground on one side, and a fenced dog park on the other. All the surrounding benches were taken, some by city dwellers oblivious to what was unfolding nearby, and others taken by clandestine agents with concealed weapons. Who was who, however, was anybody's guess, because the agents were experienced field operatives who specialized in blending-in among civilian populations. This sort of arrangement assured that neither side would attempt to break the terms of arrangement.

The older of the two men started the conversation, his eyes on a bench from which a young couple showed particular interest in the two men.

"I suppose there's no point asking who your new friends are?"

He went on when no answer followed his first question, "Do you even know who your friends are?"

"Shall we skip the foreplay?" the younger man suggested through his clenched teeth.

"Andrew, Andrew, Andrew… Are you sure you want to do this? It is not too late to turn things around, you know. You've done nothing that can't be undone. With well thought out, and extenuating circumstances, you may even be able to keep your job with little more than a slap on the hand. I was young, too; I know what love does to the strongest of us."

"Do you think that it's all it is about? Love?"

"For you own sake — yes, I hope that's all it is about." The older man accentuated his words.

Andrew said nothing. He realized that the station chief probably meant it. He was always a decent boss to operatives under his command, and for some reason took to liking Andrew in particular. For a long time the sentiment was mutual.

"I should've known better," the chief continued. "Assigning you to a young, beautiful, and smart woman, had to've affected your judgment."

"You're right, and wrong. Getting to know her affected me, but it did not change my judgment. Something else did. Getting to know her father, and his work, did it."

The chief said with almost fatherly concern, "Careful there, Andrew; don't say what you might regret."

"I'd rather not regret things, which I could've done, but didn't. They tend to stick in my head like a sore point."

"You've become a philosopher. It's dangerous for an agent in the field."

"You're wrong. Thinking may just be the most powerful weapon."

"Is that it, then? You've come armed? There can only be one reason for it — to fight. Do you want a fight, Andrew?"

"I doesn't have to come to that, Dick. I want Amanda."

The station chief watched him closely, not a muscle moved on his face, but a well-skilled observer would have noticed the sudden change in his pupils. This, in turn, would have provided more answers than the longest interrogation.

"You've come to bargain, then," the chief said at last; it was a statement. "What are your terms?"

Andrew sneered. "Don't tell me you haven't set the price."

"Name your terms. Perhaps I'm feeling generous."

"What is the point in this bartering," Andrew said angrily, and immediately scolded himself for showing it. He checked himself, and added "We both know what we came for."

Dick Verso watched him closely, and said, "Tell me, Andy. How long since you've reported to the station? Weeks, anyway."

Weeks? Andrew looked at him with puzzled eyes.

This time the station chief was baffled and made no effort to conceal it.

"We tried to contact you. We couldn't even locate you. Your microchip must be dead."

Andrew listened to him dumbfounded.

"Weeks?" he repeated.

With his eyes on his agent, the station chief said, "You disappeared off the radar."

Andrew could not help it. His head turned to a bench across the park alley, where one of Kalgun's teams sat at the ready. The look in Andrew's eyes did not spell the need for help. On the contrary, an entirely new emotion was present in them.

He started cautiously, his voice barely above a whisper, "Yesterday. The operation to raid the apartment, to seize Allende."

The station chief returned a bland look. "We lost Allende some weeks ago. There was a fire in a mansion he was hiding in. We assumed he realized he was being watched, staged the fire, and fled. But now, I see—"

"Don't play with me, Dick!" Andrew warned.

"Do you even know what game's at play?" Dick Verso's eyes darted to the bench occupied by Soba Kalgun's team.

Andrew followed his gaze, and suddenly the world reeled in front of his eyes. His mind was working frantically. This cannot be! It cannot!

The chief watched him closely. "Let me ask you something. What happened to your I.D. chip? Have you deactivated it, or removed altogether?"

Deactivated? Removed? Andrew was at a loss.

The chief looked at him indulgently.

His chip had been deactivated, despite a clear agreement to the contrary. Andrew turned pale. Everything became clear. He had allowed himself to be duped. With the realization came calm, and calm brought clarity to his mind. Of one thing he was now certain: He was on the path of no return, in a maze from which only decisive and determined action could lead to an exit. This was neither time for regrets, nor for doubts.

"What's happened to you, Andy?"

Andrew expounded in quick, short sentences, "I'm done with the CIA. One way or another. I want out. For what it's worth — my conscience is clear. I did nothing to harm the Company, or the United States. Not yet... If anything — I am the one who was harmed. Or rather — it was my soul. It became possessed by the evil that grips the world in its bloodied claws. Then I learned about Damian Allende. I studied his work and became convinced that not only a different I, but a whole new world, was possible. I saw that it wasn't too late, that I still had a chance to redeem myself. The more I learned about the man and his work, the more I understood my own place in this new world. Meanwhile, I fell in love with the woman who's now been taken away from me—" Andrew broke up, the confession too emotional. He could not finish.

The station chief listened intently. He turned to the young man, an expression of fatherly concern on his face. He had seen too many agents become burned out.

"Oh, Andy, how I wish you'd come to me earlier."

The soft words roused Andrew. He wiped his forehead, and said, "You should not have lied to me."

Dick Verso raised his brows, not comprehending.

"You knew Allende's whereabouts after his arrival from Reykjavik, and you kept me in the dark."

"It wasn't my decision."

"Why was it even an option? And don't give me the paygrade treatment."

The station chief weighed his words carefully before replying. "The headquarters thought it best if Allende could continue his work... unhindered."

"Why such interest to let him go on with it?"

"I couldn't tell."

They studied each other's faces for a while.

"Andy—"

"Dick—"

They were at a lack for words, so close, yet so far away, separated as though by a world of irreconcilable differences.

Andrew was angered by what he read as pity in his interlocutor's eyes. He felt weary and betrayed, the betrayal escaping his ability to comprehend its source and meaning. It all came on down on him so suddenly, crushing with unbearable weight. Too heavy, and too fast to build up defenses. He wanted nothing more but to end this painful meeting.

The station chief continued in the pitying tone, "What did you mean when you said you have done nothing to harm the CIA... yet?"

He replied wearily, as though to himself, "They teach us to always carry a bargaining chip in this job, don't they? I've got mine. I want Amanda in exchange."

Something in his voice alerted the station chief. Sensing that the young man was about to cross the point of no return, he warned, "Don't, Andrew."

"I told you. Amanda is more important to me than anything—"

"Andy, I don't—"

"The London station database."

The station chief exhaled a long breath, as though life left his mortal coil.

He said in a grave voice, "I've been trying to tell you that we don't have Amanda. We've had nothing to do with her disappearance. We had no hand in raiding Allende yesterday, as you suggested. I told you — we lost him some weeks ago. If we'd known his new whereabouts we would've offered him discreet protection, all within the distance of deniability, as these are our instructions from Langley."

The silence that followed was explosive; the smallest spark could ignite it. They looked at one another as only a mentor and a determined disciple do, and they understood — they had both been played.

30

It was not difficult to realize what had actually transpired. Andrew gazed to the park bench where Kalgun's team kept a close watch on his meeting with the station chief. The intensity of their gaze convinced him that the conversation was being picked up by remote microphones, and wirelessly transmitted to the team. The expectancy of something on their faces told him that they awaited a trigger in the conversation. What was it? He could not tell without knowing their objectives, but it reiterated the necessity to proceed with caution and to carefully consider every word. And careful Andrew would be in any instance, for he did not spend nearly six years in the CIA's employ to plunge into blindly believing the chief. The fact that both of them faced a common adversary did not make them allies, contrary to the popular proverb. On the path Andrew had chosen, he had to carefully consider his friends. Who were those friends? The chief's question was still ringing in his ears, but the connotation was not what the chief had intended. Andrew knew better than to seek friends among the spies. They were survivors, to be sure, but their loyalty knew no allegiance. The intelligence community was able to survive many ups, and even more downs, because it operated on the verge of said and unsaid. It was a chameleon without set colors, adaptive to the circumstances. Was it aware of the colors it was conceived with? Was it aware of whom it served? These were questions that did not matter, for the only objective of a service whose members' existence depended entirely on the whim of the changing policy, was — survival. Ambiguity and seeming servitude to the current masters was only a part of the game. It was ingrown. To understand it was to play the game according with rules of survival. Did Andrew understand the game? He was aware of its intricacies enough to know that the Agency as a whole, and its every member in particular, participated in the game with own objectives in mind. For this reason it helped to always carry an ace up one's sleeve. Andrew brought such an ace prior to the meeting with the station chief. He had already played it. It was time to find out if the card was strong enough.

Andrew said, "Tell me, Dick, what would you do if the station database ended up on the whistleblower portal?"

The station chief gazed at his young companion with a sad expression in his eyes.

"I don't know what I'd do, Andy. But I do know, that you and Damian Allende would end up in the same boat."

"A boat to Gitmo? Or a boat that has the CIA providing its protection, running it?"

The station chief did not reply. His silence was the more ominous. Andrew tried to find the answer on the chief's face. It was useless. The chief was an experienced field operative. He was an old bird, with over three decades of experience in the art of deception and treachery. He knew all about the art of microexpression. Like a mime, or a clown, he studied, and spent countless hours, training his facial muscles. As a result of it his face was expressionless, as that of a dead man. Andrew realized the impossibility of the task he had embarked on. How could he have imagined to play against the chief? He was doomed to lose from the start. For his excuse he could offer only one word — love. Love did not look at obstacles other than as hurdles that had to be overcome. Love was driving Andrew now. Love gave him wings, and love would guide him on. He relaxed at the thought.

"I guess we're at a stalemate then," he said.

"The Company can forgive a lot of sins, but not when someone acts against it."

It was pointless to circle around the subject. Andrew said, "Help me get Amanda back, or I let the database loose."

"Don't burn the last bridge, Andrew. It may be your only way back."

"There's no going back. I'm on a one way street."

"Don't miss the exit, then. I'm telling you this as a friend."

"As a friend you should see that I am out of options."

"On the contrary. You always held the strongest card."

Andrew looked closer into the chief's eyes. He thought he caught something in the pupils.

"Damian Allende?"

"He is more valuable now, then ever, but the Company must not be implicated."

Andrew was puzzled. He had heard the same from Kalgun, and he thought he understood the Russian's rationale, but of what possible importance was Damian for the CIA?

Before he could ask the question, the chief hurried on, as though eager to avert the subject, "There is a reason I agreed to meet you. Two, actually. Firstly — I hoped you came to your senses and wanted back. See, I knew about the database breach. Our boys discovered it when it was in progress, but were unable to prevent you from downloading the material. Secondly — the Company doesn't know, yet. Only I do, and two of our communications boys. Do the right thing, Andy, and I can close my eyes. Leak the database to Allende and you'll be lost."

Andrew's head drooped to his chest. It was the first time that Andrew felt a pinch of guilt. While, until this moment, he only considered himself against the system that created a skewed world, he was now faced with a personal dilemma. Because of his actions the station chief would be held responsible for having reared a traitor. There would be consequences. Someone else would have to pay for Andrew's actions. What right had he to act this selfishly, without any regard for the others? Then he remembered something the chief once told him after a black operation that went bad; it was not cleared with the British side, and would not have received clearance, as it was not conducted with Britain's interest in mind, and in which an agent had died. The circumstances did not permit to claim the body of the agent, nor to admit to the terribly bungled operation. The worst of it was that the death could have been prevented, but at a cost — they would have had to expose, to their hosts, what they were up to. The chief decided against it. The op was swept under the rug, and the inter-agency relations avoided serious straining. The chief said then to Andrew, "Some day you may find yourself in a situation when you'll have to make a similar decision. Someone's future, maybe even life, will depend upon your decision. Do you owe that much to your country? You, and only you, will have to answer that question."

Andrew stood up. He looked into the chief's eyes. "Of one thing I can assure you: I shall do the right thing."

31

The atmosphere in the vehicle was tense. In order to deliver their cargo safely, Kalgun's men took no chances, and employed the usual techniques of escape and evasion. As a result of it the return to the safe site was excruciatingly long for Andrew's agitated mind. At a loss about the true motivations that drove the Russian, he was burning with desire to share the results of the meeting with Damian. Together they might decipher the script to the play, in which they had been unwitting actors.

Soba Kalgun acted every bit as oblivious to the doubts that must have stricken the American after the chat with the station chief. Only a barely discernible smirk in the corner of his lips betrayed his satisfaction as he listened to the account of the meeting. Something in his eyes told Andrew that the oligarch expected the outcome; that something was challenging Andrew, as though throwing a ball into his court, with the expectation that the game would not turn into full-contact confrontation. This was to be a game that would be played according to the rules of the old-school espionage, a game of cat-and-mouse.

To Andrew's surprise, Damian took the news of failure to secure his daughter's release with stride that bordered on foreknowledge of the outcome. Had something transpired during Andrew's absence that facilitated such a reaction? He longed to ask a million questions, but how to do it under Kalgun's omnipresent eyes and ears?

Andrew turned to Damian, and said cautiously, "You don't seem surprised by the outcome."

"No."

The reply was expressionless, yet Andrew thought he caught something in Allende's eyes — a peculiar spark that alerted his senses.

Damian sent him on the right track. He said, "I should've known the price would be too low. We failed to agree on the right terms. That's all."

Andrew replied instinctively, "In retrospect, I suppose it was a low-ball offer, considering the value of the object of barter."

They knew instantly that they hit the spot. Soba Kalgun was nodding his head, seemingly engrossed in listening to the exchange of ideas; it resembled the warmer-warmer-hot encouragement in the game of hot-cold.

Andrew reiterated, his goal to clarify Kalgun's intentions, "Everyone has a sense of value."

The nodding increased, as though saying — warmer, warmer, warmer.

"But how to determine the right price?" Damian edged on.

"Is there a price too high to set Amanda free?" Andrew asked rhetorically.

"No, there isn't."

"It is obvious, then, that the station database was too low a price."

"Hence, the obvious conclusion is that we must raise the offer."

Kalgun's eyes softened, as anybody's would at the prospect of a fine reward.

"To the top?" Damian suggested.

"To the top." Andrew chimed along.

This time they made no effort at stealing glances at Kalgun; instead they faced him in expectation.

The oligarch did not disappoint. This was what he was waiting for. He flicked a finger, and two guards appeared at his sides, each carrying several objects in his hands.

Andrew addressed Damian, his eyes on the Russian. "What if we fail?"

Allende replied, "Failure is not an option when Amanda's safety is concerned."

Soba Kalgun grinned appreciatively. He said nothing.

No words were necessary, as all three understood each other. They turned on their heels, and followed the two guards who entered one of the cubes, and began installing two laptop computers, and various other equipment. Two chairs faced each other from across an aluminum table, which became a workspace for two hackers with unique skills and abilities. And so it happened that what was obscured thus far, suddenly became clear. They understood how it came to be that the two of them had found themselves together, working side-by-side. Everything had a reason. Everything that had happened to them since the night in Reykjavik had a reason: to pull off a job that could be done only by combined effort. What was that job? Andrew knew it now, as did Damian, though neither expressed it in words. They had all the clues they needed: Reykjavik, Amanda's kidnapping, and the CIA Station database being a too low a price — it was hanging in front of their noses all along, like a carrot in front of a hare's den.

There was but one thing to do. Damian and Andrew sat at the two opposing aluminum chairs. They cracked their knuckles, and began to tap on their keyboards.

Soba Kalgun smiled. *At last*, he thought.

32

The two computers were interlinked to work together. It took each man a brief moment to realize that someone else was eavesdropping; every keystroke they made was monitored, and, likely, recorded. They proceeded cautiously. The initiative belonged to Andrew, who possessed the codes and the necessary knowledge of security barriers that flanked the servers they would shortly attempt to penetrate. Yet, to his surprise, Damian noticed that Andrew was tiptoeing on the screen. No hacker would make such erratic movements unless he wanted attention drawn to himself. It worked. Damian recognized his own code being used to mimic an attack on a server located in Langley, Virginia. The code, while well copied, was so ill executed that it immediately drew Damian's attention to what hid behind such a blatant attempt at being noticed. He studied the bits of data, and from scattered and fractured commands he extracted what warranted a raised brow of awed impression.

Andrew was sending Damian encoded messages. He knew he was playing a risky game. He knew his worth, though; he knew he was good at what he did, but a successful operative ought to be mindful of a superior or equal opponent. Andrew had to consider that Kalgun had on his staff an equally skilled operator, someone who was monitoring every step made on the screen. His advantage was in having intimate knowledge of Damian's working environment, the result of close studies conducted while investigating, and eventually following the work of a man whose life he infiltrated. He found out that Damian wrote his own codes, preferring the security of multiple protection schemes from the simple ones, as used by most amateur hackers. Damian not only wrote his code, but he encrypted it, too. Andrew broke the encryption. He used it now to pass on what he suspected and found out about the case that bound them together.

They worked fearlessly, their laptops cramming the small space of the aluminum tabletop, the vibrations felt with their wrists and elbows. Facing one another, they avoided eye contact lest it be used to read what the quick keystrokes hid. Andrew, whose seat faced the Russians, could observe with the corner of his eye, that attempts were being made at deciphering what went on between the two men in the mesh cube. The Russians were all centered around a desk, behind a pile of bagged cement, seemingly engaged in a casual chat. The chat, inanimate, was only a play. Even at the distance, and without making it obvious that he observed them, Andrew could tell that their eyes were centered on computer screens. He could see the glow in the pupils. It told him that time was of the essence, and that sooner or later, they might catch up to what he was up to. He doubled his efforts, passing on messages and reading ones in return, all in a form of shorthand understood only between hackers who shared a code and an encryption.

They confirmed each other's suspicions, and came to realize that they had stumbled upon a game of the mighty. The stakes sent shivers down their spines. They found themselves between the proverbial rock and a hard place, and had to come up with a solution, not only to save the woman they loved, but to stop what could only lead to a catastrophe. Unless they found a way to avert it, the calamity that loomed would be linked to Damian — the scapegoat of convenience.

They set out to work again. Two hours later their combined efforts allowed them to break the firewalls and other security measures guarding the servers of the Central Intelligence Agency. No one cheered, no one congratulated them, least of all themselves. They knew the game was not over. Breaking in was always the easy part. Knowing where to look for the cache was the challenge, as was the care required in avoiding detection. What awaited now was a long arduous work, made the more onerous for the concentration it required.

It was that concentration, the need to carefully consider every letter of the code, that consumed Andrew's attention, and was the reason why Damian sudden dry cough, one usually associated with verbal exhaustion, had startled him.

Without halting his work, Damian called out, "Hey, you! Brings us some water, will you!" He did not have to raise his voice, speaking casually, and audibly enough for Andrew, but certain the Russian watchers would catch it too.

They did. Someone stood up and approached the cooler, where bottled water and soft drinks were kept. No one pretended anymore. Andrew and Damian knew they were being watched and listened to. The Russians knew that they knew. It was a cruel game, not unlike a hunt for a cornered animal. By no means was the outcome decided, though. Every experienced hunter knows that no animal is more dangerous than one who is cornered; and wounded, if only at heart, as were the two men who fought for the life of the woman they loved.

Startled by Damian's call, Andrew raised his eyes, first at the man across the desk, and then to the men across the floor. Though his inattention lasted only a moment, by the time his eyes returned to the screen a whole lot had happened. Suddenly a new code was in use, and Andrew was lost behind. In the short space of time that it took to call for the drinks, Damian took over the lead, and was now performing his mastery on the keyboard, his fingers dancing like those of a pianist, creating beautiful sounds from a movement too fast for the naked eye. Andrew struggled to keep up, the changed code setting him back, too fast to grasp what was happening. Of course there was the scene familiar to all hackers — the commands, the covering of tracks, the setting up of traps, and false paths. Commonplace for those in the trade, there was art to it. For a laic, as all art was, Damian's work was incomprehensible.

Andrew was not a laic. Soon his trained eye began to see the messages in the gibberish of code, and his face paled at the realization of what was in store. He frantically composed and dispatched a coded message. Then another. Damian ignored all cues. In the end Andrew kicked him imperceptibly under the table. When this did not help, he murmured, audibly enough to be heard over the white noise of the keystrokes, "What are you doing?"

Damian went on unperturbed.

There was nothing Andrew could do. There was nothing anyone could do. Damian was the unquestioned, unchallenged master, the Demon of the keyboard. What he was doing could destroy any chance to save Amanda, and it could set the world ablaze. Damian had risked everything. The only chance was in the Russians not catching Damian's intentions.

Oddly, it was Andrew who led Kalgun's men to suspect that something unexpected was in the works. Andrew stopped using the keyboard. It was pointless, anyway. He could not catch up with Damian, though he could no longer doubt that, which was developing under Damian's fingertips. Andrew stopped his participation in the hacking efforts, sat idly at his side of the desk. Only his eyes were glued to the screen. His attention was sporadically broken to scan the Russians. With his heart beating faster he awaited the results of the race. Would Damian succeed before the Russians caught up to him? Noticing the tense attention exhibited across the floor, seeing as eyes darted between computer screens and the meshed cubes, Andrew realized that the Russians were alerted. It roused him to action. The least he could do was stall them. He put his fingers to work. He doubled his efforts. His fingers were the tiptoes of a ballerina. He barely touched the keys, skimming their surface, giving the impression of hovering above them.

Two codes were applied simultaneously to the work in progress. Only one was the working code. The confusion was enough to send the Russians on a goose chase. When they realized what had happened someone raised a mobile phone to his ear. Several heads rose above the barricade of cement bags, watching the two hackers in speechless awe. It was a quiet admiration of a respecting opponent. They had lost. They could only watch Damian's concentrated attention set firmly on the screen, his eyes set on the objective, its contours drawing shape with every keystroke.

From the distance Andrew caught some Russian words. They called for disconnecting the computers from the network, but it was no use. It was too late. What Damian was doing had no impact on what had been put in motion. Disconnecting the computers now could not stop the commands that were being executed from remote servers.

Damian had done what no one achieved before him, though many had tried.

Andrew was panting, his glowing eyes set firmly on Damian's face. He saw a cool face, almost bored, like that of an office worker on a Friday afternoon, stuck in front of a computer, awaiting the clock to ring the day, while playing solitaire. Damian was in fact playing solitaire. Only now and then a spark in his eyes told Andrew that the man who achieved what no single hacker had ever done, was not at all cool, or bored. The barely perceptible trembling of the finger sliding the cards across the screen told Andrew that Damian was reacting to the tremendous emotional stress — the pressure of hours passed, and the pressure of the unknown that lay ahead.

33

Minutes later Soba Kalgun stormed in. Away for the past two hours, he had been called back by his worried lieutenant. Appraised of what had transpired, he struggled to contain his rage. He was too experienced a spy and a businessman to allow himself to explode, knowing that it would not advance the suddenly precarious position he found himself in, and his anger, though silent, was directed at the men he left in charge — the lightning in his eyes spelled severe punishment.

Damian lifted his wrists off the keyboard. Slowly, very slowly, he leaned against the hard aluminum back. Allowing his sore wrists to thaw, he did neck stretches until the creaking stopped. Physically and emotionally drained, he froze with his head pointed upward, resting on the mesh wall, eyes on the ceiling — a man tired by a day's work.

Andrew was not paying attention to the developments taking place outside of the cube, his eyes reviewing Damian's code. What he saw, what unraveled on the screen, every bit of code, line-by-line, made him see the man across the desk for what he was — an unsurpassed master of the keyboard who had made the most daring of raids, and in the process had set the world on the spiral of destruction.

"I have what you always wanted," Damian said to the ceiling, the sound wave of his words traveling to the ears of the Russian.

"If anyone could do it, I knew it would be you," Kalgun replied, while forcing himself to remain calm.

Damian turned his head. He stretched and stood up. He approached the mesh wall and said, "Let's make a deal."

"Let's," Agreed Kalgun.

Andrew turned from the screen, his eyes following Damian in stupefaction, his mind still processing the implications of the newly confirmed discovery.

Kalgun turned to his men. Someone replied in Russian from behind the pile of cement.

Kalgun said to Damian. "The password to open the file."

"Don't think me naïve. The file is out of the vaults. Your computer whiz can verify it. If you want to know what's in it, though, you have to agree to my terms."

The Russian ground his teeth, but bowed slightly. "I'm listening," he said.

"I want you to bring my daughter to a busy public place. She and I will leave. When, and if, I'm satisfied that we are not being followed, I will give you the password."

"What guarantee do I have that you will?"

"What guarantee do I have that you'll let us go?"

They observed one another for a time.

At last the tension on Kalgun's face lessened. He glanced to his men, as though awaiting some news.

Meanwhile, he said, "My agreeing to your terms is the guarantee you seek. Otherwise I would simply put my men to work, to crack the password. I can wait, you know. I've waited for it for a decade; what is another year, or two, or however long it would take to break it."

"I hesitate to operate in such final terms, but a chance exists that as technology develops along the way, the encryption and the password may be cracked. Do you want to risk that some kid with a knack for programming will stumble upon the file, and give it a try?"

"Then we are both interested in expediency." Kalgun glanced to his men again. This time someone returned a nod.

"So, the file is genuine—" Kalgun started and was about to add something when one of his men departed the pile of cement and approached hastily. He said something to his boss. Kalgun's face turned pale.

The Russian's eyes locked with Damian's.

The latter said, "Did I mention that while I acquired what you were after, I also got me what I consider to be a life insurance policy?"

Kalgun's man said something to his boss. The Russian ground his teeth.

Damian continued, "By now, files from both servers have been copied to mirror sites. Both are encrypted and password protected. As all other files stored on the whistleblower portal, they too may be made accessible to anyone with a computer and an Internet connection. Need I remind you that at any given moment millions of visitors come to the site looking for truth? The files will become available to them automatically within two hours, unless you do what I said. Right now these visitors are eagerly awaiting the key to open the files. They will receive it should something happen to me or my daughter, or if my terms are not met within three hours."

"I could shut down the whistleblower portal."

"Others have tried. They failed, and so will you."

"Tsk, tsk." Kalgun constrained his anger. Not used to defeat, he struggled to regain his trademark cold facial expression. He said through his tightly clenched teeth, "You are everything they say about you. And then some."

Damian bowed his head in modesty.

Kalgun went on, "I hope we can still work together, despite what happened. We could turn the world around, the right side up."

"You kidnapped my daughter."

"Put yourself in my shoes."

"Perhaps it is how oligarch ex-KGB agents secure deals. You're a ruthless son-of-a-bitch, whereas I'm more of an artist. It would never work."

Kalgun took the answer in stride. He pondered it in silence, then said, "We're not really that different, though, are we? You're a formidable opponent yourself, and your hands are not nearly as clean, as your image would suggest. Who knows which one of us would pass your online trial if tried side-by-side?"

Damian caught a worried expression in Andrew's eyes. He winked to the young man, and said, "That's not a bad idea, spoken by a true player. It ups the ante, would you say?"

Andrew dared not contradict.

The oligarch might have regretted his hasty words, but did not back down. He stared at Damian, as he used to at his opponents, from a height of his mighty position.

Damian said, "Neither of us is in a position to cast moral judgments. It's not for you or me to decide what is right and what is wrong. Let the people decide. Are you ready to face them as I am?"

"I'm not afraid, Mr. Allende. I stood in front of a firing squad, literally. So, let us not argue, for we both know the outcome of such a trial. We both know that people's votes can be manipulated at will. What you do with your teary online trials, reaching to people based on carefully manipulated data, mine and any other publications do every day. We're the same. We both want to reach our audiences. The only thing different is the goal that guides us. In time, I thought, even those differences could be overcome—"

"You forfeited that chance when you lifted a finger against my daughter."

"Would it make any difference if I assured you that no harm would ever have happened to her?"

"No harm will happen to her, and not because of your word, but because of what I acquired today."

Kalgun digested Damian's words. He realized that no amount of reasoning would do.

"Alright," he said at last. "Your daughter will be delivered to the location of your choosing. Both of you will walk away, provided that you release the password. But, forgive me if I remain skeptical. I shall require a collateral." With the last words Kalgun gazed to Andrew.

"Oh-h-h!" Andrew exhaled. "You've got to be kidding!"

The Russian's eyes were ice-cold, when he said, "You will pay me company until Mr. Allende lives up to the agreement."

"If he doesn't?" Andrew cried.

"Then you shall be the first to face the judgment day," Kalgun replied with a derisive grin.

34

The public location Damian chose was a busy pedestrian bridge over the River Thames. Andrew and Damian were driven to it in the company of two tensely silent Russian agents. Undoubtedly Kalgun would have used additional manpower to secure the exchange, though it would likely not be a show of force, since the location, with only two exit points, offered him the unparalleled advantage. What spoke in Damian's favor was the public space, though, it being past business hours when they arrived, the bridge was not as busy as Damian had hoped. Still, people strolled it in good numbers, beckoned by the Eye. It would have to do.

Damian was left alone at the entrance to the bridge. He exchanged a silent gaze with Andrew before the latter was driven away. Away? Damian doubted that the Russians went very far. He felt their eyes on his back as he slowly walked off. He reached the middle of the bridge, where he was promised to find his daughter. She was not here. All he could do was wait. He glanced into the eyes of the passersby. None seemed to harbor hostile intentions, yet in his imagination they were all secret agents. It was not beyond Kalgun to try and break the agreement, and knowledge of it was unnerving, bringing out the deepest fears. It took a great deal of self control to not give in to doubt, while the waiting magnified his doubts exponentially. He clenched his fists, the knuckles turning white, but refused to shout. He would not give Kalgun that satisfaction.

At last he saw her. Amanda was approaching slowly, striding toward him, alone, from the direction of the Eye, the wheel behind her turning, giving the impression of a hypnotist's tool.

"Amy!" Damian said softly as she nearly passed by, not expecting him.

"Dad!" She was startled, her nerves stretched to the limits.

They embraced.

"Did they hurt you?" Damian asked, while his eyes scanned the bridge over her shoulder.

"N-no, but how did you—"

"Not now. Come." He slid his hand under her elbow. He led the way toward the Ferris wheel.

The mobile phone given to him by Kalgun rang in his pocket. Damian drew it out, answered.

"The password," demanded the familiar voice with the Russian accent.

"Not yet!" Damian said sharply and switched off the phone.

They were watching him. Somewhere out there were agents, watching his every move. He scanned the area, his eyes darting from person to person, like a cornered elk assessing a pack of wolves.

"How many drove with you?" he asked his daughter.

"Two," she replied immediately.

It meant nothing. More could be lurking in the shadows.

They neared the end of the bridge, and Damian's grip tightened around Amanda's elbow. Whatever was going to happen would happen soon, he reasoned. With his eyes prodding the twilight for suspicious activity, or faces of persons who did not belong in this place, he walked briskly. Then he saw them. Several men and women in long overcoats; they pushed away from the shadows, began to encircle the prey, like pieces in the game of checkers.

The phone rang again. He answered it.

"The password!" the same voice repeated, sharply.

"Call off your goons!" he shot back.

"The password!"

"That's not the agreement we made."

"I've just amended it."

Damian showed no anxiety, as though expecting no less from the devious oligarch. He said, "Then so shall I. Release Andrew. Now. And call off your goons. Do it, or your file goes viral online."

"I can't do it, Damian. For the same reason you won't give me the password — neither of us trusts the other."

"Tell you what. We'll make it a hand-to-hand exchange. Call off your people. Send only one, with Andrew. Hand Andrew over, and you'll get the password."

No reply followed, and Damian's back covered with cold sweat. He said with audible anxiety, "Time is ticking."

Kalgun sensed his opponent's angst. It reassured him that no foul play was afoot.

Moments later the men and women in long overcoats began to retreat. Some two minutes passed before two men emerged from the shadows, one of them Andrew. The man escorting him was wearing a long coat, his right hand in the deep pocket. A bulge in the crotch left no doubt as to what the hand was gripping.

The four met face-to-face.

The phone rang again.

"It's your turn, Mr. Allende."

"Don't do it, Damian!" Andrew said heroically. "You can't trust him!"

"Trust!" Amanda sneered. She said with contempt, her eyes on Andrew, "Whatever it is about, *this* man is not worth it!"

Damian ignored both. He said to the mobile phone, "Your man makes me nervous. Make him remove his hand from his pocket."

Seconds passed. The escort took three steps back, and removed his hand from the coat pocket, but remained at the ready, his eyes on the targets.

"Come closer, Andrew," Damian said. When the American approached, he spoke to the phone, "Alright. The password is—"

A commotion erupted before Damian could finish the sentence. What transpired could not be a coincidence. It was a call to immediate action for some, a mortifying stupefaction for others. It all started when several couples, who hovered nearby in romantic embraces, suddenly dropped their façades. The roses in the women's hands suddenly turned into semiautomatic pistols; the hands of the men were gripping steel butts of weapons of choice. Everything happened fast and in complete silence. The Russian escort remained unmoved, which likely saved his life, and avoided an all out shootout. He was too experienced to start a war when outnumbered and doomed to fail, to say nothing of the lack of orders to proceed otherwise. It was evident, however, that some exchange of commands was in the wireless spectrum, as his head kept nodding, his mouth engaged in a conversation with a remote agent. Whatever was said did not require him to offer resistance. He simply stood, and watched, as the two men and the woman were suddenly surrounded by an armed group, and ushered away in a defensive formation. Numerous other figures dressed in long overcoats emerged from the shadows, as though in a show of force. They too participated only in passive observation of the events that unfolded.

It could have turned ugly, Andrew recalled later. In his thoughts he praised Kalgun for acting cool in a tense situation that cost him all of his assets. The Russian shrewdly avoided violence, which promised nothing, and in all likelihood would have forever erased any hope at returning to the playing field. Andrew attributed it to Kalgun's shark business skills and his KGB background, both responsible for a well trained, and sharp mind, used to making quick decisions. It allowed the oligarch to make the only logical decision in the circumstances when someone else might have acted on emotion. He watched as Amanda, Damian, and Andrew were being escorted out by well-armed agents, and smiled in the knowledge that not all was over.

Time would prove that Kalgun's hopes for a chance to regain the upper hand where not entirely unfounded. A man of his background and means was used to getting anything he desired, short of turning back time.

35

"It was quite the trick you pulled," Andrew said about an hour later, taking advantage of being left alone with Damian and Amanda, in his voice professional admiration. "Honest to God, I've no idea when or how. I was there, I watched your every keystroke, and yet I saw nothing."

"Simple multitasking," Damian shrugged off the praise.

"All the same, I'd love to retrace your code, step by step. It isn't often one gets to witness such artistry, and learn the labor behind it. It was more than multitasking, more like multi-multitasking. The way you broke into two different systems, while simultaneously covering your traces, sending coded messages, and staying ahead of the hounds who were breathing down your neck—"

"What was the break-in I heard about?" the station chief asked, his ears perked up. He had returned to the room, a bottle of scotch — single-malt — in one hand, four glasses in the other.

Damian and Andrew exchanged glances. Neither answered the question.

They were sitting around an elongated table at an empty office space used as a safe house for the Central Intelligence Agency. Three men and one woman. All four were still thawing from the tense stand off. Perhaps none was as deserving of the peaceful opportunity to rest and recuperate as the one whose artistry ensured the successful completion of the exchange.

Indeed, Damian had every reason to be satisfied. Yet he did not rejoice. Not yet. He looked out the window where, at a distance, the contours of the lit Ferris wheel could be seen against the cloudless sky. The view was pacifying, yet peace was not coming. Damian was conscious of the troubles that still lay ahead. While he succeeded this evening in freeing his daughter from one foe, it was only the first step in the string of battles that awaited ahead. He was under no illusion that he and Amanda were safe. They had merely escaped one evil, with the second, and by no means a lesser one, still looming over them. Damian was a realist, but he could not help but hope that if he played his cards just right they may succeed in breaking free altogether. Free enough to start a new chapter in their lives, together.

Damian glanced at his daughter. She sat opposite him, a bottle of water in her hands. She seemed calm, but the father knew that it came at a great price. As strong as the circumstances in life had forced her to grow up, Amanda was a frail woman, a girl, really, for a girl she would always be to him. Damian could see it in the tense way she was sitting, and the way she drank from the bottle — short and frequent gulps, putting down the bottle, and picking it up a moment later — that she struggled to keep up the appearance. Nonetheless, he commended her in his thoughts, for she appeared to understood what awaited them still.

Amanda was making great effort to remain calm. Her eyes crossed with those of the man sitting next to her father — the man who had hurt her so badly, yet whom she still loved with all her heart. Could she have been wrong about him? Was Andrew really working with her father, as the events appeared to confirm? God knew, that her desires wanted it to be true, yet how could she ever reconcile it with the image of a man who had spun a web of lies to get close to her?

The station chief broke the silence. He persisted, "Tell me all about that break-in."

"It's all water under the bridge," Damian tried to brush it off.

The chief would not let go, lest the situation slip out from under his control. "I know you're hiding something from me. It has something to do with Kalgun. You had to offer him something in exchange for your daughter. What was it?"

It was that very question expressed in Amanda's eyes that prompted Damian to answer.

"The mere suggestion that Amanda's life has a price tag attached is appalling. Only someone for whom life is a commodity, something that can be bartered, taken, or given, could ask it."

"Yet, that is what happened, wasn't it?" Dick Verso said coldly. "Your daughter's life was priced, and you paid. How much?"

Damian hesitated before replying. Was it an attempt to drive a wedge between the daughter and father? He could not discard the possibility. The move was crude, befitting the player who used it. Could it actually work? Would his daughter think any less of him for having bartered her safety?

The station chief appeared to read his mind. He said, "We all would have done it, if placed in your situation. With Soba Kalgun being one of the players in the game we all are a part of, I'm interested in what it was that prompted him to allow you to leave the controlled environment that was his safe house?"

Damian exhaled. So, this was all that bothered the chief. It was one of the two cards he acquired for such an occasion when all other options were explored. He had used it to secure Amanda's release. He saw no harm in sharing it now, when something told him that he could use it again, lest his second card prove not as strong as he had banked on.

He said, "Soba Kalgun is the sort of man who would have bartered his own daughter to retrieve what I had acquired from under his nose."

Dick Verso weighed the answer in his mind. He seemed to understand what had transpired in the Russians' safe house. He asked with caution, "What sort of man is that?"

"A man for whom family means the service he devoted his life's work to. A man who would do anything to see to it that his work did not go to waste."

"Something the two of you have in common, then."

Damian ignored the remark, confident that his daughter would not fall for such obvious provocation. "The question is: Are you that kind of a man, Mr. Verso?"

"Are you making me an offer?"

"A choice. One that should not be difficult to make. Andrew, a young and passionate man that he is, had appropriated the London station database. He was acting out of noble reasons — out of love, but it can, ultimately, lead him to a prison. So, I am offering you a choice — forget about Andrew's passionate move, hush up the station database breach, and I'll let you have a peak into that, which your agency never could lay its hands on, that which Soba Kalgun agreed to swap for my daughter. The file containing Russian intelligence operatives working under non-official cover in the West."

The question went unanswered, and the chief's eyes danced from face to face. His fingers tapped a tune on the table top. It was not a happy tune. The chief was reeling. Despite the successful exchange on the bridge, he felt that success was not his to enjoy. He could not help the sensation that he was being played. When the station received the coded message from Damian Allende, he of course sprung into action. He would have ignored it had it pertained only to the most wanted man on Earth — in accordance with instructions from the headquarters — but he could not ignore the fact that his officer was in danger, and in the hands of a foreign, and never so friendly, intelligence service. The chief sent his men to the exchange place, and in the process he went against the headquarters' directive, by intervening with Damian Allende. It was unavoidable, yet not beyond the standard of deniability. Langley will not be pleased when the incident gets reported, but that was not what worried the chief. Something else kept his tension up. He felt through his skin that something much worse was about to fall on his head.

Dick Verso suppressed his angst, and turned to Andrew. "I'll pass it on to Langley. Meanwhile let us go back to the other file — the station database. Has it been released?"

Andrew said lightly, "There hasn't been such a necessity, yet."

"Yet? Are you still planning to blackmail the CIA?"

Amanda looked up, suddenly aroused by the accusatory voice. Were her ears not deceiving her? Was there animosity between Andrew and his boss? What was the blackmail the chief had in mind? She looked at the young man with a puzzled expression.

Andrew caught her gaze. He saw hope in those two vividly blue eyes. It gave him courage to withstand the pressure from his former boss, but more importantly — it filled his heart with the strength necessary to fight for the woman he loved.

His eyes sent sparkles when he said, "I did it for love, not out of malice. I hope you can understand this, Dick. I fell in love with the woman whose father was our target. He was in danger, and by extension so was she—"

The station chief cut him off, "The CIA has no interest in Damian Allende!"

36

"The CIA has no interest in Damian Allende?" Andrew repeated after his boss. "Come now, Dick. I know the subtle difference between the official line and what happens in the shadows. And I know the Company well enough to read between the lines when orders suddenly change. That's why I extracted the station database. I acted on emotions, to be sure — something the Company doesn't believe in, and teaches its operatives to suppress. Well, I could not. What I felt for Amy was stronger. I could not allow anything to happen to her. The database was my collateral."

Andrew's eyes locked with Amanda's. The woman's face blushed.

The admittance made an emotional impact on the chief, too. Dick Verso genuinely liked his young agent in whose feisty integrity he often saw the reflection of his younger self. He cleared his throat so as not to show this weakness, and said, "I won't beat around the bush, Andrew. You've committed a punishable offence, whatever the circumstances. Seeing, however, as we've known each other for some time, and I know that you would not betray your country, and provided that you have not turned the database to Kalgun, in exchange for Mr. Allende or his daughter, and that it hasn't wound up on the whistleblower servers, I am willing to turn a blind eye on your emotional lack of judgment."

Andrew took his time before replying. For all the transformation that happened in his heart and mind since he came into contact with Damian Allende and his daughter, he still held his boss in high esteem. The London station being his first major assignment, he grew attached to this veteran CIA officer, who ate his teeth in the old Cold War days, when the known enemy made the rules of the game clear-cut, and conduct of agents on both sides was governed by unwritten rules. It was more often a war of wits, rather than fists, where respect for the opposing side garnered respect in return. That respect was the modus operandi of the old officer, it was directed to the enemy, as well as toward the officers under his command. It was for this characteristic that Andrew felt attached to his boss more than to any policy. He could not tell the exact timing, but was aware that over time, as he matured and learned to think independently, the regard for his immediate superior was the only drive that kept him employed in the agency and the government that preached good, but did the opposite. The assignment to infiltrate the life of the daughter of the most wanted, and perhaps most revered, man in the world, proved to be the final step in the transformation of the young mind. Andrew fell in love, and his talent found a new way to express itself. Which came first — the love, or the newly discovered desire to affect change in the world? It did not matter, for one was not exclusive of the other.

Andrew's eyes gazed from the daughter to the father. If only he could tell what they made of him, especially Amanda, the one who affected his heart. Whereas compatibility of thought made him nearly certain of a lasting partnership with Damian Allende, the same could not be said about the sphere of the heart. Amanda had every right to be cross with him for the way he came to know her. He should have let her know his true motives for asking her out that first time, when at last he confessed his feelings toward her. He did not, and for the most trivial of reasons, ones not foreign to any infatuated boy: Having the slightest inkling that his feelings might not be returned, Andrew was afraid to tell the truth, lest it spoil the happy moment. Of course, from the perspective of time, he understood that he should have done it right away, to tell about the assignment, and if he understood better the love of a woman, he would have known that her heart was capable of forgiving and accepting even the most heart-wrenching episodes. But for all his twenty six years Andrew was just a boy who fell in love with a girl. He was, however, old and mature enough to know that a love like that was worth fighting for, and defending until the last breath. No weapons would be excluded in saving the love of his life, and stealing the station database was one of them.

"What do you plan to do with them?" Andrew asked the chief while nodding to the father and daughter.

"This should not have any impact on your duty, Andrew," replied the chief.

"My only duty now is to protect the ones I love and admire."

"Hand over the database, Andrew." Damian seconded the chief. He added in an assertive tone, "It is no longer needed."

"It's not that simple!" barged in the station chief. "I need guarantees that the database was not uploaded to the whistleblower servers, or handed over to Kalgun."

It would have been easy to assure the chief of what he wanted to hear. Given the friendship and mutual reverence, it was not inconceivable to expect that the veteran officer would accept the younger man's word as proof. Andrew, however, did not want to deceive. The prospect of staying in the ranks of the CIA, as suggested earlier by the chief, held no hold over him. If he did not offer the empty assurances, it was only due to respect he felt for the chief. He knew, too, that the chief made the offer to retain Andrew in the CIA only out of consideration for the special rapport between the two of them. He knew that it did not come easy to the chief. These old birds lived by rules that could not be affected by personal feelings, and the fact that the chief allowed himself to bend the rules was a sign of weakness. They both understood it, as well as the fact that sooner or later the effect of the chief's human emotion would have to come into play. In the world, and in the organization where human emotion had no place, it could only turn into resentment. Neither wanted to see the moment when the respect they felt for one another would be eroded. It was thus that Andrew had to sever the old friendship here and now, while it still existed. Good friendship, if short, was better from one that turned two men into enemies.

Andrew faced the chief, in his eyes the cruel and final answer.

Damian Allende understood the young man's state of mind. Turning to the station chief he said, "Andrew acted on the spur of his heart. It wasn't an act of malice. It was an act of love. It caused no harm, perhaps acting as a buffer against evil. Ha-ha! Isn't it how the Cold War worked, with weapon stockpiles acting as mutual deterrents? Your database was such a weapon of defense, never deployed."

"What guarantees do I have?"

Damian took a deep breath before replying. "I give you my word that Andrew did not upload it to the whistleblower portal."

37

The station chief whistled.

Amanda looked up, wide-eyed.

"I suppose there's no point denying the fact anymore," Damian said simply.

"No, there isn't," the station chief agreed. "Of course, the CIA knew for some time that the whistleblower portal and you are one."

"Does it also explain the special protection the CIA offered me? See, I knew that you monitored my whereabouts from the moment I boarded that plane in Reykjavik. And I knew you'd do nothing to stop me from running the next online court."

"You knew?" Andrew could not hide surprise. "How?"

"Thanks to conscientious government servants, naturally."

The answer took a moment to sink in.

"Someone leaked the CIA orders to the whistleblower servers!"

"Why did you not publicize it?" the station chief asked through his clenched teeth.

"Somehow, I thought you'd rather if it did not see the light of day."

"If only you'd shown such restraint with all the leaked government files, instead of spreading them around the Internet."

"Oh, I don't know. I have an idea that the CIA is not as displeased about it as it now wants to appear." Damian lifted his hand and, in a gesture of scolding, he waved his index finger at the station chief.

The two men studied one another in silence, their eyes engaged in an exchange of messages that tongues withheld. Though speechless, it was by no means an exchange devoid of substance. The young man and a woman could tell that messages exchanged thus were profound, though neither understood their nature. Observing the two men was not unlike watching a wrestling match. Both players' faces were tense as though under a strenuous struggle. At last one of the players relaxed visibly, only his words told that the match was not over.

The station chief spoke slowly, accentuating his every word, "As the founder of the whistleblower portal you are most credible to back Andrew's guarantees. At the same time it makes me wonder why you'd give up such a prize as the station database?"

With his eyes on the opponent's, Damian replied, "Sometimes the prize is not worth playing the game."

"Right." The chief stood up. He uncorked the scotch, and poured it into all four glasses. He sat down, took one glass; he lifted it up, as though to admire the color of the liquid, and said. "Tell me then: What made it worth it for Kalgun to agree to let you, and your daughter, from his hold? The prize had to've been perceived as worth it, no?"

"Didn't someone say that everyone has a price?"

"Yes. There's considerable skill involved in knowing the right price, given all the pressure, particularly when, quite often, one gets a single shot at it."

"When you play with predictable players over time you get to read them quite well. You get to know their price before they even enter the game. Would you like me to tell you yours?"

"Mine?" The station chief raised his brows in poorly mocked surprise. "Am I in the game?"

The two men continued to wrestle in silence again.

It was too much for Amanda, who did not understand the nature of the sparring.

Andrew was beginning to understand. The realization of what was at stake frightened him. His stealing the station database paled in comparison with what was brewing. He said, in an effort to lighten the tension, and to steer the conversation away from the explosive revelation that Damian held up his sleeve, as a card sharp would, "Forgive me for barging in on your telepathic duel. Let me clarify something before you put one another to sleep. The database is not Damian's to dispose of. I stole it initially to protect Amy—"

"Is the young lady in any danger, Andrew?" the chief cut him off, impatiently. "Kalgun's hands don't reach this far. You can return it."

"It isn't only Kalgun that I am concerned about. It wasn't because of him that I downloaded the database in the first place, remember?"

"Damian Allende and his daughter have nothing to be afraid of. The Company has no interest in seeing them hurt."

"I don't know what the Company is plotting, but I know enough to smell a rat. The database is an insurance policy. I won't release it, unless I'm forced to. It's non-negotiable, although, if truth be told, I'd rather it were different. I'd rather the information contained in it saw the light of day. The world deserves to see the games the CIA is playing."

The chief said in an ice cold voice, "I'll pretend I did not hear it."

Damian added in a like voice, "Be careful, Andrew. Think of your future."

"That's exactly what's on my mind."

"It doesn't look bright, not after you broke-in and stole the CIA database. Take my advice, and give it up, while the Chief offers you a clean exit."

"Is this the way to affect change? To give up at the first sign of pressure? Let me ask you this, Damian: Did you give up when state after state, and intelligence agency after intelligence agency, threatened you for exposing their secrets?"

"There is a difference. I'm only the messenger. I did not steal any of the documents that I published. They were sent to me by whistleblowers. You will become one if you go any further. It is, of course, a brave and laudable act, but can you bear the consequences? Don't answer it yet, because I'm sure that you think you can. But have you thought about those close to you?"

Andrew glanced to Amanda. The woman blushed but did not turn her gleaming eyes.

"I'd like to think that those who love me will accept and appreciate the principles I stand for."

"That's what I thought when I first combined hacking with activism," Damian was now talking to both young people. The woman who loved me accepted my activism as being a part of me. She would have followed me to the end of the world if that's what the work called for. The road was not a pretty one. I could not put her through it. I left her. Now there isn't a day that I do not regret my decision. If I carry on regardless, it is because I want to convince myself that it was worth it."

"You did not let her decide for herself," Amanda replied after a period of silence that followed Damian's words. "Pretty, or not; comfortable, or bumpy, the road does not matter, as long as you tread it together. She would have followed you, not as a baggage, but as a partner, one who would help you carry the burden."

The father's and daughter's eyes met. Both glistened.

Damian swallowed hard. He said, "I don't want you, kids, making the same mistakes that I made."

"Your mistake was not in what you undertook, dad! Your mistake was that you did not believe in mom. She would have followed you everywhere, whatever it took, for better or for worse. You doubted her love. That is not a mistake I will make."

"Do you— Do you believe that I am a mistake?"

"No, dad. I don't think that you're mistake. I don't know what you are. I don't know who you are. I learn something new about you everyday. Today I learned, as in passing, that you are the founder of the whistleblower portal. Tomorrow... Who knows? That's the point. I want to get to know you better, and closer. I want to be a part of you, as mum wanted too. For better or for worse. You're a hero to many, a villain to some. It won't stop me from loving you. It never did. You are my dad, whoever you might be to others. You will always be my dad..."

38

Damian's heart came to his throat. He struggled to hold the tears that wanted to pour out. It was no time to give in to emotions. These two kids, for that was what they were, needed guidance. Who better than a father to give it?

"You can both affect change without breaking the law. Andrew doesn't need to be the whistleblower. It's a laudable move, but with short prospects. You're young, and with all due respect, with little experience, and a rather limited access to truly significant information. It doesn't mean, however, that there is no place for you. Help those who have the access to truly worthy material to deliver it to the world. Help them expose it."

"Are you offering us to join you, then?" Andrew asked.

"If that's what it takes to make you give up that damn, yet insignificant, database, then so be it."

"Now, hold on a second!" the station chief interjected. "Tread carefully, Andrew." He turned to Damian, and said in a peculiar tone, one giving encouragement, while his words were scolding, "What you're suggesting is illegal."

"Only people like you and your masters can think of truth as illegal and in need of hiding."

Their eyes sparred again.

The vehemence in Damian's words and on his face prompted Andrew to pull back. He understood the significance of what Amanda's father tried to accomplish by insisting that Andrew part amicably with his employer. Returning the file, along with assurances, to a partial boss, could mean a clean start. And he understood why Damian was willing to give up the file. He watched the master of the keyboard pull out, almost invisibly, from the most secure servers in the world, a card of his own. What Damian had done could secure the free passage for all three of them. It could give them time to disappear. But would they ever? What Damian had done would not be forgiven, certainly not forgotten. If the card was played, instead of Andrew's database, it would, undoubtedly, lead to severe response. All three of them would then be tracked, and killed mercilessly. Andrew knew what card Damian had pulled from the servers, and while he believed it the strongest possible card in the game, he also knew that it was only strong as long as it remained unused, serving as a deterrent from taking on a hostile action against its holder. It was a dangerous game, one that could just as well unleash a deadly conflict between two powerful opponents who had the means to obliterate one another. All that was needed was a spark that could ignite the conflict. It occurred to him that his own action — the stealing of the station database — might be that spark. In a tense situation anything could work as an igniter. It was thus that he realized that he ought not to make things worse. Yet, Andrew was desperate to prove his worth to the father, and, especially, to the daughter. He wanted to, he needed to make the decisive step to convince Amanda that since meeting her, under however unfortunate circumstances, he was always on her side. Stealing the database, he thought, would have done it. He glanced at her now, and what he saw in her eyes told him that no additional steps were necessary. She believed him. He had proved his worth already.

He said, "Alright. I'll return the database."

Momentary consternation befell upon the others.

"It's the right thing to do," Damian Allende said.

The station chief asked, "No conditions?"

"The word of a friend ought to be enough."

The chief agreed. "Return the database along with assurances and it ends here."

"Pass me a laptop," Andrew said.

The station chief drew out a mobile phone and sped-dialed a number. He gave instructions to the handset and moments later an agent walked in, a laptop in his hand.

Andrew took the machine, and set it on the coffee table in front of him.

"You can watch the whole thing over my shoulder," he said to his boss.

"I intend to."

Andrew stretched his fingers, making his knuckles crack. He then set out to work on the keyboard. He directed the web browser to a popular file sharing portal.

"Here it is."

"The image?"

"Just a simple steganography decoy — a hidden message embedded in an innocuous file. In it you'll find the URL to the cache. It's the only copy."

"And the threat to go viral if your demands weren't met?"

"Ha-ha! Did it work?"

"As you can see. I could not take the risk."

"Alright. Now you have it back. What next?"

The station chief said sincerely, "I'll do my best to shove it under the carpet, provided that no damage was done. As for your employment—"

Andrew did not let him finish. "Consider this my notice, effective immediately."

"I am sad to let you go, Andrew, but in the circumstances—"

He did not finish. The door opened and the same agent walked in briskly. He motioned to the boss. The station chief stood up with a sigh, and approached his agent. He listened for some time, his face turning pale.

Damian Allende watched the scene with the corner of his eye. The time has come, he realized, and shifted in the sofa to a more firm position. He watched as Dick Verso waved off the agent, and said nothing, only the crease between his eyes showing that he was thinking intensely. Suddenly he turned to the three people, focusing on one.

"Now I understand why you were so eager to let Andrew give up the database. It pales in comparison with what you'd done."

Damian replied as though he expected this time to come, "Some form of insurance policy was just too tempting to forgo, given the interest the CIA shows in my work. It makes me very nervous, particularly in light of all the examples of your country's one time friends becoming designated enemies at the whim of the changing policy. Today the CIA sweeps the sidewalk before my feet; who knows what they'll make of me tomorrow."

"You're the tailor of your own destiny."

"I've always thought so. And then the CIA and others came along. All of a sudden, my destiny was being sawn at the vaults of Langley, Moscow, Tel Aviv... I wouldn't make much of it — after all, we are, all of us on this planet, interdependent. But my daughter, you see, I could not bear that her fortunes might be tied to mine, not after all that she has already been through. While I accepted long ago that it is a risk that goes with the ideals for which I stand, I just could not allow any harm to come my daughter's way. And so, earlier today, I allowed myself to peruse the digital vaults of the department of operations of the CIA, among other places. Ah, the riches! I wish I had more time to scrutinize them, but with the Russian agents breathing down my neck I can be excused for having to cut the visit to minimum. Nonetheless I did have a good look round. I took a snapshot, according with the saying that a picture will last longer. In fact I took many snapshots. Hundreds of thousands, nearly two million, to be precise. Lots of files, plenty of very interesting information, not limited to the notorious spy agency, but containing many signatures on various executive orders. I thought it important enough to save the loot offsite. I think it's reasonable to call it a very good insurance policy for my daughter and me. I think there's enough in it to cover Andrew, too. If only you knew what I saw, you'd agree with me. Oh, and before you answer, there's one more thing: Unlike Andrew, I am fully prepared to make use of the material. Don't bother trying to shut it down. By now it is available in hundreds, perhaps thousands of mirror sites of the original whistleblower portal, undoubtedly downloaded many times over. All that's needed to make it readable by everyone with a computer is a password. It's known to several of my associates, who will monitor my wellbeing. What will happen when they can't verify that I am well, should be pretty obvious."

In an effort to minimize the damage, the station chief attacked Damian through the only weak point he knew. He turned to Amanda, and said, "I was hoping that it would not come to this; no point spreading the dirt in such an ugly, almost gossipy, fashion, but alas — this is the way your father wants to play. Since this is the night of truths, we may as well make it the whole truth. You should know that your father is not only responsible for the online court, and the whistleblower portal. He is also a murderer. Your father, Amanda, operates a network of killers who commit assassinations based on material he publishes on the whistleblower portal, and then uses it to justify the killings through the sham he calls a people's court, or WikiJustice."

39

Damian's reaction was not what the station chief might have expected. Instead of blushing, or turning pale, his face was graced with a ironic smile. He said in a voice that matched the expression on his face, "It would be convenient for the CIA, if I was the killer, or a ringleader of an assassin cell, wouldn't it?"

Dick Verso charged, "Are you not? Isn't the whistleblower portal a bridge to your online court, which in turn serves as your justification for calls to murder?"

Damian turned to Amanda. "Don't listen to him. He's trying to drive a wedge between us, that is all." To the station chief he said, "Spare us your game. We know how it works. Spreading lies laced with facts to ruin opponents is a sort of CIA trademark, isn't it? From setting up paramilitary organizations disguised as opposition groups, only to topple governments not subservient enough to Washington, to concocting evidence against foreign intelligence services for alleged assassinations, or attempted assassinations, the history of your agency is indeed ripe with examples of what you are trying to accomplish right now. The whistleblower portal provides enough documents exposing such disinformation operations to write an entire encyclopedia of alternative history."

"Dad!" Amanda said, exhaustion in her voice.

The station chief took advantage of her emotional fatigue. He addressed Amanda, "Your father's list of accomplishments will certainly land him an entry in an encyclopedia, however, it won't be the result of the public persona he's created, but the invisible one, that of a brainmaster behind some of the most egregious murders in history —

from union leaders, to police officers, to political organizers, to heads of state—"

Damian remained unmoved. "This isn't the 1960s. You can't stage a false flag operation and expect the people to swallow it. You've lost all credibility — not that you ever enjoyed any — no one believes your lies, anymore."

The station chief studied Damian's face, uncertain of the source of the confidence his opponent was not in short supply of. Not finding a satisfactory answer, he tried again, by reaching through the daughter. "Can you convince your daughter that you're not the instigator of these murders?"

"I don't need convincing. I believe my father!" Amanda replied sharply.

The chief waved her comment as though it was a pesky fly. He shot out to Damian, barely able to contain his anger, "Such partiality is expected, but can the same be said about your audiences, those gullible millions?"

"That's not a bad idea!" Damian's face lit up, as though struck with a sudden thought. "I wonder whom they would believe — the word of an agency, whose weapons are deception, or documents which contradict the official lies?"

The station chief hung his gaze on Damian; an ordinary person might have bowed under its weight, but Damian was anything but ordinary — he was used to sparring with heavyweights of all stripes.

"You don't have to do this!" Andrew warned.

Damian turned to him. He asked, "Was it not your condition that I put myself on trial?"

"A trial?" Andrew glanced at his former boss, and then back at Damian. A trial in these circumstances, with the CIA breathing down Allende's neck, could not be conducted.

Damian did not let him ponder. He said, "I think the trial is a splendid idea, perhaps even necessary, now that so much evil has been attributed to me. Whatever you may think of your employer, Andrew, one thing is undeniable — the CIA, as any intelligence service, is a master of deception. The lies spread about me are making ever wider circles. The people expect me to take a stand, to clarify the allegations once and for all. They are right. I cannot expect them to participate in online trials when my own integrity is in question. I shall give my audience the opportunity to vet my ability to conduct further trials."

"You don't have to do this. Truth needs not be defended. It simply is."

Damian replied with forcefulness that surprised all, "It is the agreement we made, and I intend to keep it."

Andrew saw that it was no use. In the last attempt to dissuade Damian from going online, knowing that the crusader for openness would turn to his explosive card to make his case, he addressed the station chief. "What about it Dick? What if Damian receives a blessing from his audience? Will the CIA sit idly by as more classified information is being used to discredit our policy and diplomats?"

"This is out of my hands. The CIA will not to interfere with the WikiJustice trials."

Three sets of eyes focused on his lips.

Damian said, "And?"

Amanda and Andrew exchanged puzzled glances.

Damian continued, "There is more. Come on, spell it out, unless you would prefer if I pulled the instructions bearing the official CIA seal."

"You're playing with fire," the station chief said quietly.

"That's what the insurance policy is for. Insurance against assurance. Ha-ha! Now, that's irony!"

Andrew looked at Dick Verso. "What's this about?"

The station chief gave up pretenses. "We've received orders to offer Mr. Allende our protection, in case some rogue entities wanted to prevent the online trial from going on." It was evident from his tone of voice that the chief was not pleased with the orders bestowed upon him.

"And you don't think it smells?"

"That's the trouble with the CIA these days — too many agents think too much, instead of doing their job."

"I wish I'd opened my eyes sooner."

"You'd've become Damian's little helper? Oh, Andy!" The chief shook his head. "Take my advice and stay out of this man's affairs. Damian Allende's fortunes can turn very quickly."

"Not if more people like us help open the eyes of others."

"People like us?"

"Yes, Dick, people like us, with the inner scoop on the wrongs that ail the world."

"Do not cross the line. You do not have to betray your country only because your service has ended."

"That's just the thing, Dick. I wasn't serving your country. I was serving the regime. These are two different things."

"Let us stop here, because it doesn't serve either of us to be getting so hung up on politics. It has ruined many a friendship; it is also destroying the Company."

"The filth that is politics will not disappear if we stop talking about it."

"Perhaps, but staying clear of it allows us to do our jobs."

Andrew looked closer into his boss's yes. Did he see regret in them?

He said, "Sometimes I wish I could be like you, like most people. I'm not. I can't go on as if I'm blind and deaf to the true state of the world."

"You're not alone, Andrew. You're just in the small minority who haven't yet figured out that the only way to retain your sanity, and to survive in this world, is by being able to develop selective hearing and sight. It is that collective human ability that allows this suicidal species to go on against all odds."

Damian Allende cut in, "I know just the way to settle your dispute. You're both welcome to stand trial, alongside me. Who's better, than the recipients of your efforts and convictions, to decide whether these are welcome or not?"

They looked at him with consternation.

Andrew was the first to reply, "I'm ready, even now." He shot a challenging look at his old friend and boss.

"You're bound by secrecy," the chief said simply.

"Excessive secrecy is turning the people away from their government. It's time to bring openness—"

"You're way over your head, Andrew!" The chief realized that his protégé was serious. "No intelligence agency can operate in the open."

"No. But governments ought to. The Company has become intertwined with the government, or vice versa. We're virtually indistinguishable when diplomats are spying, gathering secret information. What's next for them? Stabbing people in the back, in dark alleys?"

"I won't be able to protect you if you go ahead with this." The chief warned.

"You're not my nanny."

The chief tried from a different angle. "I can't permit it as long as you're within my field of operations."

"What are you afraid of, Dick? Too many skeletons in your closet?"

The chief shrugged. "You can't expect the CIA to cover your back while you're sabotaging the agency."

Damian said, "No jury would accept a trial where the CIA was breathing down my neck, anyway. You too have to stand trial if my own is to remain objective."

"As though your trials were objective! These single-track cases you build around your victims, the selective and alleged proof of crimes, without council, are nothing more than a prop for kangaroo courts. Why not have your day in the court of justice?"

"You mean — institutionalized justice. But what justice can there be when the judges are political appointees, and the jury is pre-screened and cherry picked? I offer the defendants as just a system as it gets. I do not control who takes part in the online court. All they have to do is convince enough people that what they are accused of was in fact right and just."

"Do you offer them that opportunity?"

"The crimes they are accused of were committed a long time ago, and often they went on for years. That's ample time to prepare their case. Nobody should be surprised when they are called to account for their actions. They are, to use your words, the tailors of their own destiny."

"What you have done is build a fail-proof conviction machine."

"Ha-ha! If only! Perhaps it would be the answer to putting an end to abuse? Alas, I am afraid, human nature is such that no threat of consequences will stop those who see gains, from abusing others. So, to answer your suggestion — it is not a conviction machine that I've created, but a platform for the voiceless to be heard. Judging by the response — the message has been delivered."

The chief shook his head. "You're living on borrowed, the CIA's time. The fact that you were granted protection by the CIA should tell you that you are the most wanted man, Mr. Allende. The killers are stalking the streets of London as we speak, waiting for the first opportunity to drive a dagger into your heart, or a bullet between your eyes. You're a walking dead, because sooner or later those whom you've crossed will catch up with you, and the CIA will not be there to save your ass."

"It seems my ass is a valuable commodity. There seem to be as many who want to whip it, as those who will kiss it. Who would've thought the such long-time adversaries as the CIA and the Russians would be found among the latter?

"The Russians!" Dick Verso snarled.

"I hear the Chinese are interested, too. It seems that the most powerful world players consider me more valuable alive than dead. I wonder why this might be?"

Andrew rubbed his temples with his knuckles. He murmured to himself, but others could hear it, "It can't end well."

"What are they plotting, dad?" Amanda asked, worried.

"Plotting. It's a good choice of an expression. Of course, thought, it is not a part of vocabulary between friends." Damian glanced at the station chief.

"But this is most extraordinary." Amanda disregarded the sarcasm.

"Not at all. In fact, it's rather inevitable. I've been a fool not to see it coming."

"What?"

"I should've considered it when the first murder occurred. But then other events came into play, and drew my attention. It was only in the past several weeks that I devoted all of my energy to figuring out the sudden friendliness on behalf of those who consider themselves targeted by the whistleblower portal, and especially the online court. Step by step I found out why the United States prefers me being alive, and continuing with the court, to being dead. If I were a better chess player I would have predicted the move. I would have guessed that the Russians, and the Chinese, would want in on the game."

"The game?" Amanda and Andrew were nonplussed.

The chief was unable to hide a smirk on his lips.

Damian said, "Oh, yes — it is a game. A game of life and death, where the latter is the only objective, the most desirable prize."

40

"Life should be peachy with such friends as the CIA and the Russians," Andrew said some hours later.

"Peaches and cream." Damian caught the sarcasm.

"Yet, judging by your faces, it's more of a sweet and sour dip." Amanda concluded.

"It isn't often that one receives an offer of protection from both — the Russians, and the CIA," Andrew said.

Damian added, "One doesn't know whether to rejoice, or to run for cover."

"Why do I get the feeling that we are going straight into the mouth of a lion," Amanda commented. Seeing as every traffic light brought them closer to the dangerous point, she was conscious of the time, hoping to persuade both men to change their minds before it was too late.

They were in a van, part of a cavalcade of three vehicles on the way to the only place safe enough to conduct the most anticipated online event in recent months. Sitting in the back of the van allowed the three to conduct a private conversation, away from the prying ears of the heavily armed agents who resembled guards rather than escorts.

"If you can't trust people—" Damian started.

"Trust?" she cut him off. "Trust the Russians?"

The Russians, or the Americans, as if there were any difference, Damian thought. He said, "I was going to say: If you can't trust people, then you must rely on your own instincts. Those instincts, fortified by research I've done over that past weeks, tell me that I'm useful to them — to the Russians, the CIA, and to a growing number of other shadowy organizations. They need me today; tomorrow I may become a liability. It's the way it is with these people."

"Why test your fate? Why not try for it? We've eluded them for months. We could try it again."

"You cannot escape your fate, but you can effect it—"

"Effect it, then, away from these people!"

"For how long? Another week, a month, or two? That would be postponing the inevitable. We need a clean start. There is only one way to achieve it."

"How?" Amanda asked.

Andrew turned his ears. While he was aware of the bases of Damian's confidence, seeing in it a potential benefit — at least in theory — he could not begin to fathom how it could be achieved in practice.

Damian replied, cryptically, "The best way to defeat the enemy is to wait for him to provide the opportunity."

Amanda looked at him, wide-eyed. "In other words — you do not have a plan."

A plan? It was more of an ad hoc decision to seize the situation. He was wanted by some of the most notorious spy services in the world. How could he ever hope to defeat them? Yet, that was what differentiated Damian from many ordinary people — the prospect of defeat was not an obstacle, but rather, it worked as a stimuli to overcome what seemed a foregone conclusion. Being in the grips of the most powerful spy agencies was not a reason to give up hope. To the contrary — it told him to keep trying to break free. In his view, defeated was only he who did nothing to try to change the outcome. How? It was the last conversation with the station chief that gave him the idea. Damian was suspicious of the CIA's protection for weeks, and the continuing string of murders had propelled him to determine the reasons. In the process he discovered something that made his hair stand up high. He found a pattern spanning several weeks. He found proof of it in the files he appropriated while Kalgun watched helplessly, unable to stop him. The discovery was as stunning as anything ever uploaded by whistleblowers to the eponymous portal. It was the proof that a sinister plot was enacted. Its severity was such that, in Damian's eyes, it justified any and all means of exposing it. Damian was determined to do just that, even at the price of his own freedom, but he knew that despite his best efforts and talent, he could not hope to succeed, not when the powerful perpetrators were threatened with exposure, and thus ready to do everything in their power to stop him. This was the reason why Damian shared none of his research with Amanda and Andrew, lest it be uncovered by his new protectors. He knew he would only have one chance, and even then to hope to succeed and come out unscathed, he required a safe place. There was only one such place, and the perpetrators of the devious plot would provide his security for him, albeit unwittingly.

"Turn left at the next lights," Damian directed the driver.

Sitting in the back seat, behind the father and daughter, Andrew murmured to Damian when the destination appeared at the distance, "You're playing a dangerous game."

Amanda seconded his words, resigned now that she could not dissuade her father from carrying on, "Dad, I hope you know what you're doing."

"Despite your reservations, this really is the safest place," Damian replied when the caravan drew up to the curb in front of a building under construction, with scaffolding and tarps covering it from the ground to the rooftop.

The CIA agents emerged from the vehicles, their hawkish eyes scanning the area; they deemed it safe for the civilian passengers to leave the van and traverse the some dozen feet to the building.

They were expected. Three plain-clad men appeared from behind the tarps. They had no weapons, but confidence in their eyes told that the situation was under their control.

Damian said louder than was required to be heard by the three men, "I thought it only appropriate that my two guardian angels should get acquainted, at last."

His words were heard elsewhere. One of the tarps rustled and lifted, and an impeccably dressed, and well-groomed man had emerged.

"The United States and Russia find many shared interests these days," Soba Kalgun opened.

"We have many common friends as well as enemies," the station chief replied amicably, yet warily.

"As the old saying goes — an enemy of my enemy, and a friend of my friend, and so on." Damian said jovially, and with a spice of irony. "Need I introduce you?"

"Hello, Soba." The station chief bowed slightly.

Soba Kalgun returned the cordiality. "Hello, Dick."

"Long time no see."

"It is strange that we should see less of one another, now that relations between our countries are so much more civil."

"I'm glad to provide the opportunity for you two to catch up," Damian said.

"Always glad to see an old adversary," the Russian replied.

"Not very surprised, though. Are you, Soba?" Dick Verso asked.

"If I were surprised, it would only be for the length of time it took for us to meet again."

"Blame it on all this tiptoeing around Mr. Allende."

"Ah, but it couldn't be helped. The days of the iron fist are over. Certain finesse can accomplish so much more."

"Did it?"

"That's a good question. I'm sure Mr. Allende won't keep us guessing for much longer."

"I'm glad I don't have to waste my breath explaining what brings the three of us together," Damian replied. "I have something you both want. While you may wish me no harm, as you profess so readily, the truth is that you want it so badly, that I might be hurt while handing it to you; unintentionally perhaps, as one sometimes gets injured when feeding a hungry dog. Well, I am hoping that the presence of both of you will work as restraint on your mutual appetites."

The prolonged silence of the two leaders of the opposing groups was broken by Andrew. He said barely above a whisper, "May I have a word with you? On the side." They withdrew several steps. Andrew said, "You're going to get us killed!"

"You're being overly dramatic."

"Am I? I know what you're up to. I now understand it. For whatever reason you were given the license to live. You're useful to them, for now, but what you're about to do will make you useless, even dangerous, and thus slated for quick removal."

Amanda joined in. She did not understand the intricacy of the unraveling events, but her instincts were on the right track. "Dad, have you not wondered why they agreed to let you get this far? Not long ago they would have killed you to stop you from running the trials. Now they let you carry on, and offer a safe environment to do it. There is something very fishy about it. You cannot trust them!" A deep crease of concern showed on her forehead.

Damian grasped them by their arms, and pulled close enough to feel one another's breath. "I do not trust either of them, but I'm banking that they do not trust one another, either, and their mutual mistrust will work as a deterrent, and a shield for us."

Andrew was not having it. "What you're about to do is tantamount to enraging a beast by injuring it."

Amanda added, "And you cannot possibly know how an angry and injured beast will react!"

"On the contrary, my darling. In the case of these two beasts we can predict their action with a great deal of accuracy."

"Dad—"

"I saw into the heart of the beast, and I know what makes it tick. Beside — we cannot turn around now."

"Damian!" Andrew tried once more. "What makes you think they'll ever let you go ahead with it?"

"Trust me — if there's one thing they want, it's that the online trials continue on, unhindered."

41

Certain steps were required to ensure that the hastily assembled plan stood a chance of being carried out successfully. According to Damian's instructions, Andrew and Amanda set out with a shopping list; they were accompanied by a security team composed of a mixed group of American and Russian agents. Meanwhile, Damian used the time to prepare the site. He surveyed the grounds, and assembled some material that he found lying around, as it often does at building sites. Kalgun's men offered no obstacles, as their orders made it clear that Damian's project, the WikiJustice, must go on. Dick Verso, while suspicious, had no choice but to go along — the orders from the headquarters were clear about providing Damian's security, and the latter's blackmail compelled him to see to it that the situation got resolved in the Company's favor. Both teams — the Russians, and the Americans, were in constant communication with their respective bosses, as well as with agents in the field, who were securing the site. The overall havoc, not unlike that which precedes every major operations, provided Damian with a certain edge. He seized the opportunity to slip in several unknown cards into the deck of cards that was tightly controlled by his two powerful opponents. Time would tell whether he would be able to use them to his advantage.

At last Amanda and Andrew returned with the equipment purchased in nearby stores.

"What is this?" Kalgun pointed to a device that, judging by the effort it took Andrew to carry, was a heavy item. He read the label on the box. "Backup power? You needn't worry about it. We are wired here for any eventuality."

"This may be so, but I cannot underestimate the desire of the ill-wishers to shut me down." Damian's voice left no doubt that he intended to operate his court independently.

Setting up the stage took the better part of the day, with Andrew and Damian working tirelessly and without break, on preparing the equipment, while Amanda made preparations for the exclusive interview she would be conducting with the man of the year. She allowed neither the Russian, nor the American agents, to lend her a hand in furnishing the cube; she positioned the chairs, and strapped the mesh walls with a blue tarp that Damian found somewhere; she positioned the video camera, and the microphones; and ensured that no outside intervention could interfere with the delivery of the host's message.

Andrew took care of most of the fine details. He downloaded the software necessary to conduct the online court, and installed the security measures required to withstand attacks — while ensuring the security of the equipment was his task, the server-side operation belonged to Damian. Andrew worked as if he was in a trance. Now that Damian's plan was actually being carried out, he discarded all reservations, and plunged into it with his whole heart and expertise. He could scarcely believe it was actually happening, that he was part of the historical and groundbreaking event, one responsible for such profound changes in his life. He resisted the urge to pinch his cheeks — such was the surreal sensation of watching his former CIA colleagues work alongside the Russians. What made the scene the more fantastic was that neither side fully understood the game they were engaged in, and whose rules were written by the quiet man of angelic appearance. Andrew was in awe of Damian's ability to maneuver calmly and confidently through the web of high stakes and even higher risks, as he concentrated on preparing the trial under the watchful eye of the two powerful spy agencies. Andrew could not help but wonder if he was the only one who worried, as he watched Amy fully engrossed in preparation for the interview, by brushing up on all those of her father's activities that lead to the establishment of the first online court. In her calm Andrew found similarity to her father. They were indeed very much alike — methodical yet passionate, and entirely lost in the project they devoted their attention to. Andrew was no stranger to working under pressure, yet in the circumstances as they were, he could not help but suffer extraordinary anxiety; how could he not, knowing all he knew about the agency he was a part of for years? With this intimate knowledge he was preconditioned to expect a hidden agenda in the CIA's readiness to assist the founder of the online court, to ensure that nothing would interfere with the launching of the next installment. He was overcome with Damian's calm in the circumstances, given that Amanda's father must have been equally aware of the danger of exposure of classified documents of the American intelligence community, and with its members standing at arm's length; he must have known that no government would stand idly by, particularly when its agents were in the position to stop such breach of security; yet knowing it all, he went ahead with the preparations, and behaved as though the presence of the heavily armed men was the most natural thing under the sun. Andrew admired such self control, while at the same time he cursed his own lack there of. He felt as though the others unloaded their stress onto him, leaving it up to him to worry and to take appropriate steps to avert what seemed inevitable.

Amanda broke Andrew's reverie.

"Everything's ready here," she announced. She entered the cube where the two men were working in focused silence. She was wearing a business casual top, and matching pants, the attire purchased along with the technical equipment. In her hands was a small parcel wrapped in clear plastic. She opened the packaging, removed the pins, and unraveled what was Damian Allende's trademark white shirt, with wide arms and crisp, nearly hard cuffs. She handed the shirt to her father.

Damian took it with his eyes on his daughter's. He asked, "Are *you* ready, though?"

"I'll let you in on a secret, dad," she replied as lightly as she could. "I'm never fully ready for an interview. It's helpful in retaining interest in a subject that often isn't... well — very interesting. But regardless of the depth of preparation I am always nervous, trembling in my knees, nearly sick to my stomach, regardless of who the interview is with, and on what topic. It passes. I draw the strength from the person I'm interviewing. Their confidence passes on to me. So you see, I should be asking the same of you. Are you ready, dad?"

"Am I confident? Confidence is as much a matter of knowledge as it is conviction of being right. I know that I am doing the right thing and, yes — I have the confidence for the both of us. I expect that it will transfer to the audience and the jurors, too."

"They don't need performance," Andrew chimed in. "All they need is the authentic raw data to support the case against the accused."

Damian shook his head. "They need more than that. They need to believe that what they do matters. This cannot be done by presenting them with cold facts and expecting them to act upon it. For many of them these leaked classified documents are a fact of daily life; they do not need to see a file, or a piece of paper documenting the wrongdoing. They see it on the streets, they feel it through their skins, they hear it, and they see it, every day, day after day, often for years on end. What they need is someone to show them that it can change, that they can change it, that they can make the difference. They may not be able to achieve it through a vote, or a rebellion — how does one affect a change when the guilty is a foreign politician, or a corporation headquartered thousands of miles away, under a whole different jurisdiction? — but, they need the confidence that the distance, or the inability to cast votes in democratic elections, or to stage a street protest, do not pose an obstruction to affecting the change."

Amanda said with glistening eyes, "You are it, dad! You bring the change. You are the change."

Damian replied with sadness in his voice, "Am I? So far not one policy was changed, and not one corporation, or a government entity, or even a person, changed the way they do business, as could be expected a result of the publication of leaked documents proving abuses, lies, corruption, exploitation, even murder."

"You've given people hope."

"Hope? Or ill-understood guidance? Last year, after the first trial, a police officer was killed by the victims of a raid his troops conducted against unarmed and peaceful villagers. His guilt was proved beyond any doubt, and thousands voted him guilty. But was killing him the right way to affect change? Does the killing of those who carry out harmful orders change the policy that allows the harm to continue?"

Andrew suggested, "Perhaps by killing the guilty, the victims believed that justice was served; they showed thus that no one stands above the law of public opinion?"

Damian shook his head. "I wouldn't have expected it from you, Andrew. After all you came to me demanding that I put myself on trial for having, allegedly, inspired violence."

"I'm not saying that it is the answer. I'm merely suggesting that some may find it the only way to right the evils that go unpunished."

Amanda asked, "Is it right to take life, whatever the justification?"

"Self-defense?" Andrew suggested.

They both watched Damian, awaiting his reply.

He stopped what he was doing, to face them, and said, "Every killer must face his own demons, as does everyone who issues orders to kill. Killing goes on, and will go on under a multitude of pretexts. Nothing I do will prevent it. I can, however, protest when it is done in my name, as all wars are, and as all capital punishments are. No excuse makes it right to kill, whether it is done in a supposed effort to protect my freedoms, or for the safety of the society I live in, or in response to a guilty verdict passed by a judge."

Amanda approached her father, took his hand, and put it in hers. She said, her eyes on his, "Dad, it is terrible that your work was used to launch this… vigilante-style justice. Maybe it was sparked by frustration of not being able to achieve justice by other means? Maybe it was an ejaculation of a deranged mind? Whatever the case — these are extremes shared by a few, a minority. Remember that there are thousands upon thousands of others, and they are many, the majority, for whom the mere ability to cast a vote in your poll is all they need to fuel their desire to go on living, even if living under most oppressive conditions."

Damian replied, with his hands gently caressing hers, "Do not presume that I am stricken by doubt. If anything, I am convinced that the online court must continue, now more than ever. It must, if only because of all those murders that were attributed to the verdicts. The online court was used to justify the killings, making me the one who made murder a justifiable option, something that is utterly abhorrent to me, and on every level. I must make it clear that no person can make such a determination."

Andrew asked, "Who, then? God? Is this how you justify it from now on? And what about those who do not believe in God? What if God does not exist?"

"In the absence of God, the people as a whole, those who create the canon of what is right and wrong, are God. The online court must take place, if only one more time, for the people to decide whether I and the polls, ought to continue at all."

42

The launch of the latest edition of the online court was scheduled to commence within minutes. Inside one of the two mesh cubes, sitting at a small, Parisian sidewalk café-style aluminum table, were the founder of the most-talked about event in the recent years, and a young woman, whose facial features somewhat resembled the man's. A plain blue tarp hanging behind them formed a backdrop adorned with the familiar logo of the online court, though the logo was only perceptible to online viewers, as it was digitally superimposed by a man invisible to the camera. He was separated from the two main actors by a tripod topped with a digital camera, and a small wood desk that was crammed with electronic equipment; his fingers were busy, switching between two keyboards that were connected to two laptop computers, and hidden under the table top, on retractable trays — the setup was necessary to conceal the keystrokes from possible video recording equipment, whereas a small, white noise emitter protected the keystrokes from being decoded by audio-listening devices.

Behind the mesh walls of the cube, at the far end of a — mostly empty — concrete floor, was a group of eight men, who were gathered around a large aluminum table; sitting on matching aluminum chairs, their eyes were focused on the screen of a tablet computer; their attention was broken occasionally to observe another group of men, who were gathered across the floor, behind a pile of bags of cement. Both groups chose their location so as to keep an all-encompassing view of the floor, and to remain far enough from the cube, and out of site of the video camera's lens.

The leader of the group that communicated in American English turned to one of his men, and asked, "You are confident that the broadcast can be severed at any moment?"

The answer was reassuring. "It is only a matter of a cell phone signal sent to our men who are awaiting orders outside."

The station chief was inquisitive — he learned that a boss's watchful eye was the best guarantor of a job well done. He asked, "How will this be achieved?"

"The cube itself is impenetrable to scanners, but the satellite connection requires a clear view of the sky. As soon as the outside transmitter becomes operational our team will locate and jam the signal."

"Can we stop transmission by tapping into the signal, and breaking into their computers?"

"This method, given the encryption, would require too much time to be effective."

"Can we break into Allende's computers to find the location of the files?"

"Our team will do their best, Chief, but lets remember that Walker is— was our best technical operator in such matters."

"Can the Russians beat us to it?"

"No reason to suspect that they have such an advantage."

The station chief said in a fatherly tone, "We won the Cold War precisely by anticipating the Soviet advantage. The fact that they were far behind us on every level — financial, technological, or military — made no difference." He finished with his eyes darting across the floor, "It is always better to overestimate your opponent, that it is to underestimate him."

Seven pairs of eyes followed his gaze to the cement fort, behind which the Russian team hovered over a bank of computers.

The leader of the Russian group, a man dressed in a tailor-made suit, and bearing that exuded power and confidence, asked his men, "How are they able to send a signal outside the cube?"

"It's quite ingenious in its simplicity," replied a man whose task it was to monitor the said signal. "Those wires that reach the ceiling and protrude ever so slightly, are actually custom fitted router antennas."

Soba Kalgun said in a voice not devoid of certain reverence, "A couple of pound sterling worth of wires found on the floor defeats tens of thousands of pounds worth of equipment." He shook his head, as though in disbelief, and added, "It is often the simplest solutions that work; that's why those who rely on the latest gadgets, thrusting all their efforts into technology, suffer so many defeats — our intelligence services not excluded." He turned to his men, and shot out in a voice that demanded an answer according to his expectation, "Have you located the relays?"

"We're still working on it," replied the man who was in charge of the technical operation of the safe house. He refrained from the temptation to explain how challenging a task it was to find a small device that could be fitted into a small crevice of the large building site.

"What about the frequency? Can you tap into the signal?"

"The transmission has not began. When it does it will take some time."

"Have you found any other way to determine the location of the files?"

The man shook his head, unable to bring himself to offer yet another negative answer.

Kalgun was not pleased, which showed in his voice, as he said, "In other words — we have no advantage over the Americans."

Another agent replied, "Actually, there is something. We've spotted an American team outside. We've detected their scanners. They are standing by to tap in, or to jam the signal. We can prevent them from doing both."

Kalgun said, "That's something. We're a step ahead of the Americans." He turned his eyes from his agents, and focused on the cube. "But it remains unacceptable that Allende should be able to beat us on our own turf."

His agents' eyes followed his gaze to the cube, where Andrew Walker announced, "Five minutes to launch. I'm going online, notifying the social media."

Damian Allende reached for the bottle that stood under the table, and filled two glasses, placing one in front of his daughter, and drinking from the second one; when his glass was empty he refilled it, and placed it on table top. His eyes locked with those of his daughter's. Neither said anything, but in their silence was the pent-up tension that could not be concealed.

"Sixty seconds to go," said Andrew. "The networking sites are abuzz. We have traffic building up. The word is spreading very quickly." He was speaking fast, cutting off the last syllables, unable to control his excitement. Counting seconds under his breath, his fingers were dancing on the keyboard, while his eyes furiously scanned both computer screens.

"Ten seconds." Andrew's last announcement was delivered at the height of excitement that precedes that calm that comes when the anticipated moment arrives at last, and could be heard by the Americans.

The station chief asked his men, his voice animated by the excitement reverberating from his former agent, "Anything yet?"

One of his men replied, his index finger pressing to the microphone located in his ear, "They are jumping frequencies, very fast—"

"What does that mean?"

"It means that it may not be possible to isolate and jam the connection without disrupting it for the entire neighborhood."

"Can we do it online? Can we trace him and stop him in his tracks?"

With the finger at his ear, the agent replied, "They're jumping servers. … Fast. … Very fast. … It will take time." He finished with his finger on the tablet computer, "Meanwhile they're broadcasting."

The Americans leaned over the small screen, their eyes glued to the presentation of the founding of the whistleblower portal — from meek beginnings, to becoming a repository of millions of classified documents from government offices, and intelligence agencies' secret vaults, and headquarters of multinational corporations. It went on to describe the portal's mission to end the culture of governmental secrecy, and followed to illustrate its impact on the news publishing industry, boasting — and the sheer number of files supported the claim — of reporting more newsworthy stories than the world's media combined. From the profile of the document-leaking site, it was a natural transition to the online court, as it relied on documents procured by the former. Here the focus was on giving the voice to the voiceless, to the majority of the world's population — the some 99% of people who were locked in the shackles of the remaining 1% comprising of plutocrats, and dictators, and the thugs at their disposal. The presentation went on to point up the importance of the mass participation of ordinary citizens from varying geographical locations, differing cultural backgrounds, experiences, and points of view, on the objectivism of the verdicts reached on the bases of facts supported by the documents, as well as photos, and video files hosted by the whistleblower portal.

The presentation ended with the voice of the narrator, a voice eerily similar to that of the man behind the keyboard, "And now to the latest edition of WikiJustice, the only place where your voice, the voice of the ordinary people, still matters."

Computer screens around the world were filled with the image of Damian Allende. Slowly, the camera zoomed out to include the interviewer, who, unbeknownst to most viewers, was his daughter.

43

The woman's youthful appearance contrasted with the gravity of her words; her somber voice reminded every viewer that what they were about to witness, and participate in, was equally important for the young and the old, as it was for men and for women.

Sitting in a simple aluminum chair, she was speaking with clarity, and, though used to appearing in public venues, with some trepidation, "Welcome to the third edition of WikiJustice — the online court where ordinary people voice their opinion on what is just and unjust for them, their families, their community, municipality, region, country, and the world at large. Here people from all walks of life, people like you, whether from Africa, or Australia, Asia, the Americas, or Europe, whether you are Black, or White, Yellow, or Red, poor or rich, a city dweller, or a farmer, a believer, or an atheist, a voter, or an anarchist, a communist, or a fascist, a woman, or a man, whether you suffer under a tyrannical regime, or are drowned in blissful ignorance of the so-called democracy, here you are all equal and free to express your mind." Passion grew in her voice with every word. Her eyes glistened with exhilaration. Her body language showed explosive energy, as though she was ready to leap out of her seat. While she spoke, her words were transcribed into text that appeared on computer screens, with viewers having the option to translate it into their language of choice. In the bottom right corner of every screen was a number that grew rapidly, from hundreds, to thousands, to tens of thousands.

As viewers were flocking to the portal in droves, the young woman continued, "For most of you the introduction is not necessary; for others who may have stumbled here quite by accident, or for whom access to this medium was previously restricted, I would like to introduce the man who made this project possible. Damian Allende."

Computer screens around the world were filled with the image of the white-haired man who bowed slightly, as though embarrassed, to the camera, and smiled his trademark pacifying smile that made him so alluring.

"Damian, will you briefly describe for us what the project — WikiJustice — is about?"

"Thank you, Amy," the man replied in his gentle, and pacifying voice. He proceeded in like manner, speaking clearly, his protruding eyes directly on the camera, reaching each viewer individually, "What is a Wiki? In the connected world, a Wiki refers to a collaboration of numerous individuals brought together by common interest, or concerns. From creating encyclopedia entries, to writing manuals, blueprints, and software applications, to transcribing and translating texts, and building online databases, people have been coming together to build better communities. They have been doing this for years. They unite, and participate together in areas common to their interests, and interests of a larger community. The Internet made it possible to overcome restrictions, to cross previously impenetrable boundaries, whether political, religious, racial, class, or other. For the first time in history we are able to communicate and work together, without the restrictive chains, shackled upon us by the ever-narrowing elites. Together we are discovering each other, learning that the world, not so long ago considered a vast space, is in fact small and finite. A wind that gathers in one area can, and will be, felt in another. Same is true with political, social, military, or business decisions. What happens in one part of the world is not without consequences for people, and other living organisms from across the globe, who neither caused it, nor desired it. Those people often have no recourse to disasters caused in their backyard by someone, or some entity, located thousands of miles away, in a different, often corrupt, or complicit, jurisdiction. The reasons for the lack of recourse are many — it may be the distance, it may be fear, or disbelief in the ability of a single voice to affect change. Crimes and abuses go on, and on, and on, unpunished. Well, today it all changes. Today you have the opportunity to join others who are just like you — abused, shunned, and voiceless. Today you can join others like you, thousands, tens of thousands, hundreds of thousands, perhaps millions. Today you are not alone. Today you can be heard. You can make the difference. Today your voice will be heard. Make it roar."

As Damian Allende went on in similar vein, the station chief gazed around the table, to the faces of his agents. All remained unmoved, with their eyes on the screen of the tablet computer, listening as congregation does to a sermon in a church — with one ear, letting the words out the other. It was clear to the chief that their minds were not poisoned, that they would not succumb. He smiled in his mind, and thought: These are agents one can count on, dependable and patriotic to the last breath.

Meanwhile Damian Allende continued, "Soon you will be presented with the latest cases of documented abuses of power and public office, of corruption, and decisions made contrary to mandate, or to the interest of the public good. You will be able to examine the files documenting the actions that were, and are, harmful, that are wasteful, and punishing on your pocket, to your health, and to the wellbeing of your community, region, or the planet. You will examine documents obtained directly from the secret vaults of individuals, governments, institutions, and corporations, that issued and initiated these decisions, and orders. But before you examine these documents, before you cast your judgments upon those who are named in the documents, you must decide one more thing. As you may have heard, certain allegations have been raised against me, and the service in which you are about to participate—"

The station chief said to his agents, "Ready or not, be prepared to shut him down."

In the opposite end of the floor, Soba Kalgun said to his agents, "Stand by, wait for my orders."

Damian Allende continued, "The allegations made against me also express reservations as to your ability to determine what is right, and what is wrong, for you, for your family, or for the community as a whole. I shall not comment on these allegations, as is my policy in regards to all that is presented here, in this court of the people. You shall determine and decide whether these allegations are founded. I want to remind you that your decisions shall not be cast on the legality of the online court, as any suggestions to the contrary are purely laughable, for there is no higher court than the court of public opinion. This is the one fundamental human right that no one, no jurisdiction, whether civil, religious, or military, has the right to deny. What you shall decide, is whether I am guilty of these allegations, and fit to organize, and to conduct the online court in which you participate today, as so many of you have taken part in the past. You will determine whether there is any merit to the allegations circulating in the corporate media, and sparked by those who control them. It has been alleged that the polls you participated in in the past were the cause of certain reactions directed at the individuals and entities whom you found guilty of harm, as determined by undeniable evidence. It has been alleged that I, as the founder of the service that allows you to voice your opinion, am guilty of the fate that struck those who were placed on trial, and thus that I have no moral right to provide the service to you, any longer. These allegations are serious indeed. They point a finger at me as the culprit behind the attacks against the property of those who were found guilty, even of their deaths. These allegation cannot be left unanswered. I am prepared to stand trial before you, to prove that neither I, nor any volunteers who helped in the creation of this service, had anything to do with these acts."

Damian caught the look in Andrew's eyes. It was a mix of hope and doubt. It saddened him to see doubt in the eyes of the man who had become so close to him. He had only himself to blame for it. He should have worked closer with Andrew since they parted in Reykjavik. He should have made Andrew a partner in all the research he had done since — and the doubt he was observing in these grey eyes would not be there.

Damian looked straight into the camera, and said, "As is the custom of these online trials, you will be presented with hard evidence that proves beyond any doubt the identity of the killers who purport to act on your, and mine, behalf. You shall have the opportunity to cast your judgment, to decide whether I, and, by extension, whether you have the moral capacity to participate in any further trials."

"What the heck!" the station chief murmured under his nose. He sprung to his feet, and stared through the mesh screen of the cube, to the man in the white shirt. With his eyes on Damian Allende, he raised his mobile phone to his ear. He pressed a key, and waited for the signal. When nothing happened, he tried again. "What in the Hell!" He cursed out loud. Turning to his agents he asked in a sharp voice, "Have you a signal?"

One by one they tried their mobile phones, to no avail.

The station chief raised his head, and gazed across the floor, to where the two black eyes of Soba Kalgun were staring back at him.

"That son-of-a-bitch!" the chief cried out. He turned to his agents to issue orders, when the voice from the tablet computer caught his attention.

"What you see on your screen are classified documents obtained by the whistleblower portal. You may read them online or download them to your computers. Not only do these documents prove beyond any doubt that I am not responsible for the deaths, but they also point to those who had ordered them."

"Oh, no, you won't!" the station chief roared. He turned to his agents. "Stop him! Stop this man!"

They all rose to their feet, and rushed to the cube. Two of the agents attempted to storm the mesh doors. It was latched from the inside, using wire string that Damian found on the floor. They failed. The chief was behind them, shouting, "Don't just stand there! Do something!" He watched as Damian Allende stood up from his chair, approached the camera, and with one swift move he turned the lens to the chief and his agents.

Damian said, the microphone capturing his voice, "Here stand the guilty ones, the agents of the agency where the documents you are seeing originated. Here you see agents of the spy agency that has been killing people whom you found guilty, but killing them selectively, targeting only those who were inconvenient for the administration, and for the superpower. Study the documents, read about the high level wheeling-dealing that went on in the corridors of the spy agency. Find out the true identities of those who wanted to use your votes to settle their own agendas."

"Stop him!" the furious station chief yelled at his men. "Now!"

The agents drew out their pistols. They looked at their boss, awaiting confirmation. They received it. The agents aimed at the man holding the camera in his arms. A cacophony of shots followed, but the bullets did not reach the target; their impact was visible on the mesh wall, and the act was captured by the camera, streamed live to hundreds of thousands of computers scattered around the World Wide Web.

Seeing as the bullets were useless, the station chief turned to the corner of the floor occupied by the Russians.

He cried, "Put an end to it, you hear me!"

An ironic grin on Kalgun's face told the chief that his wish would not be accommodated.

The chief raised his pistol, and aimed at the oligarch.

Several Russian agents immediately surrounded their boss, pistols in their hands, aiming at the Americans.

"What are you trying to do?" the chief cried, his voice a dagger. "Do you suppose I don't know that you're streaming those images in your media too? Do you suppose I don't know that you want to destroy years of thaw between our two countries?"

Kalgun's slightly squinted eyes were all the answer the chief would receive.

Dick Verso could not hold back his anger. "You son-of-a-bitch! Are you doing this in cahoots with Moscow, or for your own gains? Have you staged all this? Don't you see that it will have consequences? America cannot stand by and allow this to go on! There will be consequences, I tell you!"

He was met with the same eyes, the ironic expression magnified by the gaping holes of gun barrels in the Russian agents' hands.

The chief was at a loss, frozen by the standoff. Unable to effect his orders, he turned back to the cube where the source of his trouble was speaking to the camera.

"Consider the preceding footage as supporting material. Study the documents, review the footage, and come back with your verdict. Am I guilty? Am I morally unfit to provide the service that allows you to judge people, such as those you just saw, who used me and you, for their political gains? Am I wrong to provide a vessel by which you can judge the system that allows such acts to happen? When you have decided, and the majority of voices find me not guilty, the service shall continue. You will move on to the next case. You will see lots of cases of abuses of power, of corruption, lies, and harm perpetrated in the name of national security, or some other reason of convenience. Consider each case carefully, and cast your judgment for every individual and every entity named in the documents. Judge according to facts and evidence, and remember that the future of humanity and the planet lies within you, as does hope. You *can* make the difference."

THE END

ABOUT THE AUTHOR

As a former top-secret government courier, Jack King was privy to all the ins and outs of covert maneuvering on a global scale. He has turned his work experience into a series of novels that resonate with authenticity. The corridors of power, with their backstabbing, greed, and corruption, are the focus points of Jack's books.

Connect with Jack: SpyWriter.com.